Dezember 1987

DEATH OF AN OUTSIDER

She had been born and brought up in the village but had married someone outside it and had left, returning only recently, a mere seven days before her death, in fact. Was she, too, considered as an outsider who had posed some threat to the little community she had abandoned?

They were closing ranks against the idea of murder, shutting it out, because if they admitted to themselves that murder was a possibility, then they had to admit to something else – that someone from the village could be the killer.

But Inspector Finch did not believe it was an accident.

THE DARK STREAM

June Thomson

SPHERE BOOKS LIMITED

Sphere Books Limited, 27 Wrights Lane, London w8 5tz

First published in Great Britain by Constable & Company 1986
Published by Sphere Books Limited 1987
Copyright © 1986 by June Thomson

TRADE
MARK

Photoset in Linotron Trump by
Rowland Phototypesetting Limited
Bury St Edmunds, Suffolk

Printed and bound in Great Britain by
Cox & Wyman Ltd, Reading

ONE _____

'I'm going out to the post office,' Madge Bingham announced, putting her head round the door of the waiting-room. 'I shan't be long. Has Gordon gone?'

She hoped he had, otherwise he might have offered to post the letter for her while he was out on his afternoon house visits which would have defeated the object of the outing for the letter was only an excuse. There was little chance of Mrs Locke making a similar offer. She lived in the opposite direction to the village.

But how unnecessarily complex such subterfuges became! Madge thought, waving the letter in Mrs Locke's direction to show how genuine the trip was; not that Mrs Locke could see it was only the electricity bill, arrived that morning, which could have waited at least another day.

Mrs Locke was re-arranging her little cubicle which overlooked the waiting-room, putting away patients' files from morning surgery and placing her notebook and pencil just so on the counter top. She put her head through the hatch opening.

'Yes, Mrs Bingham. Doctor left about ten minutes ago. I'm just tidying up before I go. If you won't be in, I'll switch the telephone to the answering machine, shall I?'

It was one of Mrs Locke's exasperating qualities that, although she had been Gordon's secretary-receptionist for many years and carried out her duties efficiently, she still seemed to think it necessary to defer to Madge's opinion if she happened, as on an occasion such as this, to come into the surgery. It was this touch of servility in her manner which had prevented them from ever becoming on first name terms.

Seeing her face through the hatch with its pendulous

cheeks, freshly powdered because she was going home, and that faintly deferential smile, the features topped off by tightly permed grey hair, Madge had an overwhelming urge to shock her.

She thought, supposing I said, 'I'm not only going to the post office, Mrs Locke. That's only an excuse. The real reason is I'm hoping to see that man who's just moved into the caravan in Waterend Lane. He looks interesting.'?

She had thought so on first meeting him four days earlier in the village shop. It had been the briefest of confrontations as he had been on the point of leaving as she entered. In fact, he had held the door open for her and smiled as she thanked him. And it hadn't been mere civility either. She noticed that he had registered her appearance, taking in her well-cut clothes and her still trim though middle-aged figure with a look of quizzical admiration which she hadn't excited in a man for years; certainly not in Gordon.

As for the man – Alec Lawson, as Mrs Hunnicutt who ran the shop had informed her – she had, in turn, found him attractive. There was something loose and casual about him which she had liked. In his forties, he had one of those creased faces, humorous and different, suggesting an amused, perhaps even a dangerous, disregard for convention.

A free soul, she remembered thinking, her mind hardly on ordering groceries, and felt something flutter in her own breast as if answering an unspoken urging to break out.

But how absurd! she told herself, closing the door on Mrs Locke and returning down the hall to the private part of the house. I'm forty-eight and happily married. As the doctor's wife, I'm regarded as a pillar of the community. I'm a school governor, a Parish Councillor and chairwoman of the Ladies' Church Guild. I serve in the Oxfam shop in Studham once a week and help organise the Old Folks' Wednesday socials.

I am also the mother of two children whose photographs smile down at me from the drawing-room mantelpiece.

Lovely children, Mrs Bingham, and such a credit to you! And so they are, she thought, opening the drawing-room door and crossing to the fireplace. Claire and Richard, both now at University, Claire reading English, Richard Psychology, and neither of them really needing her any longer: not in the same way they used to when they were small.

So I fill my life with other duties – with committees and charitable works, with caring for Gordon who no longer notices me as a person, and with painting very fourth-rate water colours which my friends pretend to admire.

But, for the first time for years, I am going to make an adventure for myself which involves no-one except me, Madge, my sole self. Although not an affair, she thought, looking past the photographs of her children to the mirror above the mantelpiece as she arranged the red and cream silk scarf at the neck of her Jaeger coat. I'm too fond of Gordon and besides it isn't what I'm looking for. What I want is contact with someone different, a glimpse through a door into another kind of world which I haven't known since my student days.

All the same, it wasn't that easy to escape.

Locking the back door, she saw Bartlett, the gardener, come limping across the kitchen garden towards her between the rows of newly planted lettuce seedlings and beans, signalling to her with one arm as if she were a bus.

'I thought I'd light up a bonfire, Mrs Bingham. There's a lot of rubbish needs clearing and the wind's right.'

He's as bad as Mrs Locke, Madge thought. Can't he make a decision about lighting his silly fire without asking me first?

'What a good idea!' she said brightly.

'That is, if you'll be around to keep an eye on it,' he added. 'Only I was going to make a start on the shrubbery in the front. It needs trimming back.'

'I was just going out,' Madge replied, thinking: Damn his fire! Why should I alter my plans to suit the gardener, for God's sake? Aren't there enough little threads to keep me role-bound without Bartlett trying to bind me down still further? But seeing his long, lugubrious face – poor old Bartlett who'd probably never had an adventure in his life – she heard herself saying, 'I shan't be long. I'm only going down to the post office. Why don't you leave the shrubbery until the next time you come and find something to do in the back garden instead? That way, you'll be able to watch the fire yourself.'

'Right you are!' Bartlett agreed, pleased that the decision had been made for him. As he moved off to where his jacket was hanging over the handles of the wheelbarrow, she called out after him, 'I'll make some tea when I get back.'

He acknowledged the offer by raising his hand.

As she left, he was going through his jacket pockets, searching for his matches.

It was only when she was half-way down the road towards the village that she realised she had left the electricity bill on the mantelpiece under Richard's photograph and stopped, wondering whether to turn back and fetch it.

Over the top of the budding hedges, a tall white column of smoke was visible from Bartlett's bonfire, rising quite straight into the still, damp March air and, seeing it, she made up her mind.

I'll go anyway, she decided. I'll simply knock on the door and say, 'I'm Madge Bingham, the doctor's wife. I just happened to be passing and I wondered if there's anything either my husband or I can do to help you settle in?' I shall be friendly and welcoming in my best Ladies' Church Guild manner.

I might even ask him to tea one afternoon. Wouldn't that surprise Gordon?

Waterend Lane was a turning off to the left before the main centre of the village if the two shops, the general store cum post office and the butcher's, together with the straggle of houses and cottages between the church at the far end and the Goat on the nearer outskirts, could be described in so grandiose a term.

The lane ran behind the Goat, the only public house in the village, skirting its car-park and continuing in a straight line for a short distance before twisting this way and that

4

for about half a mile as it followed the irregular outlines of the surrounding fields. Just before the ford came into sight, the lane swung round in a sharp S bend and began to dip down to where the stream ran across the hard surface, rising and turning again on the far side to begin the long, slow incline towards Macey's farm, out of sight beyond the brow of the hill.

Madge walked briskly, enjoying the outing. It took a mere ten minutes to cover the distance from the village to the ford, a local beauty spot in summer, and once past the first bend, the public house and the clustered houses were no longer visible. Here the real countryside began. All along the verges the signs of spring were apparent in the clumps of pale primroses and brighter celandines studding the banks and in the new leaves emerging like little vivid green claws, sharp-edged and tightly rolled, which thrust out from the dense mass of winter twigs on the trees and hedges. The air had a buoyancy to it, fresh with the tang of new growth.

The caravan was also out of sight, tucked away on the far side of the ford in a corner of one of Macey's fields. It had been placed there originally to house the Harpers, Macey's former employee and his wife, who the year before had moved to another farm over in Riddleton where they'd been offered a decent, modernised cottage. Since then it had been empty until Alec Lawson's recent occupation of it.

It was reached across a narrow, raised footbridge which spanned the ford on the left-hand side, with worn concrete steps leading up to it at both ends and a handrail rubbed smooth by many generations of palms, the water beneath it running quite high and fast after the spring rains; picturesque with its surrounding trees and moist banks but a hazard in Madge's opinion, especially to children who tended to gather there in the summer to paddle. She had raised the matter several times at Parish Council meetings only to have her advice overruled.

On the far side of the ford, a sign-post, with a stile beside it, pointed across the fields to a public footpath leading to the church -- Waterend Lane, the main village street and the path thus forming the three sides of a triangle.

Crossing the worn planks of the bridge, she continued up the lane for another hundred yards before coming to an opening in the high hawthorn hedge, closed off with a rickety wooden gate. Behind it stood the caravan on its concrete base, surrounded by a derelict patch of garden which dated back to the Harpers' time.

The door of the caravan was set open, so Alec Lawson was at home. In fact, as the gate clicked shut behind her, she saw a head appear at one of the small windows. The next moment, he had come out to stand at the top of the steps, watching her approach with an amused air and a disconcerting lack of surprise as if he had expected her to come.

She began her piece.

'I'm Madge Bingham, the doctor's wife . . .' But she got no further.

'Come in,' he said and, turning his back, re-entered the caravan, giving her no choice but to follow.

Its interior dismayed her. It was furnished to the Maceys' taste, she imagined, not his, like a suburban sitting-room in flowered fabric with a black and yellow fitted nylon carpet which did not match, all the woodwork varnished a sticky, bright brown. A flap table, covered in speckled plastic, on which stood a portable typewriter and some paper, was set up in front of a cushioned bench seat which she assumed could be let down at night to form a bed.

'I'm sorry,' she said. 'I see I'm interrupting your work.'

'Coffee?' he suggested, ignoring her remark.

'No, I really mustn't stop. I was just passing and I wondered if my husband . . .'

'The doctor,' he put in.

It suddenly occurred to her that he was deliberately trying to put her out of countenance, for quite what reason she wasn't sure but she felt foolish standing there, an unfamiliar and disconcerting experience.

As if aware of it himself, he changed tactics, smiled

charmingly and said, indicating the bench seat, 'Won't you sit down?'

She perched herself on the end, sitting with her legs turned sideways to avoid the table top.

'I only wanted to say,' she continued, making her tone more brisk and business-like, 'that if there's anything we can do to help you settle in, you only have to ask. There's quite a lot going on in the village, the Men's Club on Monday evenings and the Dramatic Society . . .'

'I'm only here for a short time,' he replied, his head tilted to regard her, his expression still amused.

Seeing him close to and for a longer time than on their first brief meeting, she realised that he was younger than she had imagined – probably no more than in his late thirties – and this realisation together with his reply took her off guard.

'Oh?' she said. 'Why is that?'

'I'm opening a bookshop in Studham. As soon as the lease is finalised, I shall be moving in there. So I'm afraid I'm unlikely to make much use of the village activities, delightful though they sound. But it was enormously kind of you to take the trouble to walk all the way down here to tell me about them.'

Feeling the colour rise in her face at the irony in his voice, Madge said hurriedly, 'I had to go to the post office anyway,' and then remembered too late that she hadn't even that excuse for being there.

She got to her feet, feeling oddly humiliated.

'Then I shan't keep you any longer,' she replied.

He said nothing, only smiled again as he stood aside to let her move past him towards the door, looking at her with the same quizzical glance with which he had first regarded her in the shop.

Madge could see now that she had been mistaken. It was neither admiring nor appreciative, merely interested in the same entirely objective manner with which she might look up from her sketch book to survey a part of the scenery she was drawing.

How stupid she'd been!

But although her anger was directed mainly at herself, she was annoyed as well by Alec Lawson's attitude. There was an arrogance about him which was offensive. She was not used to being treated in so derisive a manner.

Well, it had taught her a lesson. She would take care to avoid any contact with him in the future.

Turning out of the gate into the lane, she was surprised to come face to face with Stella Franklin whom she hadn't seen in the village for almost two years; not since her marriage to some young man from Studham whose surname she had forgotten although it didn't matter. She had known the girl for long enough to call her by her Christian name.

'Hello, Stella,' Madge said, thinking how much she had changed since the last time they had met. Although she couldn't be more than twenty-one, she already looked experienced and, not to put too fine a point on it, a little common. But, even as a child, Madge remembered, Stella had been wilful.

'A bit of a handful,' as her mother had once expressed it to Madge.

Mrs Franklin was an unassuming, decent enough woman – too soft-hearted, perhaps, especially with Stella, the youngest of the three daughters – while Mr Franklin, when he'd been alive, had been one of those uncomplaining men who would do anything for a quiet life.

As the whole family had been Gordon's patients, Madge knew them well.

In her opinion, the root of the problem with Stella lay in the fact that the girl was more intelligent than either of her parents which made it difficult for them to know how to handle her.

It had all been wasted, of course. Stella had left school as soon as she could and, after several unrewarding jobs, had got herself pregnant at the age of eighteen by the young man from Studham whom she had married, although she had miscarried the baby a couple of months after the wedding.

Not long after that, she and her husband, who had been

living with Stella's mother, had moved out of the village to a new council maisonette in Studham where Stella was working as a barmaid, or so Mrs Franklin had told Madge when they met one day in the shop.

And now here she was back in the village, looking a little defiant which made Madge suspect that the marriage was not a success. Stella had always assumed that bold air of not giving a damn when things were going badly. Madge's suspicion seemed confirmed when she added, 'And how are you?' and Stella replied, 'Oh, fine, thanks, Mrs Bingham,' showing too much gum when she smiled and swapping her satchel handbag casually to her other shoulder.

'And your mother?'

'She's fine, too.'

Nothing more was required, Madge felt. Whatever was the reason for Stella Franklin's sudden return to Wynford, it would no doubt be common knowledge sooner or later. In the meantime, it was better to show no curiosity and she walked on after saying goodbye.

It was only when she reached the footbridge over the ford that it occurred to her to wonder what Stella was doing in Waterend Lane. Apart from Macey's farm, there was no other house she might be visiting except, of course, the caravan.

One foot on the planks, she turned to glance back over her shoulder.

Although the gate was out of sight round the bend in the lane, the hill leading up to the farmhouse was visible and, if the Maceys' place had been Stella's destination, she would have had time to emerge into view and be seen walking up the slope towards it. But the road was empty. Stella, therefore, must have disappeared through the gate which led into the field.

But what on earth was she doing visiting Alec Lawson? Madge wondered. Unless, of course, they had already met in Studham. And if that were the case, it might explain Stella's unexpected re-appearance in the village so soon after Alec Lawson's arrival. If they were having an affair . . .

But it was absurd, Madge decided. Although Stella was quite capable of chasing after any man, she had imagined Lawson, despite his casual appearance, to show more discernment, but perhaps she had been wrong in her judgement of him.

As for Stella, she could be playing with fire. In the past, before they had moved to Studham, Madge had seen the husband about the village and he hadn't looked the type who'd take kindly to his wife's infidelity. It was bound to lead to trouble.

What a fool the girl is! Madge thought. It was none of her business, of course, but all the same she couldn't help feeling exasperated at the stupidity of the pair of them.

Stella said, 'It's only me. Mind if I come in?'

Alec stopped typing and glanced up. She was standing on the top step, looking in over the open half of the door, smiling and quite clearly expecting a welcome.

Although he had told her to drop in any time, she had not chosen the best afternoon to call. Not only had he hoped to finish some letters concerning the lease of the shop, work already interrupted by Mrs Bingham's visit, but he was expecting his wife to arrive with his son to discuss, he assumed, the breakdown of their marriage.

All the same, he felt he could hardly turn Stella away and he replied, 'Help yourself,' although he began rather ostentatiously to pack the typewriter up, putting on its cover and shoving the letters into the file which he flapped shut.

She took no notice, a reaction which unexpectedly pleased him. There was a frankness about her which he had liked the first time he had met her a week before in the Swan in Studham where she had been serving behind the bar. He had called in there late one lunchtime on his way back from the solicitor's and, the pub being half-empty, they had chatted together while he ate a cheese sandwich and drank a pint of bitter standing at the counter.

He remembered he had asked her her name.

'Stella,' she had replied.

'That means a star,' he had told her.

She had laughed, her upper lip lifting to show the gums, an openness of expression which he had found attractive.

'I bet my mum doesn't know that,' she had said. 'I was called after one of my aunties. Where do you live? In Studham?'

'No, although I'm going to move here soon. I'm staying temporarily in Wynford.'

He hadn't expected her to know it but she had smiled again, delighted at the coincidence.

'Wynford? I used to live there. My mum still does. You know that row of cottages near the Goat? Well, she lives in the end one. What are you doing in Studham then?'

'I've been to see my solicitor,' he had explained. 'I'm arranging to lease a shop in the town.'

He had been surprised by her reaction.

'A solicitor?' she had asked, her expression suddenly turning serious. 'I was thinking of going to see one myself. What would I have to do?'

'Just ring up and ask for an appointment,' he had replied.

The reason for her interest had become apparent two days earlier when, calling in at the Goat one evening, he was surprised to see her at the bar, talking to the landlord. With that unaffected warmth of hers, too guileless to be anything but sincere, she had welcomed him like an old friend and, after he had bought her a drink and they had taken their glasses to a quiet corner, she told him she had left her husband.

'So I'm back home with my mum,' she had explained. 'I'm going to divorce him. Look, you know about solicitors, don't you? Could you put me right? Only I'm a bit scared to go on my own, not knowing what it's all about.'

The ingenuousness of the appeal and the similarity in their situations, both of them dealing with broken marriages, had prompted him to say, 'You know where I live. Drop by any time you like and I'll try to help. As a matter of fact, I'm in the process of a divorce myself.'

So there she was, unlatching the door to let herself in

and saying breezily, 'I'm not stopping you from your work, am I?'

'No,' he lied, smiling back at her and letting down the flap of the table so that she could sit down more easily on the bench seat. 'Come in. Would you like some tea?'

'Yes, please,' she said without any hesitation. 'Do you want me to make it?'

'I think I can manage,' he said dryly, going into the tiny kitchen where he put on the kettle.

He was beginning to enjoy the situation. Stella was looking round the caravan with very much the same curiosity as Mrs Bingham had shown but without her air of surprised concern at its awfulness.

Remembering the doctor's wife, he was prompted to add over his shoulder, 'You're my second visitor this afternoon. Mrs Bingham called on me a little earlier.'

'Yes, I passed her in the lane,' Stella replied. 'What did she want?'

'To satisfy her curiosity, I suspect, although she said she came to welcome me into the village.' He still felt vaguely guilty over his reception of her although he tried to brush it to one side as a natural response to Mrs Bingham's own assumption that he would be suitably grateful for her interest. Partly out of this need for self-justification, he continued, 'I'm afraid I rather snubbed her. She was too much the lady of the manor for my liking.'

'Oh, she's all right,' Stella said offhandedly, 'although I see what you mean. She can be a bit bossy at times.'

Perfectly at home herself, she had thrown open the fur fabric jacket she was wearing and had crossed her legs in their tight jeans, showing spiky high-heeled shoes, spattered with mud from the lane.

He supposed a lot of men would find her desirable but she was too physical for him; too much breast and hip; too highly coloured with her blonde hair, her bright lipstick and iridescent eyelids. The perfume she was wearing was already permeating the caravan, making the back of his nose tickle. He preferred women who were more subtle and low key.

All the same, it amused him to see her sitting there, knowing what his wife's reaction would be.

'But she's so dreadfully common-looking!'

Joanna would, of course, immediately suspect an affair and be outraged not only at his unfaithfulness but also at his lack of taste.

It was part of his sense of freedom on leaving her that he no longer had to concern himself with her standards. He could choose his friends, his clothes, his way of life without having them subjected to her judgement of what was or was not good taste, whatever the ridiculous phrase meant. He suspected that Mrs Bingham shared much the same attitude which was one of the reasons why he had wanted to put her in her place.

'Been to the solicitor's yet?' he asked, carrying the two mugs of tea through from the kitchen.

'No, not yet. That's why I've come to see you. I didn't like to phone them up 'cos I wasn't sure what to say. I wondered if you'd help me write a letter.'

'There's no need,' he replied, guessing that she was unused to the telephone. 'I'm seeing my solicitor tomorrow. Would you like me to fix up an appointment for you? There's Mr Sanderson who I deal with – he's rather elderly – or his partner, Mr Pickering, who's much younger.'

'Oh, I'll take the young one,' Stella said and laughed. 'But would you really do that for me? I'd be ever so grateful.'

'Of course; it's no trouble. What time would suit you best?'

'Try to make it an afternoon about four o'clock. I'm starting work at the Goat on Monday behind the bar and I don't want to ask for time off. If it's late afternoon, then I can catch the twenty past three bus into Studham after the pub shuts. What should I say when I see him?'

'Just tell him what's happened and why you want a divorce. It's quite straightforward. He'll ask you any questions he thinks necessary. Sugar?' He offered the bowl, hoping to divert her attention away from the subject of her marriage which she was quite clearly going to recount in detail.

'No, ta; I'm sweet enough already.' She smiled briefly. 'I suppose it'll be all right. After all, he did knock me about; Ken, I mean. I told him the last time, if he touched me again, I'd leave. But more fool me, I suppose. I should never have married him.'

'Why did you?' Despite himself, Alec was curious. The glimpse into another type of marriage interested him.

'I nearly didn't. We'd quarrelled, you see, and I'd broken it off. Then I found I was pregnant so it was on again. Even then I needn't have bothered. I had another offer.'

'An offer?' Alec repeated.

She laughed and shrugged.

'Oh, it was daft really. I couldn't have accepted it. Anyway, my mum got on to me about marrying Ken when she found out about the baby. Her nerves were bad, you see, 'cos my dad had just died so in the end I said yes. If I'd known what was going to happen, I'd've stuck it out. You see, I lost the baby soon afterwards. We were living with my mum then, before we got the maisonette at Studham. It was after we moved that he started knocking me about.'

'I'm sorry,' Alec said. It seemed an inadequate remark to make, considering the tragic confusion of her life.

She shrugged again, lifting her shoulders as if dismissing both her own situation and his commiseration.

'He was paying me back for having chucked him over although he'd always had a temper. That's the reason I ditched him in the first place. I thought things'd be different once we were married.'

'But they weren't?'

'He seemed to think he owned me. I got fed up with it so I walked out.' She started to laugh, throwing back her hair. 'I left a pile of his dirty socks on the kitchen table with my wedding ring on top of them. What about you? What made you decide to pack up and leave?'

'Me?' He was still smiling at the image of the socks and the ring. It seemed churlish not to respond although he was careful, not knowing her capacity for discretion, to be non-committal. 'Boredom mainly. Incompatibility. I don't know.'

'Been married long?'

'Fifteen years.'

'Any kids?'

'Just the one.'

She pulled a little face.

'It's always sad, divorce, I mean, when there's kiddies involved.'

'He's nearly twelve.'

'Oh well, then it isn't as if he's too young to understand.'

'Yes,' he said.

The conversation was beginning to wind down. To give Stella her due, she seemed aware of it. Getting to her feet, she swung her bag over her shoulder and pulled the edges of her fur fabric jacket together.

'I ought to be getting along. Ta very much for the tea. You won't forget about fixing up that appointment?'

'I'll remember,' he assured her. 'I'll let you know the details later.'

'Drop by the Goat on Friday evening. I'll be in there I expect and you can tell me then. I'll treat you to a drink at the same time.'

'Thanks,' he said. 'I'll take you up on that.'

He watched her leave over the half-door, tittupping down the concrete path in her high heels towards the gate. He wondered if she might pass Joanna in the lane and what they would make of each other, that is if they troubled to look. He had already guessed Joanna's reaction. Stella's, he thought, would be more warm-hearted and admiring.

TWO

Joanna drew the car into the side of the lane just before the ford and stared at the water which swirled across the road a few feet in front of the wheels.

Alec had told her to take the turning immediately before the Goat public house but had said nothing about this particular hazard.

'Aren't you going to drive across it?' Simon asked.

He had wound down the window on the passenger's side to crane his head out.

'No,' Joanna said abruptly.

'Why not?'

'Because it looks too deep and I don't want to stall the car.'

'But if you drive very slowly and don't make waves, it should be all right,' Simon replied in his grown-up, sensible manner.

'I'm not driving through it!' Joanna retorted, raising her voice.

At times, Simon was so like Alec that she wanted to slap him. Alec had treated her with the same slightly superior rationality, making light of her worries so that they appeared even to her so trivial and of so little consequence that she was forced into unreasonableness in order to defend them.

The damned ford was a typical example. Of course it would probably be quite safe to drive through it. As it was there on a hard-surfaced lane, presumably other cars must use it. No doubt Alec drove through it every day without any difficulty. But as her own driving experience was limited to shopping trips in Chelmsford with only short excursions outside the town, crossing fords was not part of it.

Irrationally – or was it? – she could imagine the car stuck in the middle with water coming up through the floor and the engine irreparably damaged.

And wasn't the whole situation Alec's fault anyway? After all, it was he who had chosen to walk out on them both and then bury himself miles from anywhere without even a telephone.

'If you like, I could go and measure the water with a stick,' Simon offered, looking at her with that concerned expression which, at twelve years old, was too adult to be entirely natural or desirable. He was already assuming responsibility for her.

Joanna made up her mind.

'I'm leaving the car here.'

'It'll block up the lane,' Simon pointed out.

'I don't damn well care!' she exclaimed but all the same, she reversed the car a few yards before bumping it up on to the verge, hearing something scrape along the exhaust pipe as she did so.

Simon winced but kept silent apart from saying in a plaintive voice as he opened the passenger door, 'I can't get out this side. There's a ditch.'

'Then get out this side!' she said angrily.

He scrambled out, hunching his shoulders as he always did when she raised her voice at him.

Standing together in the lane, they surveyed the car which was leaning at a drunken angle in the long wet grass, a bramble caught underneath it.

God alone knew how she'd drive it away, Joanna thought. She might even overturn it in the ditch, that is if she could get the damned thing to start. The scraping noise had sounded ominous.

'It's all right, mummy,' Simon assured her although both of them knew it was a crazy place to park. The verge was too high. She'd've done better to attempt the ford.

'Oh, come on,' Joanna said wearily, turning to walk away. She felt close to tears with the despair and frustration of it all; not just the car but Alec's desertion after fifteen years of marriage, the worry about paying for the house and Simon's school fees, what she was going to say to her mother.

'How far do we have to go?' Simon asked, hurrying to catch up with her.

'How should I know?' she replied. 'I haven't been here before either. It's probably miles.'

That was an exaggeration. Alec had written in his letter: 'If you insist on coming to talk things over, although, quite frankly, I don't see the point, you'll find the caravan on the left about half a mile along Waterend Lane, a turning just before the Goat.'

As she had already driven roughly that distance, the caravan couldn't be more than a couple of hundred yards away.

'I'll ask!' Simon announced, running ahead before she could stop him towards a woman who was about to cross a narrow, raised footbridge which spanned the left-hand side of the ford, his feet clattering excitedly on the wooden boards.

Joanna waited in the lane. There was not room enough for them both to pass on the bridge and besides, she did not want to become involved with anyone from the place where Alec was now living. The woman, too, had that bold, over-confident air about her which Joanna had always found difficult to cope with when she met it in waitresses or shop assistants.

She was blonde and looked as if she would laugh too loudly and easily. A satchel handbag was slung casually across one shoulder of a fur fabric jacket worn over a V-necked blue jumper and a pair of jeans cut so tight across the hips that the front placket was stretched open to show the zip.

Her voice in answer to Simon's question could easily be heard across the few feet of water.

'It's just up there. You can't miss it. There's a gate. Visiting, are you?'

'Simon!' Joanna called out warningly but too late.

She heard him reply, 'We're going to see my father.'

'That's nice,' the woman replied, her voice indulgent, before walking on across the bridge, giving Joanna a glance and a smile as she reached the other side.

Joanna ignored her, pretending to see neither, her eyes on Simon who had run back to lean over the hand-rail.

'Mind you don't fall!' she called out, hurrying on to the bridge.

'Oh, don't be silly, mummy,' he replied. 'Look, I told you it's not very deep. You could easily have driven through it.' Glancing up at her, he added enthusiastically, 'Isn't it super here!'

She looked about her, trying to see the place through his eyes – the high hedges in small leaf, the brown water sliding under their feet, the grassy banks scattered with tiny, yellow, star-shaped flowers, but could find nothing to say in answer except, 'It's cold,' before turning up her coat collar and walking on.

The caravan was awful. Even Simon seemed subdued at the sight of it. Small, ugly, its tin sides blotched with rust, it squatted in one corner of a field with a pathetic little patch of overgrown garden round it and a plastic washing line slung between two iron posts.

'Does daddy really live here?' he asked.

Before Joanna had time to reply, Alec was at the door of the caravan and coming down the steps to ruffle Simon's hair.

'So you found me?' he asked, turning to her last of all.

'Obviously,' she replied coldly.

'But mummy wouldn't drive through the ford,' Simon announced. 'We left the car on the other side.'

'It's perfectly safe, providing you keep in bottom gear and don't take it too fast,' Alec said, addressing her over his shoulder as he led the way into the caravan with one of his maddening casual, half-amused, half-impatient glances as if the information was so damned obvious it really didn't need stating.

She guessed then that the omission to mention the ford in his letter had been deliberate. He had wanted her to face it without any warning as some kind of stupid test. Perhaps he had even hoped that the car might have broken down in the middle although she admitted that this was probably unfair. But with Alec, one could never be sure.

She felt her frustration harden into a feeling very like hatred.

'Go out and play, Simon,' she said. 'I want to talk to daddy on my own.'

He was exploring the caravan with that infuriating curiosity of his which allowed him to leave nothing alone, bouncing on the bench seat, lifting the flap of the table experimentally, pulling aside the curtain to reveal a quite squalid little kitchen fitted with ply cupboards and a tiny cooker, its white enamel top blackened with patches of burned-on grease.

'But what shall I do?' he demanded, facing her, his mouth gone square which told her he was close to tears. She understood for the first time the effect all of it was having on him and nearly wept herself.

How dare Alec do this to him? How bloody dare he?

She was pleased to see that Alec himself realised Simon's unhappiness for his face suddenly went taut.

'There's a stream just over there on the other side of the field,' he said in his kind voice, the one he only ever seemed to use now for Simon. 'Why don't you go out and have a look at it? I'll come and join you in about a quarter of an hour.'

As soon as Simon had gone, clumping down the caravan steps and walking dispiritedly away across the field, his hands in his blazer pockets, Joanna let her anger break.

'Do you realise what this is doing to him?' she demanded furiously.

'I'm sorry,' Alec replied. He wouldn't look at her but stood watching Simon through the open doorway.

Her anger seemed to release a new awareness in her so that she was able to study her husband as if he were someone she had just met, noticing with a sense of shock how much he had aged and how neglected he appeared. His hair needed cutting. It was so long at the back that it touched the collar of the open-necked plaid shirt he was wearing. He had on his old trousers, the ones he used to wear at home when he cleaned the car, the torn back pocket, which she had meant to mend but had never got round to doing, still hanging down at one side.

The sight of it seemed to feed her anger and her despair.

'Sorry?' she repeated, aware that her voice had gone shrill. 'That's typical of you! So damned glib! You walk out and expect . . .'

'Look, Joanna,' he said, swinging round to face her. 'If

you've come here hoping for a row, then you won't get one. The marriage is over. That's final as far as I'm concerned. All that's left to talk about is what arrangements we can come to. I'm sorry about Simon. I mean that quite genuinely. But I can't go on living with you and trying to keep up the pretence of being happy for his sake. He's young; he'll get over it eventually. I told you in the letter that I wanted a divorce and I'm prepared to make the best settlement I can so that you and Simon won't be too badly off; at least financially. You can have the house and the furniture. All I shall want to take is my books . . .'

'But how on earth am I expected to keep the house going and pay for Simon's school fees?' she interrupted. It was the greatest of her practical worries. After Alec had left, she had gone through the accounts which he had always dealt with, totting up the amounts – the insurance, payments to BUPA, the gas, telephone and electricity bills and these didn't include the mortgage or the weekly housekeeping expenses – and had been appalled at the total.

'Then sell the damned place!' he said impatiently. 'Get something smaller that you can afford. For God's sake, Joanna, why do you need four bedrooms and a bloody utility room? It's absurd! I told you that when we bought the place but you insisted on having it.'

'Absurd! It was you who were absurd, wanting to buy that semi-derelict farmhouse in the middle of nowhere, miles from the shops and Simon's prep school . . .'

It was an old quarrel which she thought she had won but which she saw now had been more important to him than she had realised.

He said with a shrugging, weary gesture, 'It doesn't matter any more. That's water under the bridge. We have to face the facts as they are now. If you can't afford to keep the house, then buy something you can or get a job.'

'A job!' It was so outrageous that she laughed.

'Why not?' he demanded. 'You're a qualified secretary. You were earning good money before we married.'

'But that was fifteen years ago! Things have changed since then. It's all word processors and computers now.'

'Then re-train,' he told her. 'Take a bloody course. You're not incapable and you're the one who's so keen on Women's Lib.'

He turned away in so dismissive a manner that she wanted to hit out at him with her fists. But she was too frightened of him to risk it, not knowing how this new Alec, hard, seedy, utterly unapproachable, would react.

Instead, she said, 'You're mad, you know. George Hetherington thinks so, throwing over your job like that. He came to see me the other evening. He said you could have been on the board when Mr Tolby retires.'

That, too, was something of an exaggeration. George Hetherington hadn't actually promised a directorship; he had only said it was likely. As for Alec's madness, he had not expressed that opinion quite so forcibly, merely murmuring vaguely that Alec might be passing through an emotional crisis which some men experienced at certain stages in their lives.

'Probably hormones,' he had added in an embarrassed manner.

But none of it had any effect on Alec except to amuse him.

'Really? How typical of old George! But I don't give a damn about his opinion or his directorship. As far as I'm concerned, he can stuff both of them. Can't you understand, Joanna, I've loathed that job for the past five years? Look, now you're here, let's sit down and go over the whole thing sensibly. Sit down!' he repeated sharply, as she hesitated.

As she sat down on the bench seat, she was aware of a perfume lingering on the cushions which was released from the flowered fabric. It was a cheap, musky scent which she remembered catching a trace of from that woman who had passed her in the lane.

Suddenly the whole situation was clear to her. In fact, she was surprised that she hadn't seen it before. The woman had been coming from the caravan. There was nowhere else she could have been – no other house or cottage was in sight. And that fact accounted for her interest in their own visit and the smile and glance she had given to Joanna.

The damned nerve! And here was Alec, so obviously doubly in the wrong now, talking about her selling the house and finding a job when all the time it was he who was to blame by walking out with no real reason and then picking up with that awful, common, blonde woman.

'. . . I'll get a local solicitor to act for me in Studham where I'm going to be living. That way you can still keep on Blakely who handled the house. I don't know how long the divorce will take . . .'

'Divorce?' She began to concentrate on what he was saying. The realisation about the woman had cleared her mind, leaving it quite cold and hard. Ten minutes ago she might have blurted out what she knew in anger. Now, listening to him talking to her in that infuriating reasonable tone of voice, the one she'd heard him use to his secretary on occasions, she knew she must keep that particular piece of information to herself. 'On what grounds?'

'For God's sake, Joanna, don't you ever listen to what's said to you? You can use my desertion if you like or the irrevocable breakdown of the marriage.'

'And supposing I don't want to?'

'It won't make any difference. If you don't start proceedings, then I shall. The marriage is over. I shan't be coming back. As for Simon's school fees . . .'

'It doesn't matter,' she said stiffly. 'I'll manage somehow.'

'I'm sorry. I'll try to help out with those if I can. As I said in the letter, I won't make any claims on the house. That's yours outright. It should be worth about £80,000, if not more. I'm cashing in my life insurance policy which will get me started. I'll make the other policy, the endowment, over to you although you'll have to keep up the payments on it. In addition, there's about £2000 in the building society. I'm sorry it's not more but we seemed to spend most of what I earned. Maintenance for Simon will have to be worked out when I know how much I'll be earning from the shop but it probably won't be much, at least to begin with.' Seeing her expression, he broke off to repeat, 'I'm sorry, Joanna.'

'Yes,' she said. There seemed nothing else to add. She got up, brushing her sleeve where it had come into contact with the cheap scent on the cushions.

He got up as well, looking suddenly awkward.

'I'll go and talk to Simon. Do you want to stay here? You could make yourself some tea if you like.'

As he indicated the kitchen with its filthy stove, she shook her head.

'No, thank you. Tell Simon I'll be waiting in the car.'

She walked to the door, Alec following her. He seemed disconcerted by her new, abrupt manner.

'About access to Simon,' he began.

'I'll have to speak to my solicitor about that,' she replied, turning away towards the gate.

'Joanna, please don't make any difficulties over Simon!' he called out after her.

Ignoring him, she shut the gate behind her and set off down the lane.

Simon was crouching by the side of the stream, hands on the knees of his grey, school-uniform trousers to keep his balance.

Seen like this from the back, he looked small and vulnerable especially about the nape of his neck which still had that exposed, fragile nakedness of a much younger child.

Alec said, 'Hello, there,' and squatted down beside him.

For several seconds they remained in silence, watching the water swirling past, forming miniature eddies and rapids. A twig came into sight, lodged against a stone and then, caught once more in the torrent, hurtled out of sight towards the ford.

Alec had been on the point of saying, 'Do you remember playing Pooh sticks when we were on holiday in Cornwall?' But before he could speak, Simon said without turning his head, 'Are you really not coming home any more?'

'No, Simon.'

It was better that he learned the truth.

The boy looked up, his eyes troubled.

24

'Not ever?'

'No.'

'But where will you live? Not in that caravan?'

'No. I'm going to move to Studham. I'm buying, or rather leasing, a shop there—a bookshop. You'll be able to come and visit me.'

'Will I? But how will I get there?'

'I don't know yet. Perhaps on the bus. There must be a bus. Or perhaps I can come and pick you up from home.'

'Mummy says we may have to leave the house. She cried when she told me. If we do, I'll have to give up my bedroom, won't I?'

Alec knew what was going on in his son's mind as clearly as if the thoughts had been printed on his face. Only last year, he had redecorated the boy's bedroom, fitting it up with shelves and a worktop so that he could do his model-making without disorganising the sitting-room. Funnily enough, he minded as much about its potential loss as Simon himself. Messing about with wood and screws in its construction, he had felt genuinely happy for the first time for years. But he was angered, too, by what he saw as Joanna's manipulation of the situation, wondering if the tears had been genuine or contrived.

He said, 'I don't know what will happen about the house, Simon. Nothing's been decided yet. But if it's sold, you'll have another bedroom somewhere else.'

Harsh though it was, that truth would also have to be faced but as he spoke, he saw Simon's face close over and he knew that he had already begun to lose his son. He had been a fool not to see the inevitability of it when he had decided to walk out. It was a process which, once started, could never be reversed, like decay. Each time they met from now on, the child would be a little further distanced from him. The thought of it filled him with an overwhelming sadness and a nostalgia for the past he had shared with his son – of games of football on the lawn and of teaching him to swim, his hand cupped under Simon's chin.

Simon stood up. 'I think I ought to go back now. Mummy's waiting for me, I expect.'

'Yes,' Alec replied. 'She's gone to the car.'

They started back across the field in silence which Alec found too painful to maintain.

'How's school?' he asked, aware that it would have been better to say nothing. His voice was much too bright and interested.

'All right,' the boy replied. There was a grudging air about him and they both fell silent again.

But when they parted by the steps of the caravan, neither quite certain how the farewell should be conducted, it was Simon who suddenly seized his father round the waist and buried his face in his shirt before, breaking free, he ran off towards the gate without looking back.

Joanna watched him come clattering across the footbridge towards where she was standing by the car. Returning to it from the caravan, she had at first been reduced to tears at the sight of it, frightened at the thought of having to drive it away. But, waiting for Simon to come back, her tears had dried although she could still feel the skin under her eyes taut and sore. She was aware now of a new hardness inside her. She was damned if she'd let herself be beaten!

As Simon approached, she got into the driving seat and wound down the window.

'You'll have to help me, Simon,' she told him. 'I don't want to tip the car over into the ditch.'

His face, which had been sullen and closed, took on a more interested expression.

'Do you want me to wave you out?' he asked.

'Please. Watch the wheels on the far side.'

As he walked back a few feet to take up his position, she called out, 'What did daddy say?'

'Nothing,' he replied, his back towards her.

She started the engine. He would probably tell her later. Knowing him, she guessed he would let it slip out when he was less defensive as a casual remark, spoken before he knew what he was saying.

This realisation, like the one regarding the woman, gave her an unexpected sense of power. It was a new game, the

26

rules of which she was learning faster than she had thought herself capable.

As the car edged forwards and the wheels bumped down on to the road, this feeling of triumph increased.

'Well done, mummy!' Simon was saying, using one of Alec's expressions as he scrambled into the passenger seat beside her. 'You made it!'

She gave him a smile.

Well done indeed!

THREE _____

Madge heard the front door close as Gordon returned from his house calls just as the kettle came to the boil. The timing pleased her. It proved that they – the fates, the gods, call them what you like – were on her side after all although the encounter with Alec Lawson still rankled.

Carrying the tea-tray through to the drawing-room, she found Gordon stooping down towards the fire which she had lit against the damp afternoon, still wearing his overcoat, rubbing his hands and holding them out to the blaze.

He looked flushed and rumpled as he always did after he had made his afternoon visits, a changed image of him which she generally preferred but today, for some irrational reason, it exasperated her.

A big man, he seemed suddenly too large for the room. She wanted his indoor self, calm, relaxed, unemotional; not this tall, overcoated figure, smelling of the open air and still charged up with the energy of driving from one patient to the other in a large and scattered practice.

'Good to see a fire,' he commented, adding almost immediately, 'Any messages while I was out?'

'They'll be on the answering machine,' she replied.

'Oh, I see. So you were out this afternoon?'

He didn't really expect a full explanation. He never did, which was another of his qualities she found mildly annoying. His lack of curiosity about her life, while well meant, had the effect sometimes of making it seem uninteresting even to herself.

'I went for a walk,' she said. She could have left it there but she felt the need to offer some reason, more for her own sake than his. As it was obviously better not to use the excuse of the electricity bill, still propped up on the mantelpiece, she added, 'I wanted some fresh air.' After a pause in which she watched Gordon drinking his tea, she continued, 'I met Alec Lawson while I was out.'

The statement was vague enough to imply nothing more than an accidental encounter in the village.

'Alec Lawson?' Gordon asked. 'Do I know the name?'

'I have told you about him,' Madge replied. 'He's moved into Macey's caravan, the one that's parked in the field near the ford. He was telling me he's opening a bookshop in Studham.'

'I shouldn't have thought he'd have much success there,' Gordon commented, holding out his cup to be refilled but shaking his head at the proffered ginger cake which Madge had bought in the shop on her way home.

'Why not?' she asked.

She was of the same opinion. After all, there was already one bookshop in Studham, Luckham's, and the town was hardly large enough to support two. But Gordon's sweeping statement annoyed her.

It had the desired effect. He looked at her directly for the first time.

'I don't know, Madge. Perhaps he will. I haven't met the man. He may be the world's best businessman and I'm doing him an injustice.'

'He's rather arrogant.'

As she said it, Madge felt oddly appeased, as if the whole point of the conversation had now been reached.

But Gordon, who had finished his second cup of tea and was getting to his feet, merely replied, 'In that case, he may make a huge success of it. Either way, good luck to him.'

'I met someone else while I was out,' Madge continued, beginning to pile up the tray with the used china. 'Stella Franklin, as she used to be.'

That piece of information really interested him as Madge knew it would. Stella's miscarriage following so soon after Mr Franklin's death had meant that the family had taken up a great deal of Gordon's professional care at the time.

'Stella? What's she doing back in the village? Visiting her mother?'

'I rather doubt that. You know Stella. She had that defiant look about her. I had the feeling she may have left her husband.' Madge couldn't resist adding, 'Anyway, it seems to be Alec Lawson she's visiting.'

'You shouldn't listen to gossip,' Gordon told her.

'Sometimes it's very difficult not to as you very well know yourself,' Madge retorted, stung by his attitude for he had frequently passed on to her little titbits of local news he had picked up on his rounds, usually with an amused air although sometimes with the more serious intention of informing her, in one of her more public roles as school governor or Guild chairwoman, of some cause for her concern.

At the same time, she was pleased that he had assumed that she had been told about Stella and Alec Lawson in the village, not witnessed the evidence of the relationship herself. It saved a lot of explanation.

Gordon was saying, 'I thought she'd settle down once she was married. Oh, well. I'll go and see what's on that damned machine.'

He held the door open for her as she carried the tray out.

Bartlett had been for his money. As soon as she entered the kitchen, Madge could see that the envelope that she had left on the window-sill above the sink had gone and his empty mug was standing on the draining-board.

Putting the tray down beside it, she went out to the garden to find him but he had already left. The shed door was shut and the bonfire was reduced to a few blackened twigs and a mound of white ash which the wind was blowing away.

Walking back along the path towards the house, she thought with amusement how, even if she had not known him, she might have been able to guess something of Bartlett's character simply by looking at the vegetable garden. It was neat with that slow, painstaking care he showed even when riding his bike, head bowed, as if struggling against a non-existent wind, one foot pressing down on the pedal, the other fixed because of his lame leg. Perhaps because of this, she had never seen him free-wheel, not even downhill. He merely slowed down by using his brakes, reducing it to the same rate of solemn progress.

It was because of this lack of imagination and verve that she had never allowed him to touch the flower borders. He would have staked and pruned and trimmed them into submission. Consequently, they burgeoned in a profusion of shrubs and roses and flowers which she preferred.

Seeing the lines of seedling plants, each one pricked out exactly equidistant from the next, a little wooden peg marking the end of every row, she felt an exasperated compassion for the man.

Poor old Bartlett!

Unmarried, he had lived with his widowed mother until her death, a cantankerous old woman who had been the bane of Gordon's life with her constant complaints; so goodness knows what it had been like for Bartlett sharing the same house, although he had put up with her with a dour, uncomplaining acceptance. He still occupied the same cottage near the church, unchanged since Mrs Bartlett's time down to the chipped earthenware sink in the kitchen and the old-fashioned furniture.

Quite apart from his mother when she had been alive, Bartlett had another cross to bear. An accident on a tractor had broken his leg in three places, in consequence of which he had been forced to give up work on Sutton's farm. He'd been insured, of course, and had been awarded a lump sum in compensation as well as a pension which he supplemented by acting as a jobbing gardener to a few people in the village like herself who wanted his services, including the vicar and two or three of the wealthier farmers whose interest in the land didn't extend to their own vegetable plots.

She wished she liked him better but she found him difficult to talk to. There was a melancholy air about him, understandable when one considered the circumstances of his life although even this didn't make her feel any warmer towards him.

He had a habit, too, of creeping about the place as if afraid of asserting himself which she found exasperating at times. His letting himself into the kitchen to leave his empty mug and collect his money was only one example of this. Anyone else would have called out to let her know he was there. But not Bartlett. He'd probably knocked but not loud enough to be heard because she had been in the drawing-room with Gordon.

She wondered what they'd been talking about and whether Bartlett might have been able to overhear but couldn't remember the conversation apart from her comments on Alec Lawson, which hardly mattered.

And then the silly man had crept off without a word when she had wanted to discuss with him the possibility of moving the strawberry bed to the other side of the garden where it would get more sun or, at least, lopping back some of the overhanging branches which were casting too much shade.

Now it would have to wait until she saw him the following week.

As soon as Stella turned out of Waterend Lane and crossed the road by the Goat, she saw her husband's car parked outside the house and almost went on past it. Then, shrugging, she pushed open the gate and walked up the path and round to the back door.

What else could she do? There was nowhere she could go to wait until he had left apart from the shop and she didn't fancy the thought of going in there and meeting the stares of the other women.

Besides, knowing Ken, he'd go on waiting until she did return. He never gave up easily.

Her mother must have seen her go past the front window because, by the time Stella reached the back door, she was in the kitchen, mouthing through the glass, 'Ken's here,' and jerking her head in the direction of the living-room.

Stella mouthed back, 'I know,' at the same time pulling a face to show her distaste.

'He turned up five minutes ago,' Mrs Franklin added in a massive undertone as Stella let herself into the kitchen.

'So what?' she replied in her normal voice.

No-one, not even Ken, was going to frighten her into whispering in her own home.

He was standing by the fireplace, wearing his oil-stained overalls, so he must have knocked off work early and come straight from Hubbard's garage.

'What are you doing here?' Stella asked him.

'I want to see you, Stell,' he replied.

'You've seen me,' she said dismissively, taking off her jacket and hanging it up on the peg behind the front door which opened directly into the garden. Sitting down on one of the chairs by the fire, she began poking the coals into a blaze, asserting her right to be there and leaving him standing.

She could tell by his expression that he was controlling his temper with difficulty. That taut, white look and the sharp edge to his jaw always meant trouble.

Well, she didn't care. If he started anything, she'd bloody well give him a mouthful in return. And if he laid a finger on her, she'd do what she'd threatened and charge him with assault. So let him put that in his pipe.

All the same, she couldn't help feeling sorry for him. He looked so damned awkward standing there, like some big kid who'd had his bag of sweets taken off him and didn't know whether to cry or lash out with his fists.

She said impatiently, 'Oh, for God's sake, sit down now you're here,' adding, as he took the chair opposite her, looking pleased as if the invitation were a sign of her capitulation, 'You're wasting your time though. I'm not coming back.'

He leaned forward and tried to touch her knee which she twitched away out of his reach.

'I'm sorry I hit you, Stell. I didn't mean it. I lost my temper.'

'That's no excuse. You're always bloody losing your temper. No-one's going to knock me about.'

'It won't happen again, promise.'

'No, it won't,' she said sharply, ''cos I shan't be there to let it.'

'You mean that? You're not coming back?'

He looked so surprised that she nearly burst out laughing.

'What else do you want me to do? Put it in writing for you? You can't say I didn't warn you. "You touch me again," I told you, "and I'll walk out." Which I did. Which is why I'm here now.'

Mrs Franklin came into the room at this moment, carrying a tray of tea-things which she put down, grim-mouthed, on the table under the window.

Ken turned to her in appeal.

'You talk to her.'

'I'm not interfering,' Mrs Franklin replied, rattling the cups on to their saucers. 'It's between you and her. All I'll say is this – her father never so much as raised his voice to me in all the forty-five years we was married. And I got my money regular.'

'Well, she won't get a penny out of me!' Ken retorted, his own voice getting louder.

'I don't want your bloody money,' Stella replied, looking pleased at having provoked him. 'I can pay my own way, ta very much.'

'Doing what?' Ken asked with a sneer.

'That's enough of that!' Mrs Franklin cried, the colour high in her face. 'If you can't be civil, then you're not welcome in my house.'

To emphasise her point, she banged down the jug, sending

33

a little white spurt of milk over the tray, and, marching over to the door, threw it open.

Ken went, pushing his chair back against the wall and slamming the door so violently behind him that the window rattled. A passer-by stopped to stare as, flinging himself into his car, he drove off at speed down the road.

'Bloody maniac!' Stella commented but not without a certain satisfaction in her voice.

Mrs Franklin sat down hurriedly to hide the trembling in her legs.

'That was Mrs Armitage outside. It'll be all over the village by tomorrow.'

'Who cares?' Stella said carelessly.

'I do,' her mother retorted. 'It's me who has to live here. Honestly, Stella, I don't know where you get your ideas from. Not from me nor your dad neither. He hated any unpleasantness. You seem to go out of your way to look for it.'

'No I don't.'

'You do with Ken. You ought to try and butter him up a bit more.'

'Butter him up!' Stella repeated the phrase with derisive emphasis.

'Well, you know what I mean,' Mrs Franklin replied, looking flustered. 'Give in to him sometimes; make him feel he's the boss. You know how touchy he is and no man likes to be put down, especially by a woman.'

'And what about him putting me down?' Stella demanded. '"Fetch this. Do that. Where's my bloody tea?" I'm not going to be talked to like that by anybody.'

'You always did stand up for yourself, even at school,' Mrs Franklin admitted, half admiringly, half in despair. 'I remember the fuss there was about that needlework teacher and me having to go up there to see the headmistress.'

'If you don't look out for yourself, no-one else will,' Stella said.

'I don't know where you get it from,' Mrs Franklin repeated helplessly. 'And your language, Stella. You really ought to watch that. It's got awful since you've been working in that pub. Your dad wouldn't have liked it.' Encouraged by the contrite expression on her daughter's face, she continued, 'Perhaps if you'd had the baby, things would've been different.'

Stella, who had turned away from the window, paused in the act of lifting the tea-pot as if about to say something. Then, shrugging, she finished pouring two cups of tea which she carried over to the fire.

'Here,' she said, handing one to her mother, 'drink that, mum, and have one of my ciggies to go with it.' Bending down to light the cigarette for her, Stella added, 'If I'd had the baby, where'd I be now? Even worse off. He'd've probably taken it out on the kid as well. As for me, I'd've had two mouths to feed. I'm better off on my own. Which reminds me, I haven't told you yet. I've got a job.'

'What job?' Mrs Franklin asked, puffing nervously at the cigarette.

'Barmaid over at the Goat. Fred Mitchell asked me if I'd like to work there this lunchtime when I dropped in for a drink. They've been getting a lot more casual trade and they're rushed off their feet. Eva can't cope like she used to. Anyway, I told him yes and I start there on Monday. So I don't need Ken or anybody else come to that to look after me. I can pay my own way and take care of myself.'

'I only hope to God you're right,' Mrs Franklin replied.

FOUR

On Friday evening at approximately five past seven, Stella left the house, calling out goodbye to her mother who was listening to *The Archers* on the radio while she did the ironing.

'Shan't be long, mum. I'm going over to the Goat.'

She had gone before Mrs Franklin could call out in reply.

It had stopped raining and there was a watery moon shining, dodging in and out behind low clouds which threatened further rain. Big puddles still stood in the road, reflecting lighter patches of sky, and Stella picked her way round them as she walked the short distance to the Goat where the curtains were drawn over the lighted windows and the lamp on the corner of the building shed a cone of brilliance on to the car-park, already half-full of customers' vehicles.

The interior of the public house was warm and cheerful, a log fire burning at the far end of the bar by the tables with Eva's bits of brass hanging on the wall above it, catching the glow from the flames and reflecting it. The place looked festive and Christmassy.

Smiling, pleased to be there among the crowd and the noise, Stella nodded to several regulars she knew – Ted Macey, Jim and Doreen Saltmarsh, poor old Reg Bartlett sitting morosely by himself in a corner – as she pushed her way towards the counter where Eva, looking flustered, was pulling a pint for a man in a tweed hacking jacket, one of the casuals by the look of him, who was rattling off the rest of his order before she had time to finish getting his first.

Fred, looking hot and bothered himself, his face red and his shirt collar open, came to serve her.

'By God,' he said, 'I'll be glad when you start here on Monday.'

'I'd offer to help you out now,' Stella replied, 'only I'm expecting to meet someone. Mr Lawson not in yet?'

'Lawson? Oh, him that's got Macey's caravan. No, I haven't seen him this evening although he was in here at lunchtime. Perhaps he'll drop by later. What'll you have, Stella? The usual?'

'Ta,' she said.

She stayed at the counter, drinking her gin and orange and watching the door but, although several more regulars arrived, Alec Lawson wasn't among them. One of the new arrivals, Frank Beamish, joined her at the bar, ordering a pint before turning to speak to her. She had gone out with him in the old days before she met Ken. He was married now with two kids but that didn't stop him from looking her up and down with the same leering smile, so he hadn't changed much.

'What you doing back here, Stella?' he asked, his eyes on the V neck of her jumper. 'Chucked the old man over?'

'Minding my own business, the same as you should be doing,' she told him, adding sweetly, 'How's Eileen and the kids?'

He took the hint, saying grudgingly, 'Oh, all right, I suppose,' before moving off to join his friends who were making up a darts four.

Seeing her glass was empty, Fred Mitchell came back to her.

'Want a refill?' he asked. 'On the house this time.'

'No, thanks,' Stella said. She glanced at the clock behind the bar, Fred Mitchell following her eyes. The time was nearly twenty-five past seven. 'I'll hang on until Mr Lawson arrives. I promised to stand him a drink.'

'He's usually in here by now, if he's coming. Perhaps he's forgotten,' Fred Mitchell suggested.

As he spoke, Reg Bartlett got to his feet and came towards the bar, carrying his empty glass.

Stella crushed out the cigarette she had just lit and drew the edges of her jacket together.

'Perhaps he has,' she agreed hurriedly. 'I think I'll change my mind and walk up to the caravan to see him. He's got a message for me that's important. I'll drop in again on my way back and give you a hand behind the bar.'

'See you later then,' Mitchell called out as she turned away and began edging through the crowd towards the door which swung shut behind her.

'Damn!' Gordon said, coming back into the drawing-room from having answered the telephone. He was struggling to put on his overcoat while holding his medical bag and a small white paper sack in which prescriptions were put.

'Who was it?' Madge asked.

'Mrs Baxter. Her son's had another of his asthma attacks. I'd better get over there straight away. I was saying "damn" about this though.' Putting down his bag, he held up the paper sack. 'Ted Macey's prescription. He said he'd call for it on his way back from Studham later this morning. I've just found it in the dispensary. My fault entirely. Mrs Locke did tell me he hadn't collected it. I meant to drop it off at his house while I was out on my afternoon rounds.'

'Is it important?' Madge asked.

'He evidently doesn't think so otherwise he'd've made an effort to pick it up himself. But you know Ted. He never takes that ulcer of his seriously until it starts playing him up. He probably felt better and thought he wouldn't be bothered.'

'Then I don't see why you should,' Madge said firmly. She felt Gordon was too soft with some of his patients.

'Oh, I don't know,' he replied in the vague, harassed manner he always adopted when she was critical. 'I suppose I could call there this evening on my way back from the Baxters'.'

'But it'll take you miles out of your way,' Madge pointed out. As he hesitated, torn between his sense of duty and the inconvenience of carrying it out, she made up his mind for him. 'Give it to me. I'll take it.'

'But why should you be put out?' Gordon asked.

'I could say the same for you,' she replied. 'But it'll be less of a nuisance for me. It'll only take me ten minutes to drive over to the Maceys'. Besides, I want to see Pam. I've been hoping to catch her in the village but I've missed her all week. I want her to help out with the teas at the Old Folks' socials on Wednesday afternoons. She said she would but, of course, that's as far as it's gone even though her own mother never misses a meeting. If I see her at home, I'll be able to pin her down to a definite date, especially if I've done the family a favour by delivering Ted's prescription.' Going into the hall to fetch her coat, she continued, raising her voice so that Gordon could hear her through the open door, 'Those Maceys! They contribute nothing to the village. I don't think Pam's ever offered me a thing for the Oxfam shop. As for Ted, it wouldn't surprise me in the least if he isn't down at the Goat at this very minute.'

'He'll be a fool if he is,' Gordon replied as she came back into the room, her coat on, a scarf tucked inside its collar. 'I've told him quite specifically that he must cut out any alcohol.'

'You're wasting your time,' Madge replied briskly, holding out her hand for the prescription. Putting it away in her handbag, she checked that she had her car-keys and her diary. 'There!' she said, snapping the bag shut. 'I'm ready. If you are as well, Gordon, we might as well leave together. Then I can lock up the house behind us both.'

Ken Reeve banged on the front door of Mrs Franklin's house. He knew someone was in. The lights were on and he could hear the telly, the volume of which was suddenly turned down.

'Stella!' he shouted. If she thought she was going to lie low, pretending she wasn't at home, then she had another think coming.

Mrs Franklin opened the door a mere two inches and peered round the crack.

'She's not here, Ken,' she said, 'so it's no use you banging and shouting.'

'Then where is she?' Ken demanded.

Mrs Franklin hesitated. If she said she didn't know, the chances were that he'd sit outside the house in his car which she could see parked at the gate, waiting for Stella to come home, and then start a row in the road in full view of the neighbours. It was better, perhaps, that they met in the Goat where at least Fred Mitchell would chuck Ken out if he got too loud-mouthed, not that he probably would in front of the other customers. It seemed the lesser of two evils.

'She's gone over to the pub,' Mrs Franklin said, opening the door wider to call after him as he went striding off down the path, 'And don't start any arguments over there, Ken. Mr Mitchell won't stand for it.'

He ignored her and set off across the road towards the Goat, not even bothering to get back in the car which she had hoped he would do and clear off back to Studham.

She shut the door reluctantly.

There was nothing else she could do. Stella could stand up for herself but, all the same, Mrs Franklin was concerned.

If only Stella had married someone decent, she thought, and settled down like the other two girls who had never given her a day's worry. Sometimes she had the feeling that Stella attracted trouble to herself, almost as if she needed some drama going on to add a bit of excitement to her life.

As Fred Mitchell saw the door open and Ken Reeve come in, he moved down the bar so that he could serve him. That way, he could make it quite clear to him that he wasn't going to tolerate any nonsense before it started. And if Reeve wouldn't take the hint, then he'd ban the bugger. As he'd told Stella when they'd first fixed up for her to work behind the bar, he wasn't having Ken using his pub as a place to sort out his marital problems. It'd been bad enough before they were married and he remembered one evening in particular when Ken had bawled her out in front of the other customers and she'd run outside in tears. It was because of that occasion that Stella had chucked him over but, like a fool, had married him after all when she found out the baby was on the way.

Women! he thought disgustedly. They never bloody learn.

Even so, he wasn't quite quick enough. Eva got to him first.

'Pint of bitter,' Ken Reeve told her.

No bloody please, of course, Fred Mitchell noticed. The man looked edgy, too, tapping the corner of the pound note he was holding on the counter as Eva drew his beer and looking all round the bar to check who was there, noticing, of course, that Stella wasn't.

40

When Eva handed him his glass, he spoke again, but so mildly and reasonably that she was fooled.

'Stella not in tonight? Only her mum told me I'd find her in here.'

And before Fred could stop her, Eva, the silly bitch, had said, 'No; she left about ten minutes ago. She's gone to see Mr Lawson up at the caravan.'

'Get some of those glasses cleared,' Fred Mitchell told her abruptly, at which Eva, giving him a look, lifted the counter flap and began to make the rounds of the tables, collecting up the empties.

Fred took her place at the beer pumps, ostensibly emptying the trays under them and tipping the dregs into the sink but at the same time keeping a watch on the back of Ken Reeve's head. He had turned away as if interested in the darts players at the other end of the bar. But Mitchell wasn't fooled.

Reeve was knocking back the beer as fast as he could swallow it and then, without so much as a glance in Mitchell's direction, left his empty glass on the counter and walked towards the door, hands in pockets and trying to look so damned casual and unhurried that Mitchell almost followed him outside to warn him quietly against causing any trouble.

But before he could make a move, he saw Reg Bartlett get up and also head for the door so he decided against it. Having a quiet word with Ken on his own was one thing; doing it in front of a witness when all Reeve had done so far was to drink a pint of beer was another.

Besides, Eva chose that moment to come back, fingers of both hands thrust down into the dirty glasses which she dumped in the sink. She began running water furiously over them and he took the opportunity to say to her in a low voice, 'Why the hell did you want to tell Ken Reeve where Stella's gone? Couldn't you see he's looking for trouble?'

Her sudden, startled, guilty look appeased him.

'Oh, God!' she said, putting a wet hand up to her mouth. 'I just didn't think.'

'Just watch it next time,' he told her before sauntering out to the back storeroom to bring in another crate of mixers.

Putting Eva in her place was almost as good as warning off Stella's husband.

Joanna parked the car in the yard behind the Goat and switched off the lights and the engine. Ahead of her, the back windows of the public house showed up as oblongs of brightness in its white-painted clapboard façade. A lamp, high up on the corner of the building, further illuminated the car-park, shining down on the roofs of the other vehicles already drawn up and on the puddles gleaming inkily in the asphalt. In the silence, the faint sound of voices and laughter came from the pub's interior. It comforted her.

'You'll be all right,' she assured Simon. 'Wait for me here. I shan't be long.'

'Why can't I come with you?' Simon demanded. He was sunk low in the passenger's seat, sulking at having missed his favourite programme on the television but secretly excited by the change of routine, the sudden, unexpected evening excursion and the drive through the dark country-side. It was a let-down that it had ended here in a car-park with nothing to do except look at the other cars or a distant view of trees outlined against patches of clouds.

'Because I want to talk to daddy on my own,' Joanna told him.

It was a lie, and the realisation of this added to the mixture of tension and excitement which the journey had roused in her. The situation had taken on a conspiratorial quality which was both pleasurable as well as dangerous and in which her own boldness in coming to a decision both elated and alarmed her.

Speaking to her solicitor that afternoon, she had expressed her suspicions regarding Alec and the woman she had seen in the lane and Blakely, a lawyer of the old school who still regarded adultery as the prime cause for divorce, had suggested to her that, if Alec's infidelity could be proved, the proceedings might be more straightforward.

'And possibly more advantageous to you, Mrs Lawson,' he had added, 'although, of course, the final decision must be yours.'

The idea had appealed to her. She felt that, by walking out on her, Alec had somehow put her subtly in the wrong although quite where her fault lay in the breakdown of the marriage, she wasn't herself sure. But, if it could be proved that Alec was having an affair with that woman, then the blame would rest entirely on his shoulders.

Proving it was the only difficulty. Mr Blakely had offered her the name and telephone number of a private inquiry agent should she need his services but the expense had deterred her. Frightened by the thought of the bills coming in, she had already cancelled her sunbed treatment for the following week and gone round the house turning off any unnecessary lights.

The idea of driving out to Wynford and doing her own investigation had only occurred to her that evening and she had put on her coat and bustled Simon out to the car before she had time to change her mind, excited by the thought of taking positive action in a situation which, since Alec's departure, had dwindled down to a mere waiting on events.

Now, having arrived at the village, she wasn't sure what to do next. Quite clearly she couldn't go on sitting in the car-park of the Goat.

She gathered up her handbag and headscarf.

'Stay in the car and don't talk to anybody,' she told Simon. 'I shan't be long.'

'How long?' he asked plaintively.

She glanced at her watch. It was just before ten to eight. 'I should be back in about half an hour.'

'But that's ages.'

Joanna got out of the car, bending down to look at him through the open door. He had on his hard-done-by look, quietly mutinous, the expression he assumed when he knew he wasn't going to get his own way. She hardened her heart, suddenly struck by the thought that bringing him up on her own wasn't going to be easy, especially as he grew older. Until that moment, she had seen herself and Simon sharing in adversity, both rejected by Alec, equally wronged. The idea that his loyalties were divided and that he might regard her as partly to blame for Alec's desertion came as a shock to her.

'Please, Simon, don't be difficult,' she said.

He looked up at her over the lapels of his blazer which had ridden up round his ears but he wouldn't answer. After a moment, she shut the door on him and walked towards the car-park entrance, resisting the urge to pause and look back.

He'll be all right, she assured herself. No harm could come to him in so public and well-lit a place.

It was herself she was more concerned about. She had not thought to bring a torch with her and the lane did not appear to have any lamps, a realisation which only occurred to her as she set off along it. But as the lights from the public house illuminated the first stretch, she wasn't too worried on this account.

Besides, she told herself, the caravan couldn't be far. It had taken her only a few minutes to drive there.

She had no clear idea what she would do when she got to it. Listen outside for voices? It seemed an underhand way to behave, like being a spy, and she preferred not to consider it too clearly. She would finally decide what to do when she was actually there.

For the moment, it was enough that she was taking action rather than sitting about at home.

Encouraged by this thought and by her new-found boldness, Joanna began to walk quickly away from the Goat along Waterend Lane.

FIVE _____

Alec said, opening the caravan door, 'Oh, it's you. Come in.'

He tried to sound welcoming but the sight of Stella standing on the steps didn't exactly please him. He had been to an auction that afternoon at Bedleigh where he had bought two lots of books and he had planned to spend the evening sorting them out, pricing those he could resell. Stella's arrival, especially as the floor of the caravan was taken up with the boxes and their contents, was ill-timed.

'Forgive the mess,' he added, not really meaning it, as he moved a pile of books off the cushioned seat to make room for her.

'I won't stop,' she replied, sitting down all the same and crossing her legs as if she intended settling in for a talk. 'Only I expected to see you down the Goat this evening. Remember?'

'Oh, God!' This time he was genuinely contrite. 'I'd forgotten. At least, I thought we'd arranged it for tomorrow evening, Saturday.'

'It doesn't matter. I'll buy you that drink I promised you tomorrow then,' she said, smiling, not at all put out, it seemed.

Joanna would have minded, Alec thought. She would have taken it as proof that he didn't care enough about her to remember the appointment.

'Let me give you a drink to make up for it. No, please,' he insisted when she began to protest. 'You've had to walk all this way to find me.'

'Ten minutes up the lane!' she said derisively as if it really were nothing and to her it probably wasn't. It was only townees, or ex-townees like himself, who found a ten-minute walk along a dark country road at all out of the ordinary. As for himself, he usually drove down to the village.

He realised also as he strode over the piles of books to get to the kitchen why she was there and, as he found glasses and unscrewed the cap of the gin bottle, he called out round the edge of the dividing curtain, 'I've booked an appointment for you at the solicitor's with Mr Pickering for next Thursday. It was the only afternoon he was free at four o'clock. Will that suit you?'

He meant the gin and tonic he handed her as well as the appointment and she said, 'Oh, thanks! That's lovely,' meaning both.

'You know where to find the office?' he asked. 'It's in Market Street on the left-hand side, just past the shoe shop.'

'I'll find it,' she assured him. 'I'm ever so grateful.' She paused to sip at her drink before adding, 'Ken's been round to my mum's, asking me to go back to him. He isn't going to like it, me divorcing him.'

'Then mention that to the solicitor when you see him on Thursday,' Alec advised her. 'If there's any trouble, Pickering can arrange a court order to stop your husband molesting you.'

'Yes. Well.' She didn't seem too sure of that and Alec almost offered to go with her to the solicitor's and then changed his mind. After all, he hardly knew her and it wasn't any of his business.

She changed the subject anyway, asking, as she bent down to examine the titles of the books which were nearest to her on the floor, 'Are you going to sell these in your shop?' When he nodded, she read the words on the cover of the top one with an experimental air, as if testing them out. '*Science in the Service of Industry*. Will people want to buy that?'

'They probably won't rush the doors to get their hands on it,' he agreed, amused by her commonsense and the absurdity of his own image.

She laughed with him, then added, 'Well, I shouldn't

want to read it. I like a book with a bit of love in it. If you can't promise me something with wedding bells at the end, I shan't bother.'

'Wedding bells?' he asked with a derisive lift to his eyebrows. 'Even after your experience with Ken?'

She took it in good part, smiling back at him.

'You know us women. We never give up hope of finding a tall, dark stranger and being happy ever after. Why a bookshop though? It isn't what you used to do for a living, is it?'

It was shrewd of her and he asked curiously, 'Why do you say that?'

'I could tell when you came into the Swan that dinner-time and told me about the lease. You looked so pleased and excited.'

'Did I?' He was surprised by her perception although he assumed that working behind a bar had given her a good knowledge of human nature. 'Yes, I suppose I was. I used to work for a computer firm but I got bored with it.' It was only an approximation of the truth but it would have to do. He had no intention of describing to her in detail the sense of frustration the job had roused in him, the feeling of being trapped so that there were days when he had wanted to smash the windows and let real light and air into his over-heated, artificially lit office.

'But why a bookshop?' she persisted.

'Why not?' he said dismissively. 'I like books. Over the years, I've collected up quite a lot. It seemed logical to try my hand at selling them for a change. So when the lease on the shop in Studham fell vacant, I thought I'd have a go.'

He meant to treat the subject lightly, anxious not to let her see his enthusiasm a second time but, as he spoke, he felt his excitement rise and he wanted absurdly to share it with her.

'It's a former seed-merchant's in Brook Street, just off the town centre,' he continued, 'so it's in a good position. It needs a lot doing to it which was why the lease was going cheap. I'll do most of the renovation myself to save on the costs although I'll enjoy it.' Leaning across to the corner of the table, he opened the file and drew out a sheet of paper, explaining as he handed it to her, 'These are just the rough plans. I shall have to draw up proper ones to scale once I've done the measuring. But they'll give you some idea of what I had in mind. There'll be pine shelves round the walls but the centre will be left free. I thought I'd get hold of an old table to stand there with some of the more interesting books laid out on display. I want it to look, you see, more like someone's library than a shop, with lots of plants about the place and a few lamps. Am I boring you?'

'No, of course not!' Stella protested. 'I think it sounds super. I tell you what – when you open, I'll buy you one of them cheese plants – you know the sort, with holes in their leaves? – as a present and I'll be your first customer. When do you move in?'

'I signed the lease this morning,' Alec said. He had deliberately kept this piece of news until the last, hugging it to himself although he was pleased he had someone to share it with. He had mentioned it to no-one else except the landlord of the Goat when he called in there for a celebratory drink on his way back from the solicitor's. Breaking through her exclamations of delight which he found oddly embarrassing, he added, 'But I shan't be able to open for another month. There's a lot to be done to the place; not just the shop but the rooms over it. So I'll stay on here until it's more or less ready.'

'I'm ever so pleased,' Stella repeated. She seemed to mean it genuinely. Putting down her empty glass, she glanced at her watch. 'Thanks for the drink. I think I ought to be going. I've been here for ages and I'm keeping you from working.'

'Why, what's the time?' he asked.

'Nearly eight o'clock. I told Fred Mitchell I'd drop by the Goat on my way back. They were ever so busy when I was in there earlier so I said I'd help him out behind the bar.'

'I'll see you to the gate,' Alec said, getting to his feet.

After the lighted interior of the caravan, the night

48

seemed very dark. As they walked down the path, Alec was aware of the closeness of the trees in which the wind was keeping up a low persistent roar like heavy gunfire heard at a distance. The same tumult was visible in the sky across which low banks of clouds were driven, constantly forming and reforming. A few drops of rain fell, one hitting his cheek.

They paused at the gate which he opened for her.

'So I'll see you at the Goat tomorrow evening?' Stella asked.

Alec hesitated. Although he liked her, he was beginning to regret having confided in her. It had been a mistake. He didn't want to encourage too close a relationship with her which could cause problems. Absurd though the idea was as far as he was concerned, he could imagine a time when Stella might start to consider him as a possible lover. Despite her air of independence, he guessed she was probably the type of woman who was not happy without a man in her life.

As he hesitated, he saw the headlights of a car come tipping over the brow of the hill from the direction of Macey's farm and, anxious not to be seen with her and become the subject of gossip in the village, he said hurriedly, 'I'm not sure. I may be out tomorrow evening. Perhaps I'll see you another time.' While not exactly rejecting her, the remark was vague enough to be non-committal. As she turned to go, he added, putting out his hand, 'Be careful on the verge. It's slippery.'

His haste to get rid of her was wasted anyway for, as he spoke, the car drew almost level with them.

Stella was saying, 'I'm all right.' All the same, she stumbled, then laughed as she said, 'Oh, hell!' before walking away, the sound of her high heels clipping smartly on the hard surface of the lane.

The car had gone by that time, disappearing round the corner towards the ford.

Stella, too, was out of sight within seconds, the high hedges cutting off any view of her retreating figure.

Alec returned to the caravan, aware as he entered of the

lingering, musky odour of her scent, mingled with the smell of old books and leather bindings. He left the door open behind him to clear the air, the light from the interior shining out and glittering on the raindrops which were falling more frequently now. He could hear them, too, pinging on the tin roof of the caravan.

It was only then that it occurred to him that he ought to have offered her a lift back to the village but he shrugged and let it pass. By the time he had walked to where the car was parked in the far corner of the field, opened the five-barred gate and driven down the lane, she'd be almost at the Goat anyway. Besides, to go chasing after her might give her the wrong idea.

All the same, he felt a little guilty at his negligence. Had she been Joanna or one of her friends, the courtesy would have been automatic. Because she was only Stella, he hadn't felt the need but the thought left him with the uncomfortable feeling that, despite his rejection of middle-class attitudes, there was a part of him which preserved, however subconsciously, that snobbery which he had so despised in his wife.

Madge parked the car in Macey's yard and, getting out, picked her way towards the house, thankful she was wearing her old shoes. The yard was a mess of mud and puddles.

The house wasn't much better, she noticed, as Pam Macey showed her through the hall into the sitting-room, littered with clothes and newspapers, Ted's boots lying drunkenly by the fireplace.

And yet it could have been a beautiful room. Low-ceilinged and well proportioned, it cried out for simple white walls and a few choice pieces of antique furniture, not the jazzy wallpaper and modern three piece suite which the Maceys had chosen although, remembering the interior of the caravan, Madge was not surprised at its ugliness.

''Scuse the mess,' Pam was saying, turning off the television set which was booming away in one corner and hastily grabbing up some of the scattered belongings. She was a small, harassed-looking woman with untidy, greying hair and an air of constant hurry and anxiety.

'I've brought Ted's prescription,' Madge announced. 'He forgot to pick it up from the surgery today and my husband thought he might need it.'

Getting it out of her handbag, she took the opportunity to find her diary at the same time.

'That's ever so kind of you,' Pam said. 'Ted's out at the moment.'

Madge let the remark pass without comment although it seemed to confirm her suspicion that he was probably at the Goat. In that case, he'd almost certainly need the pills before the night was over.

'Can I make you some tea?' Pam offered.

'I won't stop now,' Madge replied, 'although while I'm here I'd like to arrange a Wednesday afternoon when you could help with the teas at the Old Folks' social.' Pencil poised over the open diary, she looked at Pam and smiled encouragingly. 'Shall we say the 24th? I've only got Mrs Franklin down for that afternoon and she can't possibly manage on her own.'

The moral blackmail worked as it usually did. Her social conscience stirred and lacking the courage to say no, Pam said reluctantly, 'Oh, all right. I'll give a hand.'

'Good. I'll phone you on the morning of the social to confirm it,' Madge said.

And to remind her, she added to herself. Judging by the physical disorder in the room, she wouldn't be at all surprised if Pam's attitude to dates and appointments wasn't equally disorganised.

While she was on the subject, it seemed worthwhile to run over the arrangements so that there would be no confusion when the time came.

'. . . And you'll find clean tea-towels in the drawer by the sink,' she concluded. 'I'd be grateful if you left everything tidy before you go because there have been complaints in the past about the kitchen not being quite as clean as it should be which isn't very nice for other people. If you have any problems, ask Mrs Franklin. She knows where everything's kept.' As if it were a continuation of the same conversation, she added, 'By the way, I saw Stella, Mrs Franklin's daughter, the other day. It's so stupid of me but I can't remember her married name.'

'Reeve,' Pam said promptly. 'Her husband's Ken Reeve from Studham; works in Hubbard's garage opposite Tenby's. I know because Ted used to go there to get his van serviced only there was some row about an oil leak not being fixed properly so he goes over to Latchingham now. She's left him,' she added with apparent inconsequentiality.

'Stella, you mean?' Madge asked. Despite herself, she was interested. 'But surely they've only been married about two years?'

'So her mum told me. I was talking to her in the shop the other day and she said Stella turned up on the bus last Friday with a suitcase and said she wasn't going back.'

It was incredible, Madge thought, putting away her diary and shutting her handbag, how even someone like Pam Macey, living nearly a mile from the village, managed to hear the gossip almost as soon as it began circulating.

As Pam showed her to the door, Madge couldn't resist adding, 'How's your tenant getting on? I hear he's opening a bookshop in Studham.'

'Oh, he's all right.' Pam sounded indifferent as if Alec Lawson wasn't of much interest to her. 'I don't see a lot of him. He's out a good deal, going round the sales, buying up books. Ted's storing them for him in one of the sheds.'

'So he'll be selling second-hand books?' Madge asked, pleased to have this point cleared up. Perhaps Studham could support two bookshops after all. The other one, Luckham's, stocked mainly paperbacks. If you wanted anything else, it always took weeks before the order arrived.

Crossing the yard and getting into the car, she waved to Pam who half-raised her hand in reply as if embarrassed at making the gesture. The next moment, she had gone back into the house and shut the door.

Madge turned into the lane. As she did so, the first drops

of rain fell, starring the windscreen; not enough to make it worthwhile turning on the wipers. She drove slowly, conscious of the muddy surface and the ford at the bottom of the hill where she would have to drop down into the bottom gear.

Ahead of her, on the right, she caught a glimpse of oblongs of yellowish light, partly obscured by the hedges, which were the windows of the caravan.

The next moment, the headlights picked out two figures standing by the gate. She had passed them almost as soon as she registered their presence and recognised them. One was Alec Lawson. The other was Stella Franklin. At least, Madge was almost certain it was her. The light shone on the blonde hair of a woman who was carrying a satchel handbag over one shoulder. Madge saw it swing as the figure turned away.

It was only after she had passed them and had braked as she came to the dip in the road just before the ford that the significance of their postures struck her.

They had been quarrelling. Of that she was quite sure. Alec Lawson had been leaning forward, one hand raised, and Stella hadn't just been turning away. She had been on the point of losing her balance as if avoiding a blow.

So it would seem, Madge thought, that she was right after all. Alec Lawson and Stella had been having an affair although it seemed likely, from what she had just witnessed, that the relationship was already breaking up. Which didn't surprise her in the least.

Joanna walked quickly until she reached the S bend in the lane. She realised that the ford could not be far away for she remembered having to change down to take the double corner when she had driven to the caravan with Simon two days earlier.

Besides, she had already been walking for what seemed like hours although she knew that was an exaggeration. It couldn't be more than about ten minutes. All the same, the caravan was much further from the public house than she had imagined.

She was in real darkness now. Even the scattered lights of the village were invisible behind the high hedges and the trees which had crowded closer as the lane narrowed. She could see their branches threshing about against the sky. Everywhere there was movement and noise – the low moaning sound of the wind in the telephone wires, the creaking of branches, subdued rustlings in the hedges which could have been the stirring of dead grasses or the scuttlings of some unknown and unseen creatures.

Her resolution began to falter. She had been mad to come, she thought. Even if that woman was with Alec in the caravan, a divorce court wouldn't necessarily accept this as evidence of adultery. She would need better proof than that.

As she hesitated, it began to rain. She felt a few drops on her face. With them, the tumult in the trees seemed to intensify. The wind snatched at her silk scarf, whipping it about her head until it cracked like a sail, and tore open the skirts of her coat.

At the same moment, the headlights of a car appeared somewhere ahead of her, swooping down over the brow of a hill.

They should have reassured her. Instead, gripped by the thought of the unknown driver behind the lights, of the terror of rape at the roadside under the booming trees, Joanna turned and ran, thankful for the wind which, now behind her, thrust her along in front of it as if a huge hand were pushing against her back, urging her forward towards the lights of the village.

'Time, *if* you please!' Fred Mitchell shouted.

It was a mere ritual. People were already making for the door while Eva was darting about, collecting up the glasses as soon as the last customers emptied them, dumping them down on the counter from where Fred whisked them out of sight into the sink.

Ted Macey drained his glass and handed it to Eva as she dashed past.

'Ta,' she said distractedly, her mind already on the ash-trays and wiping down the tables.

It was time to go before she returned with a damp cloth.

Ted Macey got to his feet, wincing as he did so. He had been aware of a dull ache in his guts all evening. Now, the effort of standing seemed to set it off and he felt the pain stab viciously.

Bloody ulcer, he thought. It's really giving me gyp to-night.

He knew he shouldn't have come out drinking. The doctor had warned him to cut out the beer but a couple of pints hadn't seemed too much at the time. Besides, if he didn't come down to the Goat of an evening, what the hell else was there to do? He wasn't going to sit at home with Pam, watching some stupid programme on the telly.

As he walked to the door, he remembered he hadn't any tablets left either. He'd meant to call in at the surgery on his way back from Studham to collect his prescription and then had forgotten in his hurry to get home and finish spraying the top field.

Hell!

'Goodnight, Ted!' Fred Mitchell was shouting.

He merely grunted in reply, not even bothering to turn his head.

'He's in a mood tonight,' Eva commented, pausing in the act of wiping down the table where he had been sitting.

'Yeah,' Fred agreed, shrugging as he swilled glasses. He was put out that Stella hadn't dropped by on her way back from seeing Lawson. Another pair of hands behind the bar would have been useful, especially when it came to clearing-up time. He assumed she'd changed her mind or stayed on at Lawson's longer than she'd intended.

It crossed his mind to wonder what exactly was the relationship between Lawson and Stella. They weren't having an affair, he thought; at least, not yet. All the same, it was a bit of an odd friendship, him obviously educated and Stella – well, Stella was all right but not Lawson's type he would have thought. Not that it was any of his business.

Yawning hugely, he upturned the last glass to drain and switched off the lights in the bar.

Outside, Ted Macey paused under the porch to turn up his collar against the rain which was now falling steadily before trudging round the corner of the building to the car-park, empty now except for his van.

Climbing carefully in behind the wheel, one hand on his stomach where the pain seemed to be concentrated, he started the engine and turned into Waterend Lane.

He drove slowly, peering ahead through the windscreen wipers to look out for and avoid the pot-holes, unevenly patched with tarmac.

After the S bend which he took in second gear, he didn't bother to pick up speed. The ford was just ahead of him and it wasn't worth changing up.

Seconds later, he saw the lights of the van glittering on the water.

And on something else.

He thought at first it was a sack of rubbish thrown into the ford.

'Bloody gyppoes!' he said out loud to himself. They were always dumping their junk anywhere.

Well, whatever it was, he'd have to shift it. It was blocking up the ford.

Grimacing, he got out of the van and approached the edge.

It was only then, when the water was lapping the toes of his shoes, that he was able to make out a tangle of wet blonde hair, looking very pale against the dark stream, and a pair of legs spreadeagled in the graceless attitude of death.

SIX

Detective Chief Inspector Finch of Chelmsford CID crouched at the edge of the ford, hands on knees to keep his balance, the collar of his mackintosh turned up against the rain.

It was a hell of a night to be called out on an investigation and a hell of a place for a death to have taken place. Lit by the headlamps of the police cars drawn up along the verge, the hedges and the surface of the stream glittered blackly, made darker still by the hundreds of raindrops gathered on the twigs and by the tiny, broken eddies in the water which caught the light and refracted it, causing the shadows behind this surface brightness to seem still more dense.

Behind him he could hear voices and the tramp of feet as men set up the arc lamps and manhandled a van out of the way which had been found blocking the lane a few feet from the ford, its battery flat. A car door slammed. Someone swore.

If he were aware of these distractions, Finch showed no sign. Crouched immobile, like a small boy watching intently for minnows, he studied the body which was lying face downwards in the water, turning his head to one side to get a better view of the features seen only in profile.

She was young; he could see that much. Blonde hair was spread out, half-submerged, lifting and falling a little as the ford ran past and over it, already tangled up with the debris, pieces of twig and grass, that a stream in full spring spate brings down with it. The hip-length fur fabric jacket she was wearing was sodden with water. Below it, legs clad in jeans were lying open and both arms were extended at roughly shoulder level. She looked as if she had been suspended in the act of falling, like one of those parachutists caught on film in the seconds before the canopy opens, stretched out on the air.

He sharpened his attention to the lower part of the body, picking up a detail which he had only partly registered and which he now confirmed. The heel of the right shoe was missing, broken off at the point where it met the sole. The other shoe with its spike heel was intact, the base of it worn down.

Not exactly suitable footwear for a country lane on a wet night, he thought distractedly.

'See that?' he said to Boyce.

The Detective Sergeant, who had been standing at Finch's side, lowered his bulk cautiously into a squatting position and peered along the line of the Chief Inspector's finger. To Finch's relief, he didn't make the obvious comment but, lifting his head, looked up at the wooden footbridge which ran along the left-hand side of the ford, before glancing down again at the sprawled figure. Even before he spoke, it was possible to guess what he was thinking. Finch himself had just come to a similar conclusion.

'She could have caught her heel in the planking and lost her balance.'

If she wasn't pushed, Finch added silently.

He shouldn't even have thought it. Nothing had so far been discovered to suggest that the girl hadn't met her death accidentally, as Boyce had suggested.

And yet, there was a taint of violence about the scene which Finch couldn't rationalise but which he could sense almost as if it were an odour in the air.

He straightened up, hearing his knees crack as he did so.

'Get Bannister to make a search of that footbridge, Tom. I want a word with the local bobby.'

As if on cue, the arc lamps were suddenly switched on, flooding the scene with a strong, white light and, momentarily blinded, Finch stumbled to the edge of the lane, calling for Hadley whom he couldn't now distinguish among the huddle of uniformed and plainclothes men who were waiting about for instructions.

Hadley stepped forward. He was a tall, fresh-faced young

Constable, keen to get on but lacking some basic quality which would probably bar his promotion. Finch hadn't yet been able to define it although he suspected it was imagination. Hadley was solid, dependable, responsible; that was all.

It was evident in his answer to the Chief Inspector's first question, 'Who is she?'

'Stella Reeve, sir.'

Just the one fact which told him, Finch thought sourly, damn all.

'Go on,' he said.

Hadley seemed at a loss.

'I don't know what else you want to know, sir.'

'The lot, man,' Finch told him. 'Come on. You live in the place. You must know something about her. What's the gossip?'

'Gossip?' Hadley sounded surprised. 'You mean what people have been saying about her?'

'Exactly. How long have you been stationed here?'

'Three years, sir.'

'Then you must have heard something. So out with it.'

'Well, sir, she was married about two years ago to a chap called Ken Reeve; a bit of a tearaway from Studham. I don't know how they met but anyway there was a quarrel and the wedding was called off. Then she found she was pregnant so it was on again—a registry office do in Studham. After that, they moved in with Stella's mother, Mrs Franklin, for a couple of months while they were waiting for a council place in Studham. Ken Reeve works there in a garage, Hubbard's. But shortly before they moved, she lost the baby. There was a lot of talk at the time although it was Mrs Franklin most people felt sorry for. You see her husband had died only six months before all this happened and they felt if anyone needed sympathy it was her. Things couldn't have worked out between Stella and her husband though because she turned up in the village about a week ago and moved back in with her mother.'

'Quarrelled with her husband?' Finch suggested.

'Could be,' Hadley agreed. 'Like I said, he's a bit of a

tearaway; tends to throw his weight about especially when he's had a few jars.'

'And Stella Reeve? What's she like?' Finch asked, indicating the body, now brilliantly lit by the arc lamps which had bleached out her hair and darkened the colour of her clothes so that she looked like a black and white flash photograph permanently fixed at the moment of exposure, the water dramatically highlighted, chopped into ebony and silver stars and ribbons of shifting light and shadow.

Hadley hesitated as if choosing what to say.

'Worked as a barmaid at the Swan in Studham,' he replied at last, 'but don't get me wrong. Some people couldn't see further than what she looked like – blonde hair and tight jeans; you know the sort of thing. But there was more to Stella Reeve than that.'

'Such as?' Finch suggested as Hadley seemed at a loss for words.

'Difficult to explain, sir. She was open; she'd say what she meant but she was never unpleasant with it, at least not with me. She was good-hearted, too, provided you went half-way to meet her . . .' He broke off, paused and then tried again. 'Let me put it this way, sir. Being the local bobby, I find people tend to treat me as if I'm different. Know what I mean? If I drop in at the Goat for a drink when I'm off duty or call in at the shop, people stop talking for a moment and then make an effort to include me. Stella wasn't like that. She always spoke to me as *me*, if you get my meaning. I liked that.'

'I know exactly what you mean,' Finch replied. He meant it sincerely, too; not as a mere conversational gambit. Such frankness was rare. He himself had encountered it only occasionally, most importantly in Marion Greave, a woman doctor who had acted as locum when Pardoe, the police surgeon, had been on leave. She, too, possessed that gift of seeing people as individuals which was one of the reasons why he had fallen in love with her, however ridiculous it had seemed at the time for a middle-aged policeman like himself. Short, stocky, with the bluff features of a farmer, he hadn't thought of himself in the role of lover for years. Nor had he been willing to commit himself. A bachelor, cared for by his widowed sister, he had been content with his life which had assumed a comfortable routine he was not willing to disrupt. Selfish, perhaps; but his uncertainty had also been compounded of a sense of his own inadequacy in any deep or lasting relationship and he wasn't prepared to settle for less. The irony was that, when he had finally found the courage to declare his feelings, Marion had rejected him for precisely the same reasons.

They saw each other occasionally – as friends, although, on his part, he still felt that uncomfortable but now familiar lurch of his heart whenever he met her. He had learnt to live with it, accepting it with a patient and even good-humoured stoicism of which, two years ago when he had first fallen in love with her, he wouldn't have imagined he was capable.

Listening to Hadley's description of Stella Reeve and turning to look at the body lying face down in the dazzling black and silver water, he felt drawn to the dead woman in a manner in which, as a professional policeman, he had no right to respond. Objectivity was everything in an investigation. All the same, he was touched by the sight of the wet, blonde hair, the cheap fur fabric jacket, the ridiculously unsuitable high-heeled shoes.

As if to emphasise the connection with Marion, Pardoe chose that moment to arrive, parking his car behind the other vehicles drawn up along the lane and stumping bad-temperedly towards them, bowed against the rain, clutching his medical bag and a pair of wellington boots.

His first remark, however, removed any sentimental aura which the scene might have held for the Chief Inspector. Small, sandy, irascible, Pardoe was not the type to waste time, especially late on a wet Friday night when he might have been home in bed. Nodding briefly to Finch to acknowledge his presence, he turned to McCullum who had been photographing the body and its surroundings.

'Finished with it?' he snapped and as the tall, laconic Scotsman nodded and began picking up his equipment, ready to withdraw, Pardoe changed into his wellingtons, one hand on the shoulder of a young uniformed Constable to steady himself, before wading into the water, remarking to no-one in particular, 'God, what a place to choose!'

'Who found her?' Finch asked Hadley, getting back to his own part of the investigation.

'Ted Macey, sir. That was his van parked in front of the ford. It seems he was in the Goat until closing time and found the body on his way home. He lives on a farm about a quarter of a mile further up the lane, just over the brow of the hill. He phoned me from home.'

'So he used the bridge?' Finch asked.

'Well, yes, sir, I suppose he must have done. There's no other way of getting across the ford on foot unless you wade through it and the water's all of fourteen inches deep.'

'Damn!' Finch said softly. If, as seemed likely, the dead girl had been crossing the bridge just before she met her death, valuable evidence might have been destroyed, a point which Hadley seemed aware of for he said, 'Sorry, sir,' in a subdued voice, as if it were all his fault.

But not quite everything had been lost for, as Pardoe walked into the water and bent down over the body, Bannister called out from the footbridge that he had found something.

Indicating that he would join him shortly, Finch turned back to Hadley.

'Is that the lot?' he asked.

'Not quite, sir. Perhaps I ought to add that I had a few words with Mr Lawson while I was waiting for you to arrive. It seems he heard my car and noticed my headlamps and Ted's in the lane – Macey had forgotten to turn his off. So Lawson came down to the other side of the ford to see what was up. No,' he put in quickly as the Chief Inspector seemed about to interrupt, 'I told him not to get too close. But he said Stella Reeve had called on him this evening, leaving about eight o'clock and that he'd walked with her as far as his gate. He lives in a caravan about a hundred yards up the lane. He said that, as she left, a car passed them coming down the hill from Macey's farm but he doesn't know who was driving it. It couldn't have been Macey, sir. According to him, he left home about ten to seven to go down to the Goat and anyway, he drives a van, not a car.'

'Lawson?' Finch asked.

'Hasn't been in the village all that long,' Hadley explained. 'It seems he's setting up some shop or other in Studham and he's been renting Macey's caravan until he can take over the premises. I don't know much more about him.'

Finch nodded to Hadley, acknowledging the information and dismissing him at the same time, before walking over to the footbridge where Bannister was waiting for him.

The object which had excited the Detective Constable's attention was the heel broken off the dead woman's shoe. It was wedged in a gap between the planks, the tiny nails which had fastened it to the sole still in place.

Finch squatted down over it. Judging by its position, it appeared that the girl had been walking across the bridge in the direction of the village when the heel had become caught.

What had happened afterwards was pure speculation, of course, but it was feasible, Finch thought, getting to his feet and peering down over the handrail, that this was what had caused her to lose her balance and fall. From the slightly elevated position, for the bridge was about four feet above the ford, he could see her body lying almost directly below the place where the heel had been found, Pardoe still bent over her.

He called out to Boyce who was setting up a search of the immediate area.

'Sergeant, I'd like you and McCullum up here. Get Wylie as well.' When the three men had joined him on the footbridge, he continued, 'I want a few shots of the heel and some general views from up here as well. Wylie, you go over the handrail for prints and anything else you can find. The wood's worn smooth so you may be lucky in picking up something. After that, I want the whole of this area searched.' Drawing Boyce to one side, he added in a lower voice, 'I'll leave you in charge here, Tom. I'm going to have a word with Macey, the man who found the body, and also with a chap called Lawson. According to Hadley, Lawson told him that Stella Reeve called on him earlier this evening. I'll make the interviews short at this stage. If Pardoe's finished, I'll see to getting the body moved before I go.'

'Right,' Boyce replied before moving off to supervise the men.

Finch clumped his way back along the bridge to the edge of the ford, watching as Pardoe, with the help of two uniformed Constables, turned the body over on to its back, the doctor remarking over his shoulder to the Chief Inspector, 'See that?' with an air of satisfaction.

Finch didn't bother to reply. The bruise on the girl's forehead was too obvious to remark on. It stood out on the skin, bleached white by the bright lights, as a livid stain, matching the red lipstick and the blue eye-shadow on the closed lids like another bizarre form of make-up.

Pardoe waded forward the few feet to join him.

'I'll need to have her on the slab to make a proper examination but it looks obvious to me what happened. She fell off that bridge into the water, struck her forehead on the hard surface and was knocked unconscious. Lying as she was face downwards, she'd've drowned.'

As an explanation, it was perfectly feasible.

'No other marks on her apart from that bruise?' Finch asked.

'Not that I can see,' Pardoe replied. He looked sideways at the Chief Inspector. 'If you mean was she pushed, I can't answer that question; not for the moment anyway. As for how long she's been in the water, I'd say two or three hours at least. But that's only a guess at this stage. You can move her when you're ready.'

Her.

It was strange, Finch thought, as Pardoe walked away to his car, that the doctor had referred to the dead woman in this way and not by the more impersonal 'it' which he had used when he had first arrived. In death, Stella Reeve was still very feminine. Even the two Constables who were lifting her body from the water and carrying her to the stretcher at the side of the lane seemed to treat her body more tenderly than usual although that could have been his imagination.

The water ran from her clothes and hair, strands of which had washed across her face as they lifted her up, partly obscuring the bruise on her forehead. She might have been merely asleep or unconscious.

It was not a beautiful face. Studying it in the few seconds it lay there before the ambulancemen closed the body bag and carried the stretcher away, Finch could see a coarseness in the features. The mouth was a little too wide for real beauty, the angle of the jaw too heavy. But she had probably been attractive in life. All the face needed was animation.

He followed the stretcher as far as his own car where he changed into the wellingtons he always kept in the boot. By the time he had put them on, the ambulance had left, its tail lights disappearing down the road in the direction of the village.

Torch in hand, another piece of basic equipment he never travelled without, he walked back towards the brightly illuminated scene, curiously isolated and self-contained in the surrounding darkness, about which the figures of the men were moving as if taking part in some ritual, and, having had a last word with Boyce on the bridge, Finch set off into the darkness which lay on the other side.

He could have taken the car. Now that the body had been moved, there was no reason why he shouldn't have driven through the ford. But, despite the rain, he preferred to walk. He was wet through anyway and, on foot, he could get a better idea of the layout of the place.

Once past the ford, the lane began to rise in a long incline at the same time turning to the right so that by the time he noticed the lights of the caravan on his left, the ford was obscured by hedges although the arc lights indicated its position. Immediately in front of the caravan, the hedge was broken by a small, white-painted gate, the verge lead-ing to it trampled into mud.

Finch walked on. Lawson was evidently still up and could be interviewed later.

The lane continued to rise and, as he reached the top, Finch paused to look back. The hill was steeper than he had thought. From the brow, he had a view across dark fields towards the village where a few lights still twinkled through the rain. He'd need to look at the place in daylight, he decided, and preferably with a large-scale map in order to get an idea of the details of the area.

The patch of brightness round the ford was still clearly visible, the lights shining upwards to illuminate the trees. He could even pick out the figures moving round it.

Lights were also visible behind him on the left. Macey, too, was up, it seemed.

The farmhouse stood a little way back from the road behind a yard surrounded by a huddle of outbuildings and low-roofed barns. Seen in the darkness and the rain, it had a crouched, neglected air about it. Water pattered down from a broken gutter above the front door which was opened to him by a thin-faced, middle-aged man wearing a collarless shirt and an old V-necked sweater.

'You the police?' he demanded and when Finch an-nounced his name and produced his identification, the man replied, 'And about bloody time, too. I've been sitting up, waiting for you to come.'

Without any further comment, he started to lead the way down the dimly lit hall, clearly expecting the Chief Inspector to follow him and, with a shrug, Finch walked behind him into the sitting-room.

'Mr Macey?' he asked as he entered. It was the first opportunity the man had given him to establish his ident-ity.

Macey nodded. He had taken up a position standing in front of an open fire which had smouldered away to mere ash. As he did not invite Finch to sit down and as every chair was cluttered up with newspapers and clothes, the Chief Inspector also remained standing just inside the room. Macey evidently expected the interview to be over and done with in as short a time as possible.

The first part was, in fact, completed in a few minutes as Macey's statement regarding his own movements was straightforward.

He'd left the house about ten to seven, spent the evening in the Goat and discovered the body lying in the ford on his way back after closing time. No, he hadn't touched it, he added. He'd taken a look and then walked up to the house where he'd phoned Hadley, the village copper.

'You'll find your van's been moved to a gateway further down the lane,' Finch put in. 'The battery's flat, by the way. You left the lights on.'

'Oh, bloody hell!' Macey said gloomily. This piece of information seemed to confirm his feeling that events weren't going his way that evening.

'You recognised her?' Finch asked, ignoring Macey's comment.

'Course I did. It was Stella Franklin.'

'Franklin?'

'Well, Reeve then. She married Ken Reeve from Studham but she's been known as Stella Franklin round here for years. She was in the Goat earlier this evening so I recognised her coat as soon as I saw it.'

'What time was she in there?' Finch asked. This was new information as far as he was concerned.

'I dunno. About ten past seven, I suppose. She got there not long after me. She didn't stay much above a quarter of an hour, long enough for a drink and a chat with Fred Mitchell – the landlord,' Macey added quickly as Finch seemed about to query Mitchell's identity. 'According to him, she was due to start work behind the bar on Monday. Well, she won't now.'

It was said with morose satisfaction as if Macey found his own problems diminished by the thought of someone else's.

'No,' Finch agreed. He paused momentarily before moving on to the next part of his inquiry. 'A car was seen driving down the lane at roughly eight o'clock this evening.

It could have come from this place. Do you know if there were any callers here this evening about that time?'

'Car?' Macey seemed nonplussed for a moment and then his face cleared. 'Oh, yes. That'd be Mrs Bingham, the doctor's wife. She dropped off a prescription for me I forgot to collect from the surgery.'

'So she'd've spoken to Mrs Macey as you were at the Goat?' Finch asked.

All he had intended was to clear this point up but Macey seemed to think the Chief Inspector wanted confirmation for, pushing past him, he went out into the hall and shouted up the stairs, 'Pam! Get down here! The police want to talk to you.' Returning into the room, he added, 'She'll tell you.'

Mrs Macey appeared a few minutes later, a dressing-gown clutched about her and her hair hastily combed. She looked tired and apprehensive, glancing nervously first at her husband and then at Finch.

'It's all right, Mrs Macey,' Finch assured her. 'I only want to check the time Mrs Bingham left here.'

'It was just before eight o'clock,' Mrs Macey replied.

'You're sure?'

'Yes, because there was a serial I wanted to watch on the telly. As soon as she'd gone, I switched it on and the adverts were just finishing.'

'So you didn't miss it,' Finch said cheerfully. 'I understand she came to leave a prescription?'

'That's right. And to fix up for me to help out with the Old Folks' teas. It's no good you looking like that,' she added, turning to her husband with an unexpected flash of spirit before looking at Finch in appeal. 'I couldn't refuse, could I? My mum goes every Wednesday. It's the least I could do. Besides, she wouldn't take no for an answer.'

'Well, don't expect me to drive you down there,' Macey commented.

'Don't you bother yourself,' Mrs Macey retorted. 'I'll walk down to the village, the same as I always do.'

'What time did Mrs Bingham arrive?' Finch asked the question more to interrupt what appeared to be the airing of a long-standing grievance between husband and wife than to establish the fact although, if the case turned out to be a murder investigation, he might very well need to know the exact movements of any possible witnesses or suspects.

In the event, Mrs Macey's answer wasn't helpful.

'I'm not sure. About half past seven, I think.'

'Thank you, Mrs Macey,' Finch replied.

'Can I go back to bed now?' She directed the appeal at both men and didn't finally leave the room until Finch's nod was confirmed by a look from her husband.

'Is that the lot?' Macey demanded after she had gone.

'Just one other point,' Finch said. He tried to appear casual. Having been brought up himself in a village, he knew the capacity of local people to gossip about outsiders who were not part of the established community and he did not want to cause any problems for Lawson, whoever he was, by appearing too interested in him. But in the light of what Hadley had told him and as Macey appeared to be the man's landlord, the question would have to be asked. 'I believe you rent a caravan to a Mr Lawson.'

As he had feared, Macey bristled up at once.

'Lawson? What's he got to do with it?'

'Nothing as far as I know, except the caravan's close to the ford,' Finch said blandly. It was better, he decided, to say nothing about Stella Reeve having visited Lawson that evening. Apart from not wishing to arouse Macey's suspicions further, Finch had not yet confirmed this fact with Lawson himself.

'How did she die?' Macey countered. He had swung round to look directly at the Chief Inspector. 'Was it an accident or murder?'

'I can't answer that,' Finch said in his official voice. 'The investigation isn't finished yet.'

'But you're making an investigation?'

'Yes, as in any case of sudden death.' Finch could almost read the thought on Macey's face: no smoke without fire. Well, even if it made things difficult for Lawson, he still had to press on with the inquiry. 'About Mr Lawson . . .'

'He moved into the caravan about a fortnight ago; saw it advertised in the local paper. He wanted somewhere temporary to live while he's sorting out about a shop he's going to lease in Studham, selling second-hand books, or so he told me. I've been storing some of them for him in one of the sheds. What you want to know about him for?'

'Thank you, Mr Macey,' Finch said pleasantly, brushing aside the question. 'That's the lot for the time being. You won't object to making an official statement some time later, will you? I'll see myself out.'

All the same, Macey followed him to the front door, watching as Finch crossed the yard and set off down the lane towards the village.

SEVEN

Lawson was still up; probably waiting, like Macey, for the police to arrive to question him.

Finch trod carefully across the muddy verge towards the gate beyond which a concrete path, its surface cracked and broken, was almost as much of a hazard although the light, shining out through the thin, flowered curtains drawn across the caravan windows, made it possible for him to see to pick his way.

Lawson opened the door immediately to his knock, waving him inside impatiently as Finch hesitated on the steps.

'Come in!'

'I'm a bit wet and muddy,' Finch confessed.

'That doesn't matter,' Lawson said abruptly. 'The place is in a mess anyway.'

It was, too, although it was at least warm and dry. Books were piled everywhere and he had to step over them to get inside.

'Part of the stock,' Lawson explained. 'I've been sorting them out. Tea? Or would you prefer something stronger?'

'Tea would be fine,' Finch replied, loosening his wet raincoat and perching himself on the end of a long cushioned seat which Lawson had indicated with a wave of his hand.

'On duty, I suppose?' Lawson commented with an ironic inflection in his voice and, without waiting for a reply, disappeared into a curtained-off kitchen area where he began setting out two mugs on a tiny work surface.

'I'm Detective Chief Inspector Finch, Chelmsford CID, by the way,' Finch added, addressing Lawson's back.

Without bothering to turn round, Lawson replied, 'And I'm Alec Lawson. Now we've got the introductions out of the way, I assume we'll get down to business.'

'That's what I'm here for,' Finch replied equably.

He had met Lawson's type before. Educated, confident, still relatively young, for Lawson was only in his mid-thirties, he possessed an impatient and irreverent attitude to authority which could be offensive.

So be it, Finch thought, planting his muddy wellingtons firmly side by side on the black and yellow carpet. He was here to do a job and he'd bloody well carry it out to the best of his ability whatever Lawson's response.

Lawson came back, carrying two mugs, one of which he handed to the Chief Inspector. Finch took it gratefully, cradling his hands round its warm sides.

'I'm sorry about Stella,' Lawson said unexpectedly. He had retreated with his own mug to an upright chair on the other side of the caravan and his thin, dark face looked suddenly older. 'I liked her. She was what I suppose would be called "a good sort".'

Even so, he couldn't resist putting a wry emphasis on the last words as if deriding the compliment.

'You knew her?' Finch asked.

'Not all that well. I met her first about ten days ago. She was working as a barmaid in the Swan in Studham. I called in there one lunchtime and we got talking. I'd been to see my solicitor about the lease of a shop and she seemed interested. I knew she came originally from this village but I was surprised all the same when I saw her in the Goat one evening a few days ago.'

'Do you know why she came back here?'

'Yes, as a matter of fact I do. I suppose you'll want to hear the gossip?'

Again the sarcasm was evident in his voice.

'I need to find out about her,' Finch replied. 'I can't carry out an investigation without asking questions, Mr Lawson.'

'Point taken,' Alec Lawson conceded. 'But I need to know something first myself. Was it an accident or not?'

'If you mean was she murdered, I'm not in a position yet to say,' Finch countered. If Lawson was so keen on a confrontation for whatever motive, then let him face the unpleasant word 'murder' directly. 'So far we're treating it as a suspicious death. Even so, I still have to ask questions in order to establish exactly how she died.'

Lawson considered this comment in silence for a few moments and then appeared to come to a decision.

'All right. Stella told me that she'd left her husband and was thinking of divorcing him. She wanted my help in getting in touch with a solicitor. We got talking about it and it seems I'd arranged to meet her at the Goat this evening.'

'"Seems"?' Finch broke in, picking up the equivocation.

For the first time, Lawson looked defensive and less sure of himself.

'To be honest, I'd forgotten. It was one of those casual arrangements; nothing definite. She called here on Wednesday afternoon to ask my advice and I promised I'd arrange an appointment for her one afternoon next week with the same firm I deal with. When she left, she said something about treating me to a drink at the Goat on Friday – tonight, that is.'

'But you weren't there?'

'No, I wasn't. I'd been to a sale this afternoon and got involved in sorting out the stuff I'd bought. Then Stella turned up. It seems she called in at the Goat and, not finding me there, had walked up from the pub. She was anxious to know if I'd fixed the appointment for her. Which I had.'

'What time did she arrive?'

'God knows. I told you, I was busy. I didn't take much notice. I know she left just before eight because she looked at her watch and mentioned it.'

'And then?' Finch asked.

'As I said, she left. I went with her as far as the gate.' He paused before adding more emotionally, 'I wish to God I'd offered her a lift! It occurred to me afterwards. But it meant getting the car out and she seemed quite happy to walk. It wasn't raining all that much either. Just a few occasional spots.'

'Yes, I see,' Finch said non-committally.

All the same, he felt he knew Lawson a little better. He was not a callous man; just averagely selfish and prone, like most people, to put his own interests first. But it also occurred to him that Lawson had treated Stella Reeve with less consideration than he might have shown another woman friend simply because she was a barmaid and less educated than himself, and that he was aware of it.

Lawson certainly looked uncomfortable as if this were indeed the case.

'Are you married, sir?' Finch asked. The question wasn't as inconsequential as it appeared. He was curious to know the man's marital status.

The query caught Lawson off guard.

'Yes, but I'm separated from my wife,' he replied before adding, 'I don't see what that's got to do with Stella's death.'

'Not a lot, Mr Lawson,' Finch admitted blandly.

'If you think I was having an affair with her, then you're quite wrong,' Lawson continued.

'The idea hadn't occurred to me,' Finch replied. Interesting though, he thought, that Lawson should mention it. It suggested that the idea had crossed *his* mind in his brief relationship with the dead woman even though he might not have acted on it. 'To get back to this evening,' he went on. 'You saw her off at the gate. In what direction was she walking?'

'Towards the village.'

'Did you see her cross the ford?'

'No. There's a slight bend in the lane and the hedge is too high. Besides, it was dark.'

'And what did you do after she'd gone?'

'I came back here and got on with sorting the books.'

'I believe you mentioned to PC Hadley that you saw a car about the time Mrs Reeve left?'

'Oh, yes, that's right. I'd forgotten about it. It was coming down the hill and passed us just as Stella was on the point of leaving. I don't know who was driving it.'

Finch let it pass. It was none of Lawson's business to be told that the driver was probably the doctor's wife, especially as he hadn't yet checked this with Mrs Bingham herself.

He continued, 'And you remained here in the caravan for the rest of the evening?'

'Yes, until I went into the lane to speak to Hadley. I took some rubbish out to the dustbin and noticed lights by the ford. I thought there might have been an accident. There were two sets of headlamps, you see. So, wondering if I ought to help, I walked down there. Hadley told me what had happened. When I found out it was Stella, I mentioned she'd called on me earlier this evening. Then I cleared off back here. There was nothing I could do and Hadley didn't seem to want me trampling about the place.'

Good for Hadley, Finch thought, closing his notebook and finishing his tea which had gone cold during the interview.

'Is that all?' Lawson asked as Finch put down his mug and rose, buttoning his raincoat.

'For the time being, Mr Lawson. Thank you for your help. I may need to ask you to make an official statement at some later time.'

'Of course.' Lawson sounded distracted as he, too, got to his feet. 'I'd like to say something else, Chief Inspector, before you go.'

'Yes?' Finch paused at the door.

Even then Lawson seemed reluctant to come to the point.

'I don't usually like passing on gossip but perhaps you ought to know, just in case, that Stella had left her husband because he'd been violent to her a couple of times.'

'She told you that?' Finch inquired, intrigued by the form in which the remark had been made. Just in case of what? That Stella had been murdered? If that were so, was Lawson suggesting that the husband might be a likely suspect? It was an interesting speculation.

'You've met him?' he asked Lawson.

'No, but from what Stella told me, he wasn't the best of husbands.'

Not the best of husbands. Another curious phrase. Was that how Lawson saw himself? The man was obviously very much on the defensive.

'And?' Finch prompted.

Lawson hadn't quite finished. Almost imperceptibly, he had drawn a breath as if about to continue.

'She mentioned something else while she was here on Wednesday afternoon. I don't know if it's important. Anyway, she told me that she and Ken quarrelled before they were married and she broke it off. Then she found she was pregnant and married him after all, largely to please her mother. At least, that's the impression I got. But that's beside the point. The point is that she said she needn't have married him. She had another offer from someone else.'

'An offer?' Finch said sharply. 'You mean another man wanted to marry her?'

'She didn't explain but, whatever the offer was, she didn't seem to take it very seriously.'

'Can you remember her exact words?'

Lawson frowned in concentration.

'I'm sorry, I don't think I can. It was said almost as an aside, something along the lines of, "I needn't have married him. I had another offer." Then she went on to say, "It was stupid", although I think the exact word she used was "daft". I'm merely passing it on for what it's worth. It may mean nothing at all.'

Finch made no comment, apart from repeating, 'Thank you, Mr Lawson,' before nodding farewell and letting himself out of the caravan.

He paused by the gate to check Lawson's statement that he hadn't been able to see Stella Reeve cross the ford. In this, at least, Lawson was correct. The slight bend in the lane, apart from the hedge, even with its sparse spring foliage, cut off any view of either the ford or the footbridge. Within seconds of leaving the gate, Stella Reeve would have been out of sight.

As for the offer – Finch put that piece of information at the back of his mind for future consideration. Along with Alec Lawson's other statement, that Reeve had been violent towards his wife, it would need checking on, of course, but, for the moment, he had more urgent demands on his time, such as the search of the area where Stella Reeve's body had been found.

Boyce stepped forward as soon as Finch emerged from the darkness and crossed the bridge into the circle of light.

'So you're back, sir!' he announced, as if the Chief Inspector needed informing of this fact.

'You've found something.' Finch's remark was a statement rather than a question. Having worked with Boyce on many investigations, he knew that eager look by now.

'Two things. First this.'

Leading the way back on to the footbridge, he pointed to a section of the wooden handrail. The surface was dark with rain but the tiny tuft of brown fibres was clearly visible, caught in a rough patch where the wood was splintered.

'Off her coat?' Finch suggested.

'That's what I thought,' Boyce agreed. 'And it's in line with where the heel was found.'

He indicated a chalked circle on the planking. As Finch stepped back to get a measure of the two pieces of evidence, Boyce continued, 'She was lying immediately below so it looks as if she could have got her heel stuck, lost her balance trying to get it free and pitched head first over the rail, catching her coat as she did so.'

'Then she was facing the ford.' Finch offered the idea almost to himself.

'With her torso twisted round and her hands gripping the rail?' Boyce suggested. 'When the heel snapped off, she'd've gone forwards.'

Standing there, Finch tried the movement for himself, oblivious of the glances of a couple of uniformed men, yellow jackets gleaming in the rain, who were searching the ditch on the other side of the lane and who stopped in their task to watch.

'Possible,' Finch grunted. The movement wasn't an easy one. The waist and upper part of his body was unnaturally turned but, by holding on to the rail, he was able to maintain the position. At the same time, he wriggled his right foot backwards and forwards as if the heel of his shoe were caught and he were trying to free it.

Boyce stood back, surveying the Chief Inspector critically and, when Finch stood foursquare again, he said, 'Definitely possible,' in a tone of voice which brooked no denial.

Finch made no comment. At this early stage in the investigation, he wasn't prepared to be dogmatic about any theory.

It crossed his mind to wonder why the hell she hadn't slipped her foot out of the shoe and used her hands to wrench the heel free.

The answer, he told himself, was probably because it was beginning to rain. She wouldn't have wanted to put her bare foot down on the wet planking. Hence her attempt to free the shoe while the foot was still in it. The rest appeared to follow logically – the sudden snapping of the heel, the fall forwards, the loss of consciousness as she struck her head and the subsequent death by drowning in a mere fourteen inches of water.

An accident, in other words.

But the Chief Inspector wasn't willing to be dogmatic about that either.

'What about that other bit of evidence you mentioned?' he asked Boyce.

'It's her bag. One of the men searching the ford found it about a foot from where she had been lying.'

The handbag, a satchel type with a long strap which could be carried over one shoulder, was laid out for his inspection on the verge, the metal clasp still fastened. Finch merely stooped to look at it briefly before straightening up again. Its contents could be examined in detail later.

'Get Wylie to pack it up,' he told Boyce, 'and tell him not to get his prints on it. I want those fibres bagged up as well. They've been photographed?'

'Yes, sir. McCullum's taken some shots of them.' As he spoke, Boyce was taking a critical look round the scene. 'I reckon we've more or less finished here. The ford's been searched as well as the immediate area. I've got some men to go through the ditches on the far side of the lane.' The Sergeant was forced to raise his voice as Finch suddenly set off in that direction, Boyce loping to keep up with him, anxious that the Chief Inspector had noticed some inadequacy in the men's activity which he should have seen for himself and put right.

But it wasn't the two Constables, who were slashing at the long wet grass with sticks, which had caught the Chief Inspector's attention.

Ignoring them, he had mounted the stile where a green-painted finger post pointed across the adjacent field. White lettering on it announced: 'Public Footpath to the Church'.

A faint track led from the stile across the meadow before disappearing into the darkness.

'Just getting my bearings, Tom,' Finch explained, clambering down. He put into words the idea which had occurred to him as he had paused at the top of the hill to look back at the darkened village. 'We'll have to get a large-scale map of the area, just in case.'

As he said it, he realised with a sense of exasperation that he had used the same phrase as Lawson and was further exasperated when Boyce picked it up.

'In case of what? That it wasn't an accident?'

Finch humped his shoulders, a gesture which indicated he'd rather not explain himself, and Boyce, taking the hint, had the good sense to keep his mouth shut for once.

All the same, he couldn't resist looking up and down the lane before glancing up at the finger post to show the Chief Inspector that he had followed the drift of his thoughts.

If it wasn't an accident, these glances implied, then there were two routes which a possible murderer could have taken: along the lane itself or across the field by the footpath.

Finch was moving away.

'We'll get this lot packed up then,' he said, taking up a position in the middle of the scene.

Boyce visibly cheered up at the prospect of returning to headquarters, to hot tea and the chance to get out of his wet clothes, only to have his hopes dashed when the Chief Inspector added, 'We'll have a word with the dead girl's mother on our way back through the village. Find Hadley and get the address.'

They were met at the front door of the house, the last in a row of brick-built cottages only a short distance from the Goat, by the WPC whom Finch had despatched earlier to break the news of Stella Reeve's death to her mother as soon as Hadley had confirmed the identification.

There was no hall, the front door opening directly into the living-room, and the WPC came out on to the doorstep to confer with them briefly.

'The doctor's been and has left her a sedative to take when she goes to bed. And a neighbour's with her. She's agreed to stay the night,' she told them in a low voice before, pushing open the front door, she preceded Finch and Boyce into the room, announcing in too bright a tone, 'Detective Chief Inspector Finch is here, Mrs Franklin.'

The little living-room was hot and bright and so packed with objects and patterns that, after the starkness of the night outside, Finch was overwhelmed for a moment. Flowered curtains, flowered wallpaper, cretonne covers on a pair of low armchairs drawn up by the fireplace, potted plants and ornaments in profusion, winking brasses and a collection of framed photographs on the sideboard bewildered the eye. There were too many people as well. In addition to himself, Boyce and the WPC, two women were sitting in the fireside chairs, one plump and clearly not Mrs Franklin, judging by the look of bright-eyed curiosity she directed at the Chief Inspector and his Sergeant as they entered the room. This must be the neighbour, shocked by the news, no doubt, but enjoying the excitement of it all at the same time.

The other chair was occupied by a small woman who, as if diminished by grief, had shrunk back against the patterned fabric of the cushions, her hands in her lap, immobilised, it seemed, by the news of her daughter's death. She had a faded prettiness about her. Her soft grey hair might once have been fair and, underneath the fallen flesh, a delicate bone structure was still apparent, more refined than her daughter's for it lacked that fullness and heaviness about the mouth and jaw.

Finch said, 'I'm sorry, Mrs Franklin.'

He felt doubly ill at ease; emotionally, because he had never learned to cope with other people's grief; physically, because in the crowded room, it was impossible to approach her without stumbling into the furniture.

Boyce had the good sense to hang back in the relatively uncluttered space by the door.

The neighbour also showed some sensibility.

'I'll make some tea,' she announced, heaving herself up. 'I'm sure we could all do with a cup.'

Finch sat down in the vacated chair, feeling its seat warm from her ample backside.

'I won't keep you too long, Mrs Franklin,' he said. 'At this stage, all I want to know is the time your daughter went out this evening and if you have any idea where she was going.'

They were sitting so close together that their knees were almost touching across the hearth where a coal fire burned fiercely, adding to Finch's discomfort.

'I want to know what happened,' Mrs Franklin replied. '*She* won't tell me much.'

She indicated with a jerk of her head the WPC who had taken up the stand-easy position in front of the sideboard.

'That's because we're not sure ourselves,' Finch said in defence of the woman although he made a mental note not to use her again on a similar duty. She evidently lacked the right touch. 'We think she lost her balance and fell off the footbridge into the ford but we can't be certain until we've made further inquiries. That's why I need to know what your daughter was doing this evening.'

'Yes, I see that.' Mrs Franklin seemed to accept him, leaning forward to establish closer contact with him as she might have done the vicar, the doctor or, he liked to think, a friend. 'She left here about five past seven. I didn't see her go. I was ironing in the kitchen.' Again, she nodded her head to indicate the door through which the neighbour had gone and behind which could be heard the subdued rattle of china. 'She just called out goodbye and then I heard the front door shut.'

'You're sure of the time?'

'I was listening to *The Archers* on the radio. It'd been on for only a minute when she left.'

'And do you know where she was going?'

'Yes, over to the Goat to have a word with Fred Mitchell. She was starting work there on Monday. When she didn't come back at closing time, I thought at first she was with Ken.'

'Ken? Her husband, you mean?'

'That's right. He'd called here, you see, soon after she left, wanting to see her. I told him she'd gone to the Goat. Knowing him, I didn't want him hanging about outside the house, waiting for her. I thought if he met her over at the Goat and made a row, Fred Mitchell'd sort him out. She left him, you see; walked out about a week ago. He was round here on Wednesday, asking her to go back but she wasn't having any. She'd made up her mind to pack him in.'

'Why was that?' Finch asked. Although he already knew Lawson's version, he wanted to hear hers.

It was the same.

'Ken knocked her about a few times and Stella wasn't going to put up with it. She believed in standing up for herself. I don't say it happened often but Ken can be short-tempered, especially when he's had a bit too much to drink. Anyway, she turned up here with her things, talking about getting a divorce.'

'I see,' Finch said quietly and left it there. It wasn't the time, he felt, to question her further about Stella's marriage. That could come later at a second interview when Mrs Franklin had recovered from the first shock of her daughter's death. He would also, on this later occasion, try to find out if she knew anything about the offer which Lawson had mentioned. At the moment, he was more concerned with establishing the husband's movements earlier in the evening, Mrs Franklin's statement that Ken Reeve had been looking for his wife having opened up a new and unexpected line of inquiry.

'At what time did Ken — Mr Reeve — arrive?'

'About half an hour after Stella left. Perhaps a bit less.'

'So that would be roughly between half past seven and twenty-five to eight?'

'I suppose so. I didn't look at the clock. He'd parked his car outside and walked over to the Goat. It was still there at nine o'clock. I know that 'cos I watched the serial on the telly and I had a look out of the window just after it finished.'

Thank God for the television serial, Finch thought. Two individual timings had been established fairly accurately that evening because of its popularity.

'But you don't know what time he left?'

'No. There's quite a few cars going up and down the village, especially at closing time. I had another look at quarter to eleven but Ken's car had gone. I was ready for bed by then and thinking that Stella ought to be home soon.'

She began to cry for the first time, quietly, shamefacedly, the tears running down her face.

'Tea!' announced the plump neighbour, bustling in with the tray. At her arrival, Mrs Franklin dabbed at her eyes with a crumpled handkerchief she had been holding in her lap and accepted a cup, trying to smile her thanks.

It put an end to the interview although, swilling his own tea down hastily, Finch put one last question.

'So you don't know if your daughter and her husband met at the Goat?'

'No; you'll have to ask Fred Mitchell that,' Mrs Franklin replied.

EIGHT _____

Finch asked Mitchell the following morning, in company with Boyce.

It had stopped raining, thank God, for they were on their way to the ford to supervise the re-photographing and a further search of the area in daylight and Finch didn't relish the thought of another hour or so spent soaked to the skin.

Watery sunlight brightened up the countryside, revealing trees and hedgerows in new spiky growth and daffodils in green bud in front gardens. On such a morning, it was possible to believe that spring had actually arrived.

Thus revealed, Wynford looked pleasant enough. It was a long village, strung out along the main street, punctuated by the Goat public house at one end and the church at the other, each building forming, as it were, a bracket round its development for beyond them fields and farmland took over.

The Goat was not yet open for business although the rear door was set back with a brick and a man in shirt sleeves was carrying crates of empties out of a storeroom to pile up in the yard.

He was a middle-aged man with wide, tufty sideboards of sandy-coloured hair and a brushed-up moustache which gave his face the whiskery, amiable appearance of a character from a children's animal story – Mr Badger, perhaps, dressed in check shirt and grey terylene trousers. But his eyes had the hard, watchful look of a man who has seen it all, while the powerful forearms suggested considerable physical strength. It was no surprise that Mrs Franklin had relied on Fred Mitchell to sort out her son-in-law, as she had put it. He looked capable of dealing with a whole bar full of troublemakers if need be.

After Finch had introduced himself and Boyce, Mitchell led them into a small, private sitting-room behind the public bar where he came straight to the point.

'I've got a pub to open, Chief Inspector, so what do you want to know?'

'What time Stella Reeve arrived here yesterday evening,' Finch replied.

'Just after five past seven at a rough guess. She had a gin and orange and then she went.'

'So she wasn't here all that long?'

'Not much above fifteen minutes. It was just before twenty-five past when she left. I know that because I happened to glance at the time.'

'Have you any idea where she went?'

'Yes; she was going to call on Mr Lawson, or so she said. She seemed disappointed not to find him here. She mentioned there was something she wanted to discuss with him.'

Her appointment with the solicitor, Finch thought, although he said nothing.

'And I believe,' he continued, his voice carefully casual, 'that her husband, Mr Reeve, also called in here last night?'

'That's right. He arrived about ten minutes after Stella left. He didn't stop long either. He had a pint and then he cleared off.'

84

'He came in here looking for her?' Finch asked in the same throw-away manner.

Fred Mitchell wasn't fooled.

'Yes, he did. And looking for trouble, too. I nearly followed him outside to warn him off but another customer went out at the same time and I didn't want to show him up in front of someone else. It's a bit of a tricky business running a pub, Chief Inspector, rather like you lot controlling a crowd. You try to keep it pleasant and not go out of your way to stir things up but if anyone looks as if they're going to cause trouble then you've got to step in and stop it, preferably before it starts; nip it in the bud. You get my meaning? Well, Ken Reeve hadn't done anything I could object to but he had a look on his face which made me think he was spoiling for a row.'

'Between himself and Stella?'

'That's right. And then when Eva – that's the wife – let slip that Stella'd gone up to Lawson's caravan, it crossed my mind that Ken might go after her. He didn't though, did he? I mean, according to the rumours going round the village, she fell off the footbridge. There was no funny business?'

The last remark was in the form of an appeal which Finch responded to pleasantly without committing himself.

'So it would seem, Mr Mitchell. Even so, inquiries have to be made. I believe Mr Macey was also in the pub last night. What time did he arrive?'

'Ted? Not long before Stella turned up; say about seven o'clock. He left at closing time. Here, you don't think Ted had anything to do with it?'

'Only as a potential witness, Mr Mitchell. He found the body,' Finch pointed out, at which Mitchell nodded, satisfied with this explanation, before remarking, his face behind the sandy whiskers suddenly gloomy, 'It's a hell of a thing to happen. I liked Stella. She was a good-looker, too, and it's always an advantage to have an attractive face behind the bar. And friendly with it; the sort who enjoyed a bit of a chat and a laugh although she wouldn't stand for

85

any old acid from anyone, no matter who. God knows who I'll find to take her place. I was counting on her starting here on Monday.'

'I'm sorry,' Finch said in general commiseration as he rose to leave, adding as he went into the passage leading to the back door, 'By the way, if we need it, would you be able to give me a list of all the customers who were in the bar last night when Stella Reeve was in there?'

'All of them?' Fred Mitchell sounded outraged although he softened this initial reaction by remarking more reasonably, 'I suppose I could. Most of them were regulars anyway.'

'I'll let you know if I'll need it,' Finch said before walking away with Boyce across the car-park to where their vehicle was parked.

In the few minutes it took to drive to the ford along Waterend Lane, there wasn't much time for Boyce to comment on the interview although he remarked, 'I suppose you'll want that list in case it turns out to be murder after all.'

Finch merely grunted in reply. He was trying to keep an open mind on Stella Reeve's death and was reluctant to discuss with Boyce the flicker of doubt which had crossed his mind the night before as he had stood looking down at her body. Besides, he was more interested in studying the scene in daylight.

After running relatively straight for a short distance, the lane began to twist and narrow down between high hedges for about half a mile before swinging round in a wide S bend where it tilted down towards the ford, thirty yards ahead. On the other side, it started to rise again in the long slope which led towards Macey's farm.

Boyce drew the car on to the verge and Finch got out, strolling with his hands in his pockets towards the ford.

McCullum, the police photographer, and some of the other men were already there, a smaller group than yesterday, their cars drawn up along the edge of the lane.

When Finch had set up the task of resuming the search, he stood to one side, making his own assessment of the surroundings which he had seen only in the artificial illumination of the arc lamps the night before.

In daylight, the place looked less sinister and dramatic. The water, no longer theatrically black and silver, was tinted brown by the soil washed down into it from the surrounding fields by the spring rains.

It was a picturesque scene, or would have been in high summer with the trees and hedges in full leaf. On such a March morning of thin, chilly sunlight, it had a cold, austere beauty, only partly softened by the small, yellow stars of the celandines growing on the banks and by the new, tender grass pushing up through last year's dead growth. The bones of winter were still too visible. Even in the fields, flushed green with sprouting corn, it was possible to see under the top mantle the ribbed furrows, streaked silver with the standing water which had collected in the hollows.

Finch mounted the stile by the signpost as he had done the night before and looked out across the meadow in the direction of the village. He could now trace the line of the footpath across the grass towards the church, the tower of which stood out against the surrounding trees, still bare of foliage, it seemed, at that distance although on the nearer trees and hedges the new leaves were everywhere apparent.

Climbing down, he crossed the footbridge, pausing to look down over the handrail before walking on towards Lawson's caravan, noting again the bend in the lane and stopping at the gate to check that, from this position, the ford and bridge were now out of sight.

Lawson was probably at home. At least, glancing across, Finch could see a car, a Volvo estate, parked in the field a little distance away where a five-barred gate gave access. A window in the caravan was also open. But the Chief Inspector made no attempt to approach any nearer and, turning away, walked back towards the ford where he sought out Stapleton, the tall, slow-moving uniformed Inspector.

'I'm leaving you in charge here, George. There's a couple

of people I want to interview. But I should be back before you've finished.'

'Very good, sir,' Stapleton replied.

Beckoning to Boyce to follow, Finch returned to the car.

'Where now?' the Sergeant asked, getting in behind the wheel.

'Studham,' Finch told him. 'I want to have a chat with Ken Reeve, Stella's husband. On the way, though, we'll drop in on Mrs Bingham.'

The doctor's house was on the outskirts of the village, a large Edwardian detached residence, solid and comfortable, set back from the road behind a wide, well-kept garden of lawn, shrubbery and rose beds. A modern-looking, one-storey addition on one side with a separate entrance housed, he assumed, the surgery and waiting-room.

Finch rang the bell at the front door which was opened to him by an attractive, well-dressed woman in her forties – Mrs Bingham herself, as she acknowledged in answer to his first question. When Finch had introduced himself and Boyce, she showed them into a drawing-room at the back of the house, overlooking another broad sweep of garden, where she invited him to sit down.

Finch looked about him covertly as he lowered himself into an armchair. It was an attractive room, furnished with a mixture of comfortable, cushioned chairs and a pair of matching sofas, covered in crisp cream and blue flowered linen, combined with a few choice antiques, paintings and silver; a suitable setting for Mrs Bingham for she was a good-looking woman although a little too dominating for his taste, Finch thought, summing her up silently. She had a positive tilt to her head and fine dark eyes which regarded him with a challenging directness. Here was someone used to authority and undoubtedly intelligent although, underneath the carefully maintained image of the doctor's wife, he sensed an energy and restlessness which he detected in the movements of her hands and a rapid, rather impatient manner of speaking.

'I'm afraid I can't tell you a great deal, Chief Inspector,' she replied when Finch had explained the reason for the visit. 'I called at the Maceys' to leave a prescription which Ted Macey had forgotten or hadn't been bothered to collect from the surgery. I also wanted to arrange for Pam Macey to help with the old people's teas one Wednesday afternoon. I'm not sure what time I arrived although I left, I suppose, about eight o'clock.'

'Then I believe you must have passed the caravan on your way home just as Mrs Reeve and Mr Lawson were saying goodbye. At least, Mr Lawson spoke of seeing a car go by as they were standing at the gate. The timing would appear to coincide.'

As he spoke, he saw that Boyce, seated on the opposite side of the fireplace, had begun quietly to take notes of the conversation. Mrs Bingham, too, was aware of it for she glanced briefly in his direction before replying.

'Yes, that would have been me,' she agreed. 'As a matter of fact, I noticed them, but only briefly, in the headlights.'

'Yes?' Finch prompted.

There was something in her manner which persuaded him that this was not all she could tell him. The signs were almost imperceptible: a faint hesitation, the slightest possible upward intonation at the end of the sentence as if she had been about to add another remark.

She looked across at him and then averted her eyes.

'That's all. I only saw them for a few seconds.'

'But long enough, I think, Mrs Bingham, for you to have gained an impression. What was it?'

'It's too vague to be of any use to you, Chief Inspector. And besides, it was an accident, wasn't it?'

'So it would appear,' Finch said. 'But our inquiries aren't yet complete. I need to have as much evidence as I can before any such conclusions can be reached.'

He was aware that he was using his official, formal voice but Mrs Bingham was hardly the type of woman with whom he could settle down for a quiet chat, knee to knee, as he had done the night before with Mrs Franklin.

'I see.' There was a pause in which she seemed to consider his comment. Then she continued. 'I thought they were quarrelling. At least, that's the impression I had. As

I said, I saw them only briefly and I could be wrong.'

'But you don't think you are?' Finch persisted. When she didn't reply, he took her silence for assent, adding, 'What gave you that impression?'

'Mr Lawson had his hand raised. Stella Franklin was turning away rather abruptly, as if she were trying to keep her balance. It seemed to me they were arguing.'

'Mr Lawson was about to strike her? Is that what you're saying?' Finch asked sharply.

The question seemed to distress her. She got up from the chair in which she had been sitting and went to stand by the fireplace on the shelf above which was a collection of silver-framed photographs – of her children, Finch guessed, at various stages of their development from babies to young adults.

'Yes, that was my impression, Chief Inspector,' she replied, her face averted. 'It was only after I passed them that I realised who they were and what was happening.'

'You didn't stop?'

'No, I thought it was none of my business so I drove on.'

'Where to?'

She looked annoyed.

'Here, of course.'

Where else? she seemed to imply.

'You knew Stella Reeve?' Finch asked, shifting the subject slightly.

'Of course. We've lived in the village for twenty years. The Franklins are my husband's patients and, in a place like Wynford, you know everybody if only by sight.'

'And Mr Lawson?'

'I've only met him once or twice. But I certainly recognised him as the man I saw yesterday evening with Stella.'

There seemed nothing more to ask. Finch thanked her and rose to his feet, following her, with Boyce in tow, to the front door where she let them out of the house.

'What did you make of that?' the Sergeant asked as they got into the car and turned out of the driveway into the road.

'I don't know, Tom,' Finch replied. He genuinely didn't.

The interview had left him feeling uncomfortable, largely, he suspected, because of Mrs Bingham's attitude. Seated in her drawing-room, he had felt very much the outsider, not one of the community, asking questions which she seemed to regard as faintly impertinent.

Much of the problem arose from the case itself. If it had been a straightforward murder, he could have carried out his inquiries with complete authority but, as it had not yet been proved that Stella Reeve had met her death other than accidentally, he was aware of having to proceed more carefully and of unseen barriers going up; not just in the case of Mrs Bingham either. During the interviews with the Maceys and with Mitchell, he had had the feeling that, deep down, they wanted Stella's death to be treated as accidental and had resented, however covertly, any suggestion on his part that it might be otherwise.

Boyce was saying, voicing aloud his dilemma, 'If it turns out to be murder, Mrs Bingham's evidence about Lawson could be useful. Will you interview him again?'

Which wasn't what Finch wanted to be asked at that moment; certainly not so directly. He was aware that his own reticence about discussing the case with Boyce didn't help the situation although he could not rationalise this reluctance. If only he were seeing Marion Greave in the near future, he thought. She would understand better than Boyce, disloyal though such a comparison might be towards the Sergeant. But no such arrangements had been made and he did not like to ring her up to suggest a meeting. To do so might be pushing his luck a little too far. Since her rejection of him as a lover, he had become self-conscious about getting in touch with her even as a friend. The barriers had gone up there, too, leaving him again on the outside.

He said, 'Let's wait until we get some confirmation on that one, Tom.'

'Perhaps Pardoe will come up with something,' Boyce suggested with a helpful air.

Finch merely replied, 'Turn left at the crossroads for Studham.'

The town had begun life as a small market centre for the surrounding farms and villages and still preserved the original narrow streets, choked now with modern traffic, although the outskirts were spreading beyond the original perimeter into new housing estates and small industrial developments.

Hubbard's garage was in a side street behind a cramped forecourt allowing barely room for a motorist to draw off the road to reach the petrol pumps. The building itself was of brick and corrugated iron construction, a pair of wooden doors set open to reveal the interior, minimally equipped with an inspection pit and a ramp. The place looked badly run. A work bench was littered with tools while bits of cars, wheels, inner tubes, pieces of bodywork, were piled up along the walls.

At the far end, a small office had been knocked together out of laths and boarding where, under a dangling light bulb, Mr Hubbard was drinking tea at a desk covered with papers, discarded sparking-plugs and dirty ash-trays.

Ken Reeve, he informed them, was out in the yard and waved a negligent hand towards a door at the back.

The yard showed as much disorganisation as the workshop with cars in various stages of repair or dismantling drawn up haphazardly, although in a relatively clear area in the centre a van was standing with its bonnet up, a young man in overalls bending down over the engine.

He wasn't aware of their approach until Finch spoke to him.

'Mr Reeve?'

He straightened up and turned to face them.

Seeing him, Finch could understand both Mrs Franklin's and Mitchell's remarks which had suggested that Ken Reeve was a potential troublemaker. It was evident in his expression as he looked them over. He wasn't bad-looking in an obvious swaggering and macho manner, with black wavy hair and strong features, but the look on his face was immediately belligerent.

'You're the police,' he said with an accusing air.

'Detective Chief Inspector Finch and Detective Sergeant

Boyce,' Finch replied more equably than he felt. He recognised the type at once. Reeve, who liked to think of himself as a hard man, would consider it demeaning to be co-operative even though he knew they were there to inquire into his wife's death. He'd been informed of that fact earlier by the Studham police who'd been sent round to his address soon after the official investigation started. But the need to maintain this image of himself would prevent him from showing any grief he might feel. Or guilt, come to that, Finch realised.

'I'm sorry about your wife,' Finch said, testing out this theory. 'It must have come as a shock.'

'Yeah,' Reeve replied. He seemed about to add more but, changing his mind, kept silent.

'I'm afraid,' Finch continued in the same pleasant tone, 'that we have to ask you a few questions concerning your movements last night. I believe you were in Wynford?'

'That's right,' Reeve replied with a truculent air, as much as to say, So what?

'What exactly were you doing there?' It was Boyce who asked the question, moving forward to interpose his bulk.

Reeve, seemingly unimpressed, looked him up and down before replying.

'I called on Stella's mum.'

'At what time?'

'How the hell should I know?' As Boyce waited, massively silent, Reeve added, 'I suppose about half past seven.'

'And what happened?'

'The old bat wouldn't let me in; spoke to me on the doorstep.'

'She told you where your wife had gone?'

Finch took up the questioning this time.

Reeve glanced from one to the other of them and then laid down the spanner he had been holding on the wing of the van. The action seemed to signal some kind of truce, to Finch's relief, for when he answered he spoke more reasonably.

'Yeah, that's right. She said Stella had gone over to the

Goat. So I went over there myself, only Stella had left about ten minutes earlier, or so the woman behind the bar told me. I had a pint and then cleared off.'

'Where to?' Boyce asked.

'Back to the car,' Reeve replied. 'I'd left it parked outside Stella's mum's house. I thought I'd sit in it and wait for Stella to turn up. When she didn't, I went home.'

'But I think you knew where your wife had gone,' Finch pointed out. 'Mrs Mitchell, the landlord's wife, told you.'

Reeve shrugged indifferently.

'She might have done. I didn't take much notice. She said something about a caravan but I wasn't going to go traipsing about the place looking for it. So, like I said, I waited in the car.'

'Until when?' Finch asked.

He had a rough idea of the time from Mrs Franklin's statement. It would be interesting to see just how far Reeve told the truth.

'I don't know,' Reeve replied. 'An hour, I suppose. It could be more. I listened to the car radio and smoked a few ciggies. Then I got fed up with it and drove home.'

'Did you leave the car at any time?' Boyce asked.

'No, I bloody didn't!' Reeve raised his voice. 'It had started to rain. And what the hell's all this about anyway? I was told she'd probably had an accident. The way you're bloody questioning me, anyone'd think I'd killed her.'

'Questions have to be asked, Mr Reeve,' Finch said quietly, aware that with each interview he'd so far made the same query had been raised, and wishing to hell the case was more straightforward. 'When was the last time you saw your wife, by the way?'

Again, he knew what the answer ought to be from his interview with Mrs Franklin and he waited, keeping his expression bland, for Reeve's reply.

'About ten days ago before she cleared off,' Reeve began and then paused. 'No, hang on a minute. I called round her mum's a few days ago.'

'You'd forgotten?' Finch hinted.

Reeve gave him a strange look, half-defiant, half-shamefaced. He clearly preferred not to remember what had happened on that last occasion but whether deliberately or because he had genuinely forgotten in an attempt to protect his own self-esteem, Finch couldn't tell.

'I wasn't there much more than a quarter of an hour,' he said, avoiding Finch's eyes. 'I wanted Stella to come back.'

'But she wouldn't?' Finch asked.

Reeve turned aside and, picking up the spanner, flourished it in the direction of the van.

'Look, I've got work to do,' he said. 'I can't waste half the morning answering your fool questions. If that's all you want to know, then push off and let me get on.'

'I won't keep you much longer,' Finch replied. 'I shall need you to make a formal identification of the body. Would this afternoon at three o'clock suit you?'

He had postponed the timing of this formality in order to be present when Reeve identified his wife, curious to witness the man's reaction.

Reeve's immediate response was also interesting.

'Do I have to?' he asked.

'If you don't, it means asking Mrs Franklin which I'd rather not do. She's still in a state of shock.'

'All right then,' Reeve conceded reluctantly.

'Thank you, Mr Reeve,' Finch said courteously. 'I'll see you then this afternoon at Divisional Headquarters in Chelmsford. Ask for me at the desk.' Nodding to Boyce to follow, he picked his way back across the yard towards the garage.

'That's all you're going to ask him?' Boyce demanded as they emerged on to the forecourt. 'Nothing about the divorce? Not a word about him knocking his wife about?'

'That can come later, Tom,' Finch replied, climbing into the passenger seat of the car. 'I want to keep a few cards up my sleeve.'

'In case it turns out to be murder?' Boyce finished the sentence for him, again voicing out loud the thought which Finch would have preferred kept silent. 'Well, if it is, Reeve's capable of shoving anyone off a bridge, by my reckoning.'

It was too soon to come to such a conclusion and Finch was exasperated enough to reply, 'If it is murder, then Reeve's not the only one who could have a motive. Don't forget Mrs Bingham's statement about Lawson. According to her, he and Stella Reeve were quarrelling only a few minutes before she must have died.'

Which hardly helped in keeping an open mind on the case, Finch thought, regretting the remark as soon as he made it. But at least it had the effect of diverting Boyce's attention from the husband.

'Yes, you're right there,' he agreed, looking thoughtful, before adding more briskly, 'Where to now? Back to Wynford to see how the search is going?'

NINE _____

The arrival of a uniformed Constable at the caravan had alerted Alec Lawson to the presence of the police in the lane that morning. They were, the man explained, continuing the search in daylight and they'd be grateful if no traffic used the road into the village until the task was completed, probably in a couple of hours. He had then left on foot in the direction of Macey's farm, presumably to repeat the request.

As far as Alec Lawson was concerned, the restriction wasn't a nuisance. He had no plans to leave the caravan until later that morning anyway, having made up his mind to finish sorting through the books before putting them into boxes and taking them up to the farm where they would be stored in one of Macey's outbuildings until he could transfer them to the shop.

The arrangement was far from ideal. The shed, for which he paid an additional £5 a week on top of the rent for the caravan, was weatherproof but damp and the books could not be left there for too long without running the risk of becoming mildewed.

Now that he had the keys to the shop and the place was legally his, he could have taken the boxes there but he wanted to wait a few days in order to get the interior into some kind of fit state, a few shelves put up and the floor cleared, before he started moving in stock. As it was, he estimated that at least a fortnight's work had to be done before he could open for business.

Once the police had gone and the lane was again open to traffic, he intended driving into Studham that afternoon and making a start by ordering the materials he would need and getting an estimate for the fascia board to be repainted; nothing elaborate, of course; he hadn't the capital to waste on anything expensive. All he had envisaged was the name 'Lawson's' and the words 'Second-hand Books' in white lettering on a black background.

But only half his mind was on his long-term plans. Kneeling on the floor and opening the books in turn to examine their contents briefly before pencilling a price inside the cover, he thought of Stella.

Her death had distressed him more than he had been willing to admit to Finch or even, at the time, to himself. Although he had hardly known her, he found himself mourning her death as if she had been an old friend.

Stella, the bright star, he thought and then smiled wryly at the image. But the comparison wasn't without some validity. She had possessed a certain luminous quality of her own although the concept of the star was perhaps too pure and virginal to be entirely apt.

And, if he were honest with himself, would he have continued the relationship? Probably not. Once he had moved away from Wynford, he doubted if he would have taken the trouble to see her again although she might have dropped in at the shop occasionally as she had promised when she happened to be in Studham. That was all.

All the same, he regretted not having accompanied her as far as the ford or gone to the bother of getting the car out and driving her home. It had been thoughtless of him;

selfish even. Since walking out on Joanna and Simon, he had been aware of a hardening in his attitude to other people, a tendency he'd have to watch, he decided. There must be a middle way between being too soft and total self-interest.

At eleven o'clock, just as he was thinking of making himself coffee, he heard the sound of cars backing and turning in the lane. The police seemed to be leaving and, curious to see their departure, he walked as far as the corner where it was possible to look down the slight incline towards the ford.

Finch was aware of Lawson's presence but ignored it. He and Boyce had arrived only twenty minutes earlier to find the search almost completed. Three policemen in waders had moved from the ford itself further down the stream in the direction of the footpath leading to the village. Here, at the point where the path branched off from the bank and struck out across the field, they had halted before returning for further orders.

Stapleton looked at Finch.

'Is it worth going on?'

Finch humped his shoulders.

So far they had discovered nothing more from either the stream or the ditches than the usual sodden litter which accumulates at the side of any road, however little used. The whole operation seemed to have been a waste of time, especially since the inquiry was not yet officially designated a full-scale murder investigation. Once that fact had been established, or not, as the case might be, he'd know better whether to commit more time and men to it. In the event, they had covered the immediate vicinity. To extend the search seemed unnecessary.

'We'll pack it in for now,' he told Stapleton.

As the men began to move off, the cars and vans heading for the village, Finch noticed that Alec Lawson had strolled into view round the bend in the lane and was standing watching them.

He appeared casual and unhurried, as if he had merely sauntered down from the caravan to see how the search was progressing, unconcerned whether anyone noticed him or not.

Finch deliberately turned his back on him and caught up with Boyce who had moved away towards the car.

'Pick me up in the village,' he told the Sergeant. 'I'm going to walk back by the footpath.'

'Any particular reason?' Boyce asked nosily.

'Just to check how long it would take. Besides, I want to stretch my legs. I'll meet you outside the Goat.'

'Okay by me,' Boyce replied, getting into the car and seeming relieved that the Chief Inspector hadn't wanted his company.

Lawson was still there, Finch noticed as he mounted the stile, although he had moved to the side of the lane and was now standing up against the hedge where his presence was less obvious. Ignoring him, Finch checked his watch before climbing down on the other side and setting off along the footpath. But, as he left the bank to follow the path across the fields, he couldn't resist looking back. Lawson hadn't moved.

The walk invigorated him. He spent too much time, he decided, sitting behind a desk or in a car. It was good to be out in the fresh air.

The meadow sloped gently downwards, allowing him a panoramic view of the village which straggled along the line of the road. On his right was the white-painted clapboard gable end of the Goat and, further off still and just visible above the trees in the garden, the red-tiled roof of Mrs Bingham's house. To his left, the church tower jogged into nearer view as he approached until finally the path turned off into a narrow alley running between the churchyard wall on one side and the high boundary hedge of the vicarage garden on the other. At the end of it, he emerged into the village street.

Finch looked at his watch again. The walk had taken him nine minutes but that was in daylight and downhill. Anyone using the path at night and in the opposite direction would take longer; how much longer would have to be checked on if necessary.

If necessary. He grimaced impatiently. Surely he didn't need to use that euphemism to himself? If his instinct was right and the case turned out to be murder, he corrected himself.

The walk from the church to the Goat took altogether another five minutes. On the way, he glanced about him, taking in the details of the village which so far he'd only glimpsed briefly from the car earlier that morning – the parish hall; the war memorial, standing on a little patch of grass; the shop with a wholesaler's van parked outside; the three-gabled primary school with its asphalt playground and children's paintings Sellotaped to the classroom windows; a self-contained place very much like the village where he had spent his own childhood and in which, even with today's increased mobility, the majority of its inhabitants would spend their lives.

It was a community in which the people knew each other, better, in some cases, than members of those families who were physically separated from one another and met on only rare occasions. As a way of life, it had its disadvantages. Gossip was rife as no doubt Stella Reeve had discovered. But, at the same time, it offered protection from the outside world and, like a family, would close ranks at the first sign of danger.

He was an outsider, he realised. So, too, was Alec Lawson and, to a lesser extent, Ken Reeve. None of them really belonged to the place as the Maceys did or the Franklins. But what about Stella herself? She had been born and brought up in the village but had married someone outside it and had left, returning only recently, a mere seven days before her death, in fact. Was she, too, considered as an outsider who had posed some threat to the little community she had abandoned?

It was possible. And if that theory was right, it might account for the anxiety on the part of some of those he had interviewed – Fred Mitchell, Ted Macey and Mrs Bingham – for her death to be considered an accident. Not that he suspected them of covering up evidence of murder; that was too extreme. No, the process was more subtle than that. But they were closing ranks against the idea of murder, shutting it out, because if they admitted to themselves that murder was a possibility, then they had to admit to something else – that someone from the village could be the killer. The reaction was probably instinctive. Finch doubted if anyone had worked it out rationally. It was a collective response to danger. Better for it to be an accident than to face the alternative.

And as the thought crossed his mind, Finch was suddenly aware of the reason behind his reluctance to discuss the case with Boyce. It was not simply because he had nothing else to support his belief that Stella Reeve had probably been murdered except his own intuition, although that was bad enough. Boyce had never been sympathetic to mere supposition and quite rightly, too. It was evidence that mattered.

What also bothered him was the thought that his instinct might be wrong. For the first time in his professional life, he doubted that sixth sense on which he had so often relied. For, if he were wrong and Stella Reeve had after all died accidentally, he could, by continuing the inquiry, be uncovering old wounds which, in a small place like Wynford, could go on festering for years.

That was the crux of his dilemma, he realised. His own loyalties were divided. Part of his instinct worked on a professional level; it was the reaction of a policeman who, after years of being in the business, learns to pick up certain scents as a labrador, trained for the gun, will search out game. But, like the dog, he, too, possessed other less directed impulses which in his case had their origins much further back in time than his years as a policeman; to his childhood, in fact, spent in a village like Wynford, and to that much earlier training which had never been expressed in so many words, merely in a shake of the head or a folding of the lips but which, nevertheless, had made it quite clear that there were certain subjects which should never be discussed, certainly not with strangers.

As a child, he had never questioned this unspoken tenet or indeed attempted to put it into words himself. It was only now, as he reached the end of the village street and drew level with Mrs Franklin's cottage, that he realised he had unconsciously been sharing in the primitive and collective response of the herd under threat to group together against the danger.

The curtains in Mrs Franklin's cottage were drawn; so, too, were those of her immediate neighbours, he noticed; a sign of mourning, of course, but a symbol of something more, he felt – of that closing of the ranks and the shutting out of strangers to which that part of himself, still loyal to the old pattern of village allegiance, wanted to respond.

But how the hell did he express this dilemma to Boyce for whom such loyalties would be incomprehensible? And, more importantly still, how was he to reconcile them with his professional duties?

The answer, of course, was he couldn't. The old instincts were still there but had to be resisted. Like Stella Reeve, he had turned his back on his community but for him there was no return. As a professional policeman, his commitments lay elsewhere and, as he walked past the gate of Mrs Franklin's house, he checked his watch again, shooting back his cuff with more determination than was strictly needed for such a trivial act.

It had taken him one and a half minutes to walk from the church to the cottage; a further one and a half minutes to reach the Goat, three minutes in all, so, when these timings were added together, it gave him a total of twelve minutes to cover the distance from the ford to the public house.

The other route, on foot, from the Goat to the ford along Waterend Lane, would have to be checked another time.

Boyce was sitting in the car parked behind the pub, arms spread out over the steering wheel, reading the *Daily Mirror* which he folded up and pitched on to the back seat as Finch climbed in behind him.

'Satisfied?' he asked.

'For the time being,' Finch replied non-committally. Catching the Sergeant's glance turned expectantly towards the Goat, he added, 'No, not here, Tom. We'll stop at another pub on the way back to headquarters. We're bound to find one in the next village.'

'All right with me,' Boyce replied, starting the engine. 'I just thought you'd like to soak up a bit of the local atmosphere.'

He grinned as he said it, amused by his own disingenuousness, knowing full well that he'd made the suggestion entirely for his own benefit.

Finch smiled back although he did not explain that, as far as he was concerned, the last thing he wanted was to become too involved with the place until the exact manner in which Stella Reeve had met her death had been established. Far better not to stir up the water too much at this stage in the investigation.

Which was hardly an apt turn of phrase under the circumstances, he added to himself.

Alec Lawson watched Finch climb over the stile and set off along the footpath. The action surprised him at first. What the hell was he doing? The other policemen had all taken to their cars and driven off down the lane towards the village. One explanation was that the Chief Inspector fancied a country walk but this was not entirely satisfactory. Lawson doubted if Finch did anything for the obvious reason. Despite the man's apparently bland manner and bluff, open features, Lawson wasn't fooled. During the short interview which had taken place the previous evening, he had been aware of a quiet, watchful intelligence, suggesting that the Chief Inspector had been absorbing a great deal more than either his expression or his attitude had indicated.

So, on the basis that Finch's decision to walk back to the village across the fields had some ulterior motive behind it, Lawson moved to the side of the lane where his own presence was less obvious and from where he could watch, with less chance of being observed himself, as the short, stocky figure of the Chief Inspector went stumping off along the footpath.

He was timing the walk. As Finch mounted the stile, Lawson noticed him turn his wrist to look at his watch. And if that were the purpose behind his actions, then there was only one possible inference which could be drawn from it – Finch had reason to believe that someone had used that route to reach the ford and, given this assumption, Stella's death might not have been an accident after all. Would Finch have gone to the trouble of checking the distance and the timing unless there was some doubt in his mind?

Which left the possibility of murder.

Until the thought crossed his mind, Alec Lawson had been merely amused by the idea of watching the Chief Inspector, unobserved himself as he imagined. It was a case of the biter being bitten, a reversal of roles which had a pleasurable ironic twist to it.

But even as the idea occurred to him, Finch reached the point at which the footpath diverted from the bank of the stream to strike off across the meadow where he paused momentarily to glance back over his shoulder. It was done so casually that, had Alec Lawson not been watching closely, he might have missed it.

But that quick movement of the head in his direction made one fact uncomfortably clear to him: Finch was aware of his presence and, in turn, was keeping him under observation.

I should have known better, Lawson thought, turning away himself and walking back along the lane towards the caravan. Never underestimate the opposition.

Although quite what he meant by thinking of Finch as the enemy was not clear even to himself.

All the same, the episode disturbed him and, as he resumed the task of sorting and pricing the books, he found his thoughts turning again and again to the question of Stella's death.

Supposing it were murder? As the last person to see her alive before she met her death, wouldn't he be placed in a difficult position? The police would be bound to treat his statement with suspicion.

Come to that, what exactly was going on in Finch's mind? Had he reason to suppose someone had come across the fields and met her at the ford? If this were so and Stella had indeed been murdered, it could have been either a spur of the moment killing following an accidental meeting or a premeditated crime. In the latter case, the only assumption which could be logically drawn from that was that the killer had known she had been visiting him at the caravan and had lain in wait for her.

Lawson put down the book he had been examining and stared straight ahead.

Why the hell hadn't he offered to drive her home?

Until that moment, he had dismissed his omission as mere thoughtlessness. Now, faced with the possibility that, by offering her a lift, he might have saved her life, he realised that he could not shrug off his responsibility quite so lightly, especially when he remembered her body lying face downwards in the stream.

She had looked so damned pathetic, her blonde hair bedraggled, the cheap fur fabric coat, which had smelt of the scent she wore, dark and sodden with water.

He tried to thrust the image and his own thoughts to one side but they refused to be banished.

The real reason behind his omission was, of course, that he had wanted to punish Joanna through Stella. Let her bloody well cope on her own. I'm no longer responsible for her.

Hadn't that been at the back of his mind?

If he were totally honest with himself, the answer had to be 'yes' which left him facing the unpleasant fact that not only had he been thoughtless but callous and arrogant as well. It was not a very worthy truth to come to terms with.

He finished sorting the books, although any pleasure in the task or in opening up his own business had lost its brightness and sense of anticipation. It was all spoilt.

The job done, he made himself lunch, heating up a tin

of soup on the miniature stove, before carrying the boxes out to the car.

As he turned into the farmyard, Macey came out of the front door of the house to meet him. His presence there and his expression, not at all welcoming, warned Alec even before Macey opened his mouth.

'You planning on storing more boxes in that shed?' he asked.

'That was the idea,' Alec replied.

'Well, it don't suit me no more,' Macey retorted.

'Why not?' Alec tried to make his voice sound pleasant.

'Because I need it myself.'

'I see.' Alec paused before pointing out, 'I have paid rent on the shed, Mr Macey, which doesn't run out until Monday.'

Macey didn't reply immediately. Instead, he felt in his pocket and, producing a roll of dirty pound notes, thumbed through it before handing it over.

'You'll find twenty quid there,' he said. 'That'll cover the two days' rent on the caravan and the shed up to Monday that I'll owe you, plus a tenner for any trouble you'll be put to.'

'You want me out?' Alec demanded. It seemed a superfluous question to ask, especially as Macey had clearly had the money ready on him, but he wanted to make the man admit the fact.

Macey wouldn't meet his eyes or answer directly.

'I've changed my mind about letting them,' he said.

'And you want me to leave at once?' Alec pressed the point home.

'If you can't make it today because it's too short notice, then I'll give you till tomorrow.'

'Supposing I've nowhere else to go?'

'But you have, haven't you?' Macey countered in a jeering manner. 'Fred Mitchell said you'd told him you'd collected the keys to that shop of yours in Studham yesterday.'

Alec Lawson smiled as if amused at having to concede the point. Macey was quite right. The day before he had called in at the Goat at lunchtime on his way back from seeing the solicitor and, pleased that the lease had been signed, had confided this fact to Fred Mitchell. He had even, he remembered, got the keys to the shop out of his pocket to show the landlord and had treated both of them to a whisky on the strength of his new ownership.

Well, that would teach him not to discuss his business with others in the future.

He had, moreover, no intention of pleading his case with Macey or of explaining that, while he might be in possession of the keys to the shop, the place was hardly habitable. The electricity hadn't been switched on yet and he had no furniture to put in the place, not even a bed.

Shrugging as if Macey's decision did not affect him in the least, he said indifferently, 'It suits me, Mr Macey. I'll clear out this afternoon.' He couldn't resist adding as Macey turned away, 'Why the sudden hurry to get rid of me?'

He guessed the reason but was determined to hear it from Macey's own mouth.

In the event, Macey refused to give him that satisfaction. Walking back to the house, he pretended not to hear as he slammed the front door shut.

Inside the house, Pam Macey met him in the hall, her face anxious.

'You've told him?' she asked. 'Is he going?'

Macey made no reply but, pushing past her, went into the sitting-room where he stood at the window watching as Lawson, having opened the shed door, was beginning to carry the boxes out to his car. Pam, who had followed her husband into the room, came to stand behind him.

'He'll see you, Ted,' she protested.

'I don't give a bugger if he does,' he retorted. 'He's leaving, that's all I care.'

'Are you sure it'll be all right?' she asked. 'Only he's got a solicitor, hasn't he? He could make trouble if he wants to.'

The thought didn't seem to worry her husband.

'Then let him try. If he starts anything, I'll get a solicitor of my own and tell him straight out why I don't want Lawson on my property.'

'But you haven't got any proof,' his wife objected. 'The police seem to think it was an accident.'

'Proof!' Macey swung round to face her and she shrank back. 'She was with him yesterday evening just before she died, or so Mitchell told me. What more proof do you want? The bloody police don't know what they're at! They should have run him in this morning; stuck him behind bars. I know what I'd bloody do to him, given half a chance.'

'I'll make some tea,' Pam said uneasily, moving away from the window.

'You didn't see her lying there!' Macey shouted after her as she left the room. 'Animals like him ought to be strung up!' A sudden pain made him clutch his stomach. Half bent over, he followed her to the door. 'And fetch those bloody pills of mine while you're at it!' he added, wincing as he raised his voice.

Alec Lawson drove into the small yard behind the shop where he parked, remaining behind the wheel for a few minutes as he contemplated the back of the premises.

He had looked forward to this occasion eagerly, ever since he had first decided to take up the lease. Now everything was changed. Even the place looked different. The bars on the ground-floor windows and the rubbish littering the yard gave it the grim, dilapidated air of some abandoned institution.

At the sight of it, he felt the anger which had sustained him during the confrontation with Macey and his return to the caravan to pack up his possessions evaporate, leaving an overwhelming sense of depression.

The adventure had gone sour.

To make matters worse, it had started raining again.

You'll bloody well have to make the best of it, he told himself, climbing out of the car and crossing the yard to the back door which he unlocked.

The smell of the place came to meet him, a mingled odour of damp plaster and old food turned rancid.

Leaving the door open to let in the air, he made a tour of the interior, tramping up the uncarpeted stairs to the upper rooms which the previous occupants had used as their living accommodation and noticing details which he had not seen before when he had gone round with the estate agent or which he had discounted as unimportant.

Floorboards creaked underfoot. A sash window rattled where a broken cord hung down. The bath was stained brown under the cold tap.

The shop itself was no better. As he stood in the doorway surveying it, he wondered what the hell had persuaded him he could do anything with it. The dream he had had of pine shelves full of books, of plants and a few choice volumes displayed artistically now seemed ridiculous.

It would take weeks of work to strip out the old fitments and repaint the discoloured walls before he could open for business.

Kicking at the pile of circulars which had collected under the letter-box in the front door, he went back to the car and began to move in his belongings; first the boxes of books which he piled up in the back room behind the shop; then his personal possessions. These he carried upstairs to the room overlooking the yard which he had decided he would use as a temporary bed-sitter until he could afford to redecorate and furnish the other rooms. It was equipped with a cupboard in which he hung his clothes. Lastly, he moved in the camping gear which he had bought at Poulson's on the way there, stopping in the town centre before driving to the shop.

With the bed unfolded and the canvas chair set up by its side, the little spirit stove placed in the hearth and the Gaz lamp standing on an empty crate he had found in the yard, the room began to take on a makeshift homeliness.

But, God, what would Joanna think of it!'

He imagined her standing in the doorway, wearing that light grey coat of hers with the silver fox collar and raising her eyebrows in horrified disbelief.

Suddenly he began to laugh.

The whole situation was so absurd that laughter was the only possible reaction. Any other was unthinkable.

He'd celebrate, he decided, by buying himself a fish and chip supper and a can of lager.

Checking the money in his pocket, he found he had three pounds and sixty-seven pence, all that he possessed until the banks opened on Monday.

And he'd bloody well buy a plant, too. The market hadn't yet closed and he'd probably be able to pick up something from one of the stalls selling garden produce for a few bob.

Still laughing, he clattered down the stairs.

TEN _____

Madge was annoyed. She had expected Bartlett to arrive as usual for work on Wednesday afternoon and had spent part of the morning inspecting the kitchen garden and marking out a new site for the strawberry bed.

The far end would be best, she decided, where the ground lay in full sun for most of the day; not that Bartlett would be pleased. It was the plot he used as a nursery to raise wallflower seedlings for the herbaceous borders. But she was determined to have her own way. After all, it was her garden and Bartlett grew far too many wallflowers anyway. Every spring she was forced to give away bundles of plants to anyone who'd accept them, grateful to be rid of them.

In view of her own plans and Bartlett's normal reliability, his unexpected non-appearance was both surprising and exasperating.

She expressed her annoyance to Gordon over tea, the only time of the day when she had the opportunity to discuss her interests with him. By the time evening came, he was too exhausted to listen properly.

'He simply didn't turn up,' she explained. 'You'd think he would have sent a message. He's not ill, is he?'

'Not to my knowledge,' Gordon replied. 'At least, he's not called at the surgery or asked for a visit. No-one said anything to me either when I was in the village this afternoon. I dropped in on Mrs Franklin, by the way.'

'How is she?' Madge asked, adding as she raised the pot, 'More tea?'

'Please.' He held out his cup for her to fill. 'A little better but still shocked. That woman's aged ten years in the last few days. I feel desperately sorry for her.'

'But what can you do?' Madge asked. 'What can anybody do? One feels so helpless. I'd call myself but I don't think she'd welcome a visit. Besides, the vicar told me that her next-door neighbour, Mrs Rattney, has been staying with her practically day and night and, quite frankly, Gordon, I'm not too eager to run across her again, remembering all the fuss there was last month over the church jumble sale. As if I'd accuse her of pocketing some of the money! I simply said that wasn't it disappointing that her stall hadn't done as well as last year? That's all. But that's beside the point. Honestly, I really feel that you ought to persuade Mrs Franklin to go and stay with one of her daughters. I'm sure Helen would willingly have her. They've got that nice, modern bungalow over at Latchingham and being with the grandchildren would take her mind off the whole ghastly business. Can't you speak to her?'

'I think she prefers to stay here until the inquiry's over,' Gordon replied.

'Which will be when?' Madge demanded. 'I can't imagine what the police think they're doing although, judging by that Chief Inspector who's in charge of the case, I'm not surprised it's taking them so long. It was obviously an accident. In fact, I understand she'd been drinking at the Goat before she called on Alec Lawson. It's possible she'd had too much and that's why she fell.'

'If she did, it'll come out at the inquest,' Gordon pointed

out. 'There's bound to be a post mortem and that'll show how much alcohol was in the stomach.'

'Oh, Gordon, don't!' Madge protested, putting a hand on the front of her tweed skirt. 'For some reason, just the thought of it makes me go quite cold.'

'Sorry. I didn't realise it would upset you. You usually take such things in your stride.'

'Accidents, yes, when there's something practical one can do to help. I've never minded that. But the idea of some pathologist quite dispassionately ... oh, it doesn't bear thinking about! I don't know how anyone could seriously choose such a profession.'

'It has to be done,' Gordon put in mildly, 'although I don't mind admitting it wouldn't be my choice of a career. I prefer to work with the living rather than the dead. You'll be all right at the inquest?' he added, looking into her face with quick anxiety.

Madge shook back her hair. For some reason, his concern made her feel impatient as if he were suggesting she couldn't cope.

'Of course I shall. I imagine it'll be quite straightforward, especially if Broderick's the coroner. He usually is, isn't he? The last time I met him, at that Conservative do at Lyston Hall, he didn't strike me as being particularly formidable. Rather the opposite, I thought. Besides, I shan't have much to contribute, shall I? If I'm called at all, it will simply be because I happened to see Stella with Alec Lawson on my way back from the Maceys' which will hardly be useful except for establishing the timing.'

'But that's not all you saw,' Gordon reminded her. 'You may be asked about the rest of it – Lawson raising his hand and Stella seeming to stumble.'

'Shall I?' Madge seemed distressed at the idea. At times she regretted having told Gordon about this part of her interview with Finch although she could hardly have kept it from him. She was still angry with herself for having been tricked, as she felt, into making the admission in the first place by the Chief Inspector, who hadn't seemed capable of such subtlety nor perception. But, as Gordon had pointed out, it had been her duty to speak. To do otherwise would be to withhold evidence. 'But surely, if it's an accident, Broderick won't be interested in details like that?'

'He may ask you about it and I think you ought to be prepared in case he does. After all, we don't know what the verdict will be.'

'But it's absurd!' Madge protested. 'That bridge is notoriously dangerous. If you remember, I raised the whole question with the Parish Council only last year and if that fool of a man, Sutton, hadn't insisted on the money being spent on new equipment for the Youth Club, it could have been put right. The steps need repairing as well as the actual planking itself and another rail ought to be placed below the top one to act as an extra safeguard. It's a miracle no child has fallen into the ford. They often play there in the summer.'

'Yes. Well,' Gordon said, not committing himself. It was an old source of discussion between them and, while he agreed with her basic argument, Madge hadn't at the time handled it all that well, although he had refrained from pointing this out to her. She should have got the vicar and the PTA on her side before tackling Sutton who was a stubborn man when crossed in committee and didn't like to be defeated, especially by a woman. He ought to have talked to her about it at greater length, he felt. He had let her down. And not just over that particular subject but many others. It was his fault entirely, of course, although there never seemed enough time. Since the children had grown up and left home to go to University, he had sensed a restlessness and dissatisfaction about her. Of course, being Madge, she kept herself busy and never complained but he had the feeling that much of the village activity in which she involved herself was a mere stop-gap for something else that was missing from her life which he ought to fill but which somehow in the busy years since their courtship and the early years of marriage he had lost the knack of supplying.

To make it up a little to her now, he said, 'You were

right, of course, about the bridge. Perhaps something will be done about it.'

'When it's too late,' Madge replied with some bitterness.

'Exactly,' he agreed. 'But we've strayed rather from the main issue, Madge. The point is, if you're questioned at the inquest about Lawson, what will you say?'

'The truth, of course,' she said sharply. 'I shall tell them exactly what I saw. I'm not for a moment suggesting that Alec Lawson had anything to do with Stella Franklin's death and I shall make that quite clear although I can't imagine Broderick will raise the matter anyway. As I said before, I'm convinced it was an accident. But that doesn't alter the fact that I saw Lawson quarrelling with her.'

'It could be awkward for him if the verdict isn't accidental death,' Gordon remarked.

'But what else could it possibly be?'

'I don't know, Madge. Murder? I know it's unlikely but it depends on what other evidence the police have. Or there could be an open verdict. Either way it could make life difficult for Lawson, even if he isn't named. You know Macey's asked him to leave the caravan? More or less chucked him out as far as I can gather.'

'Who told you that?'

'Oh, I don't know, Gordon replied vaguely. 'I heard it in the village this afternoon. It seems Macey was suspicious of the part Lawson might have played in Stella's death and told him to go. It's absurd, of course, but there you are. Once the mud gets churned up, some of it's bound to stick, even on the innocent.'

'God!' Madge said furiously and began rattling the tea-things on to the tray as if finding some solace in the crash of china. 'People round here are impossible! I sometimes hate their . . .' she broke off. Gordon had never encouraged her to show emotion. A controlled man himself, he was embarrassed by such outbursts. She began again, more calmly. 'Although I didn't much like Alec Lawson, I'm sorry this has happened. I wouldn't have wished it on him for the world. I'd rather hoped he was our kind of person.'

'What do you mean by that?' Gordon asked. He had

half-risen from his chair but sat down again, looking across at her.

Madge laughed and shrugged as she continued loading the tray.

'Oh, I don't know,' she replied. 'Someone interested in books, I suppose, and art and things like that. But it doesn't matter now. Didn't you say earlier that you had a letter to write to the specialist in Chelmsford about the Baxter boy? If you'd like to get it done, Gordon, I'll post it for you in the village. I was thinking of walking down there anyway to call on Bartlett so I could put it in the box for you. Someone ought to find out what's the matter in case he's ill. Besides, I want to know if he's coming tomorrow or not. I had planned on driving into Studham to change my library books but I'd rather wait in and see him, that is if he comes. I must discuss the garden with him. What a nuisance it all is! I had tomorrow all arranged.'

Bartlett was at home. He was sitting in the kitchen with the back door open as Madge arrived, gazing morosely down the garden at the long vegetable plot where strips of old blue fertiliser bags, fixed to the top of tall canes to act as bird-scarers, fluttered over the neatly ridged earth.

He didn't look particularly ill to Madge, merely sullen, lifting his head unwillingly to look at her as she walked round the side of the cottage.

'I've come to see how you are,' she announced.

'I'm all right,' Bartlett mumbled, returning his gaze to the garden.

'Only you didn't come this afternoon,' Madge continued. She had been expecting an apology and, when Bartlett still didn't respond, she felt a further explanation was needed. 'To do the garden.'

'No,' he agreed.

'Aren't you feeling very well?' Madge asked. He had made no attempt to get up from the kitchen chair which was placed just inside the doorway or to invite her into the house and she was forced to remain standing outside on the patch of concrete by the step, looking up at him. Seen from this angle, his face looked longer than ever, the jaw sagging slackly, dragging down the corners of his mouth so that the features had the exaggerated appearance of a grotesque mask depicting melancholy.

Perhaps he was ill after all, Madge thought.

'If it's your leg that's bothering you,' she added quickly, before Bartlett had time to reply to her question, 'I could ask my husband to call or I could drive you up to the surgery myself. I'm perfectly willing to do so.'

The offer seemed to mollify Bartlett a little. He got up from the chair and carried it back to its place by the deal table which, covered with a flowered plastic cloth, took up most of the centre of the room. A jerk of his head invited her to enter. Madge mounted the step and stood just inside the door, resisting the temptation to look too closely about her at the signs of Bartlett's disorganised bachelor existence.

A grey woollen vest hung on a string over the mottled boiler, its arms dangling down, while, on the table, a loaf of bread sat among crumbs on a worn round board, the wood cut about with countless knife marks. Beside it were two slices of ham in a piece of greasy wrapping paper and a jar of Branston pickle, with its lid off, showing a dried brown crust round the rim.

'I see I'm interrupting your tea,' she added, feeling the need to say something as Bartlett remained silent.

'I'd finished,' he replied.

'Would you like my husband to call?' Madge asked again. She had noticed that, as Bartlett had carried in the chair, he had moved more stiffly than usual, one hip pushed forward as if he were attempting to take the weight off his damaged leg.

'I ain't been sleeping too well lately,' Bartlett said with apparent inconsequentiality although the remark seemed to be intended as an oblique explanation of his present physical state as well as his non-appearance that afternoon.

'If you're in pain . . .' Madge began.

'It ain't my leg,' Bartlett said. He remained standing on the other side of the table, still holding on to the back of the chair. 'It's the shock.'

'Shock?' Madge didn't understand.

'Of that girl dying.'

'Stella Franklin, you mean?'

Her first reaction was one of surprise. Why on earth should Bartlett care about Stella Franklin? Of course, he knew her as everyone else in the village did. One couldn't live in a place like Wynford without getting to know each individual by name at least. But Bartlett had never struck her as the type who would take much interest in his neighbours nor in local gossip like some she could think of. He had always seemed an uncommunicative man who had held himself aloof from any personal contacts. She could conceive of no reason why the girl's death had affected him so deeply, as it obviously had, unless the very idea of someone dying had reminded him of his own mother's death which, Madge remembered, had occurred about the same time last year. Madge had visited her in her last illness on several occasions, bringing flowers and women's magazines and grapes, the usual contributions which the healthy offer to the sick, like sacrifices made to some pagan goddess of vitality to ensure one's own continuing physical well-being, Madge had thought at the time; not that the comparison had been exactly apt in old Mrs Bartlett's case. Madge recollected a beaky nose sticking out over the bedclothes, thin white hair spreading out on the pillow and a sour-sweet smell of urine and old, unwashed flesh.

All Bartlett had said when she finally died was, 'She's well out of it.'

Madge had the impression that the relief he expressed was as much for his own sake as hers.

'Stella's death was a shock to all of us,' she remarked. She hoped Bartlett would leave it there but, now he was embarked on the subject, he seemed unable to let it go.

'I saw her last Friday night, not long before she must have died,' he continued. 'She was in the Goat. Then she left and _he_ came in.'

'Who?' Madge asked.

Bartlett couldn't possibly mean Alec Lawson, she thought. As far as she knew, Lawson had been in the caravan all evening. At least, that was the interpretation local rumour put on the events. Stella Franklin had walked up to the caravan to find him because he hadn't been in the Goat as she had expected.

'Him. Her husband,' Bartlett explained.

'Oh, I see,' Madge replied. There was not much else she could say as she still couldn't remember Stella's husband's name or much else about him except he came from Studham where he worked in a garage and was, judging from the rare occasions when she had seen him in the village after the wedding when he and Stella were still living with Mrs Franklin, a dark-haired young man with a glowering expression and a disturbing air of suppressed violence about him. 'Didn't he knock Stella about and that's why she left him?'

'She should never have married him!' Bartlett shouted in an unexpected outburst of emotion.

'Yes, of course,' Madge agreed.

But how extraordinary! she added to herself. Why in heaven's name should Bartlett feel so involved with Stella Franklin's life? Or death, come to that? Unless he was going through some emotional crisis to do with his age. He was – what? – in his fifties, she supposed, at the time of life when such disturbances were said to occur, and even Bartlett, who never gave any indication of having any interests apart from work or any real feelings except for a plodding, dogged acceptance of what could only be a dull and routine existence, must nevertheless be susceptible to hormonal changes. She remembered Gordon telling her about a farmer at Latchingham, also in his fifties, who had shot his wife and two sons before hanging himself in the barn. Gordon had attributed that fourfold tragedy to the man's age.

The memory of it made her uneasy as did Bartlett's face, pushed forward towards her, the eyes staring and the mouth open, blobs of spittle gathered at the corners of his lips, and his hands grasping the back of the chair with such force that she could see the knuckles showing yellowish-white under the skin.

She had been about to add that Stella had been forced to marry the young man from Studham, whatever his name was. After all, she'd been pregnant by him, hadn't she? But, at the sight of Bartlett's face and gripping hands, she changed her mind.

Instead, she said, 'If you're not sleeping very well, Mr Bartlett, I'm sure my husband could prescribe something for you.'

To her relief, the spasm of anger passed and his face fell back again into its normal, melancholy folds.

'I don't want no tablets,' he muttered, turning away so that she could only see his profile. 'I don't hold with dosing myself up.'

'But you should take something to help you relax, if only a nightcap.'

Opening her handbag, Madge took out her purse and extracted a five pound note which she held out to him.

'Won't you treat yourself to a bottle of whisky or brandy? I'm sure it would do you good last thing at night. Go on, take it,' she urged as Bartlett shook his head and turned even further from her and the proffered note.

'I ain't short of money,' he retorted and his head went up, showing the same beaky profile as his mother spurning the copies of *Woman's Own* and the black, hot-house grapes, an ironic expression glittering under her wrinkled lids.

'Very well,' Madge said briskly. If that was his attitude, she had no intention of pleading with him. She put the purse away and snapped the bag shut, at the same time making up her mind to speak to Gordon about the man. Clearly Bartlett was under some stress although for quite what reason she couldn't imagine. It couldn't just be caused by the girl's death. No doubt Gordon would be able to contrive a visit without it appearing too obvious when he was calling on other patients in the village.

'I'll leave you then, Mr Bartlett,' she concluded. 'I hope

you'll feel better soon. When you do, I expect I'll be seeing you back at work.'

She gave a slight interrogative lift to the last remark, inviting Bartlett's reply, but instead of saying as she had expected that he'd be round the following afternoon or early the next week, he made no comment and Madge was forced to let herself out of the cottage with no definite idea of when he would return.

It was a nuisance. She was hoping to get the new strawberry bed prepared and planted before the main work on the vegetable garden began. In a few days' time it would be April when there would be so many other jobs to be done outside and she couldn't possibly cope with them on her own. It was no good expecting Gordon to help either. He was far too busy as it was.

Damn Bartlett! she thought. He'd always been so reliable in the past. If he let her down, who could she find to replace him? There was no-one else in the village who was willing to be employed as a jobbing gardener despite the fact that several young men she could think of were out of work, such as Mrs Wilson's son, who spent all day lounging about at home when he wasn't scrounging money from his mother to go into Studham to a disco. Not that she would dream of asking him anyway. She doubted if he'd recognise a strawberry plant if he saw one.

Walking back along the village street, she was overwhelmed with the feeling that everything was changing and for the worst. Wynford wasn't the same as it had been when she and Gordon first came to live there. The children had been small then, Richard only a baby. Life had seemed so very full and rich with promise. And easier, too. There had been no problem getting help with the housework. Mrs Stone – dead now – clean, respectful, eager to earn a little extra, had come in every morning while her husband, also dead, had seen to the garden, working on it every Saturday afternoon for ten shillings, despite the fact that he had a full-time job as a farm labourer all the rest of the week. Shops had delivered. Tradesmen went out of their way to be obliging.

People were more content, too. There was none of this desperation to acquire material things. Teenagers were happy if they went to Studham on the bus once a week to the cinema. The fare then had been one and tenpence. Now the cinema was closed and turned into a bingo hall with a disco twice a week and a wine bar. God knows what the fare was these days. Over a pound, she believed.

Madge reached the end of the street and paused outside Mrs Franklin's house. As the doctor's wife, she ought to go in, she supposed. Gordon obviously expected her to pay a visit but what on earth would she say? The conventional expressions of sympathy seemed quite inadequate.

As she hesitated, the front door to the next house opened and Mrs Rattney came out, carrying something in a pudding basin covered with a white cloth, and eased herself sideways through the gap in the hedge between the two gardens. The sight of her, that formidable backside and fat, foolish face with its little turtle mouth clamped shut, decided her and as the woman let herself into Mrs Franklin's cottage, calling out 'Coo-ee!' as she did so, Madge walked on, pretending she hadn't seen her.

She had no intention of confronting Mrs Rattney; at least, not yet. There would be a more suitable opportunity at some later date at one of the Ladies' Church Guild meetings when it was Mrs Rattney's turn to supply the refreshments and Madge, by praising her scones, could make her peace with the woman.

But how stupid it all is! Madge thought suddenly. And what a waste!

Although a waste of what, she herself wasn't quite sure.

ELEVEN

It was early the following week before Finch received Pardoe's report. Until it arrived, there was little he cou do except write up his own reports and wait for Pardoe to submit his.

Meanwhile, forensic examination of the dead woman's clothing had come up with nothing positive to help the investigation. Her handbag had also proved negative for tests had shown that only Stella Reeve's fingerprints were found on it while it had contained nothing more than might have been expected—a box of matches, a half-empty packet of cigarettes, a lipstick, comb and powder compact together with a purse containing a couple of pound notes and some loose change – no vital evidence in other words.

No useful fingerprints had been found on the handrail either, only blurred smudges which it was impossible to identify.

The only positive test was on the fibres caught on the rail. These had come from Stella Reeve's coat, not that this was any help in establishing whether or not she had been murdered. In fact, if anything, it tended to support the theory of accidental death.

The body was formally identified by Ken Reeve on Saturday afternoon after Finch's return from Wynford, an arrangement he had made in order to be present to witness Reeve's reaction.

In the event, he was disappointed. It was a brief, sombre occasion, Reeve merely glancing down at the face before turning away.

'That's her,' he said.

He seemed subdued, less challenging and macho in a suit and a white shirt, his thick black hair combed flat.

And that was that.

He said nothing more, not even looking in Finch's direction as he was led away to sign the necessary statement.

Finch lingered to take a last glimpse of Stella Reeve's face before the trolley containing her body was rolled back into its refrigerated compartment. The hair had dried and, under the strip lighting, looked coarse. He noticed for the first time the dark roots and the artificial kink in the ends from a perm which was growing out and which e submersion in the water had turned frizzy. Without make-up, the features looked less well-defined while the mouth had fallen slightly open, revealing the prominent teeth and accentuating the heavy line of the jaw.

Death had not been kind to Stella Reeve as it was to some.

Seeing her, Finch felt an overwhelming sense of waste. She had been robbed, not just of life, but of some special vitality which had been uniquely hers, like a light suddenly quenched.

'How did Reeve take it?' Boyce asked when Finch returned to the office.

'He didn't confess if that's what you're hoping to hear,' Finch snapped.

He felt in low spirits, a reaction which a visit to the mortuary always roused in him although in this case it was worse than usual.

Boyce shrugged it off. Having worked with Finch over many years, he knew the Chief Inspector too well by now to be affected by his moods. The inquiry itself didn't help, of course. Until the exact circumstances of the death had been established, a question mark hung over the investigation which was inhibiting to everyone concerned but especially to Finch who was in charge of it.

'Perhaps Pardoe will come up with his report soon,' he said with a helpful air.

Ignoring him, Finch went to stand hump-shouldered at the window where he stared morosely out at the rain.

The report came three days later. Pardoe brought it himself, bustling into the office in his usual hurried manner as if the visit had interrupted much more important and pressing matters.

'As I thought when I made the preliminary examination, the cause of death was drowning,' he announced briskly. 'And the time was approximately three to four hours before I examined the body, that is between eight and nine o'clock that night. My theory that she was knocked unconscious by the fall seems to be borne out by the evidence, by the way. Forensic has identified some small pieces of gravel and debris in the wound tissue on the forehead which correspond to the sample your men collected up from the bed of the stream where the body was found.'

'Any other marks on her?' Finch asked, trying to disguise his eagerness.

'I was coming to that,' Pardoe retorted, annoyed at the interruption. 'There's bruising on the right forearm. I can't be too precise about it because the thickness of the coat she was wearing absorbed a lot of the pressure. But from the position of the marks, it looks as if someone grasped her fairly tightly just above the elbow and not long before she died either. The bruises were fresh. What you make of it is your own affair.'

And with that, he handed over his report and left the room.

'Wait a minute,' Finch said quickly as Boyce seemed about to speak. 'Don't let's jump to any conclusions. Those bruises don't necessarily mean she was murdered. They could have happened earlier in the evening.'

'At Lawson's you mean?' Boyce replied. 'That's true. Mrs Bingham said she thought Lawson and Stella Reeve were quarrelling as she drove past. You'll check with him, of course?'

'Yes; get your coat; we'll go over to Wynford straight away.'

As he put on his own coat, Finch didn't add that, as far as he was concerned, Pardoe's report had confirmed the impression which he had received when he had first viewed the body – that taint of violence which had seemed to hang over the scene. Whether or not it amounted to murder had still, as he had pointed out to Boyce, to be proved. But at least it justified a further inquiry into the exact circumstances surrounding Stella Reeve's death. It confirmed something else as well. There was now no question where his own loyalties lay. He was fully committed to his professional allegiances.

Lawson wasn't in the caravan which they found locked and, when Finch mounted the steps to peer through the glass panel in the door, stripped as well of all the man's possessions.

'It looks as if he's gone,' he announced.

Inquiries of Mrs Macey at the farm elicited the information that he'd moved to the shop in Studham.

'Sudden, wasn't it?' Finch asked.

Obviously ill at ease, Mrs Macey had nothing more to say to them except to smile nervously before closing the front door.

The reason for her embarrassment was explained later when, having driven into Studham and found the shop, they put the question to Lawson who replied, 'I got chucked out by Macey.'

'Why?' Finch demanded.

Lawson shrugged and tried to look amused.

'He didn't give a reason but I can guess. I was the last person to see Stella alive. As some mystery seems to surround her death, rumour has it she might have been murdered and I seem to be the most likely candidate for the role of killer.'

'I see,' Finch said blankly.

'I notice you don't deny the possibility,' Lawson commented.

'Our inquiries aren't yet complete,' Finch replied. In view of the reason for his visit, he felt uncomfortable and unexpectedly sorry for the man. Lawson looked exhausted and dispirited, quite unlike his usual cocky, rather self-assured manner.

Looking about him, Finch realised it wasn't hard to understand the reason for the change. The shop interior was in confusion. Chunks of plaster had fallen from the walls where the old fitments had been removed and were littering the floorboards, some of which had been torn up. Lawson himself was covered in dirt, his clothes and hands filthy, his hair full of plaster dust.

Some comment seemed called for and he remarked, 'You've got a job on your hands by the look of it. Are you tackling it yourself?'

Alec Lawson's mouth twisted with some of his former irony.

'In the absence of money to pay a builder, yes, Chief

Inspector, I am. Don't tell me I've bitten off more than I can chew which is the comment most people make when they see it. I'm well aware of it myself. We'll go upstairs to talk, shall we? I assume that's the reason why you're here. At least the floor up there is whole.'

They tramped up a narrow, uncarpeted staircase to a back room, minimally furnished with a camp bed, a canvas chair and a crate.

'Sit down,' Lawson told them.

He had recovered sufficiently to be genuinely amused at the situation, smiling broadly as Finch claimed the canvas chair while Boyce lowered himself reluctantly on to the crate. He himself remained standing, one elbow propped on the mantelpiece.

'Well?' he asked.

'I wanted to check on the statement you made on Friday evening,' Finch replied. 'You said Mrs Reeve was with you for about half an hour. Was there any quarrel or disagreement in which you grasped her by the arm?'

Lawson looked at him directly. He seemed about to lose his temper and then changed his mind.

'No,' he said evenly although Finch noticed the muscles tighten along his jaw. 'There was no quarrel and I didn't touch her.'

'Or later when you said goodbye to her at the gate?'

This time Lawson merely repeated the single negative, 'No.'

'You didn't raise your hand as if to strike her?'

Lawson paused before replying.

'Someone saw us?' he suggested at last and as Finch appeared about to open his mouth to protest, he continued, 'It's the only obvious explanation, isn't it? You wouldn't have come here asking that sort of question unless you have evidence. So there was a witness.' He made the remark musingly, half to himself. 'The driver of the car, of course! The one that passed as Stella and I were standing at the gate. Who was it?'

'I'm not prepared to divulge the witness's name,' Finch said in his best officialese.

'Just answer the question, Mr Lawson,' Boyce put in, adding his own weight to the situation, pen poised over his notebook.

Lawson looked from one to the other of them.

'It would be funny if it weren't so damned serious,' he commented. 'You know, I can see exactly how your mind's working. What are you trying to prove? Murder? Does that count higher in the crime ratings than accidental death? I don't know what the hell your witness saw in the few seconds it took for the car to pass us, in the dark, too, with only the headlamps to see by, but it wasn't a quarrel or a fight, I can assure you.'

'Your hand was raised, according to our witness,' Finch persisted. He tried to keep his voice non-committal but was aware of a growing dislike for the man. Lawson clearly had a chip on his shoulder; quite why, he wasn't sure. But for whatever reason, Lawson's bitterness seemed to find expression in attacking any form of authority as if, by doing so, he was trying to justify his own rejection of what it stood for.

For his own part, Finch realised that he had to make a conscious effort to control his antipathy in order to remain objective.

'Did I raise my hand?' Lawson was saying with pretended lightness. 'I suppose I must have done, as your witness saw me. Oh, yes.' He began laughing. 'I remember now. How absurd! The verge was muddy. I believe I did lift my hand to point this out to Stella. She was wearing ridiculous high-heeled shoes and I thought she might slip.'

There was a contemptuous note in his voice as he spoke of the shoes, dismissive not just of Stella but of all women, and, hearing it, Finch thought he understood the man a little better. The arrogance was largely defensive. For some reason, perhaps because of the breakup of his marriage, Lawson felt threatened by his own guilt and needed to strike out at others in order to protect his own self-esteem.

Which would make a good motive for murder, Finch thought, if Stella Reeve, by something she had said or done, had damaged Lawson's pride.

'I see,' he said blandly, his expression giving away nothing of what he was thinking. 'I'd like you to make an official statement, Mr Lawson. Would tomorrow afternoon at Divisional Headquarters at half past two suit you?'

'It won't but I suppose I'll be expected to put in an appearance. Is that all?' Lawson asked as Finch rose to go.

'One other point,' the Chief Inspector added almost as an afterthought. 'At the first interview, you said Stella Reeve had spoken of an offer she'd had. I'd like you to give the matter a little more thought before tomorrow so that we can include it in your statement.'

'What offer?' Boyce asked when they emerged from the shop and got into the car.

'Didn't I mention it?' Finch sounded distracted, glancing back as the car drew away from the kerb at the shop front with its dirty windows and shabby paint. He was thinking that Lawson would have a hell of a job putting the place into any sort of shape before he could open for business. He felt almost sorry for the man. 'According to him, it was something Stella Reeve said in passing. She needn't have married Reeve, she told Lawson. She had another offer. That was all.'

'So?' Boyce asked.

'So it occurred to me that someone else might have been interested in her and could have resented her marrying Reeve.'

'You think it could be a motive for murder?'

'If it's murder,' Finch pointed out.

They were coming up to the roundabout on the outskirts of Studham.

'Where to?' Boyce asked.

'Wynford,' Finch said, making up his mind. 'I think we'll have another talk with Mrs Franklin.'

'Any particular reason?'

'About the offer, among other things. She may be able to tell us if Stella had any other boyfriends before she married Reeve. I'd like to have a look at her belongings as well. You never know, she might have brought something with her when she left her husband that'll be a help in the inquiry.'

Mrs Franklin knew nothing of the offer.

'Stella never said anything to me about it,' she said in answer to Finch's question.

They were sitting together in the living-room, Mrs Franklin looking pale and a little dazed. Finch wondered if she had been prescribed tranquillisers. A small bottle of pills was standing on the mantelpiece but he couldn't see the label.

'But she had other boyfriends before she met Ken?' Finch asked. It seemed natural to use Christian names when referring to the individuals involved in the case, almost as if he were a member of the family. And indeed he felt perfectly at ease. Many of the objects around him, the potted plants on the window-sill, the picture calendar hanging on a hook by the fireplace, the crocheted chairbacks, reminded him of his own childhood home.

'Oh, yes; Stella went out with quite a few. They're all married now, though.'

'Could you let me have their names all the same?' Finch asked.

Boyce jotted them down as she went through the list. There were about five of them.

'Stella was never short of a boyfriend,' Mrs Franklin added in explanation, 'although it was generally her who chucked them over. Then she met Ken.'

'Where did they meet?'

'At a disco in Studham. Stella was working in the town then, in Baxter's on the cooked meats counter. That was before she went in for bar work. Ken had a car and he used to come over here to pick her up.'

'But I believe they quarrelled?' Finch put the question casually.

Mrs Franklin seemed to accept without resentment the fact that he had picked up some of the local gossip.

'That's right. Stella said he wanted to be too much the boss. She wouldn't stand for anyone ordering her about so she threw him over.'

'They got married though,' Finch hinted. He knew the reason, but he wanted to hear her version of the events.

'That was my doing,' Mrs Franklin confessed. 'Stella found she was expecting and it was me who pushed her into marrying him. I knew people were talking and who else would have wanted her, with another man's baby on the way? So they got married. Later, I wished to God I hadn't got on to her about it. That was after they'd moved in with me and I could see the marriage wouldn't last although I hoped once they'd got their own place over at Studham they'd make a go of things.'

'But they didn't,' Finch said. He had learnt that much from Mrs Franklin herself at the first interview.

'No,' she agreed quietly.

'You told me, Mrs Franklin, that when Stella came home she brought some of her belongings with her. Would you mind if my Sergeant and I had a look through them?'

She accepted the request without question, perhaps in the belief that this was normal procedure in a sudden death.

'She had the back room, the one where she used to sleep when she first married Ken,' Mrs Franklin explained, leading the way up a flight of steep stairs which ran from a narrow inner hallway between the kitchen and the living-room. It opened on to a tiny landing with two doors.

The bedroom was small with a sloping ceiling and was almost entirely filled by a double bed with oak head and footboards.

'I'll leave you to it,' Mrs Franklin added as she ushered them into the room.

When she had gone, Boyce squeezed himself past the end of the bed towards a wardrobe which was wedged in on the far side under the slope of the ceiling and, opening the door, began searching through the contents.

After a few minutes, he announced, 'Nothing much here except clothes and shoes.'

Finch was having no better luck with the dressing-table which stood under the window. The top two drawers were crammed with jumpers and underwear, pushed in haphazardly, although the contents of the bottom drawer, evidently her best clothes, were more carefully arranged.

Tucked under a nylon blouse with sequin embroidery, he found what he had been hoping for: a box with a picture of black kittens on the lid which had once held chocolates.

It contained, as he discovered when he carried it over to the bed to examine it, a collection of cheap jewellery underneath which were several cards – twenty-first birthday greetings mostly, inscribed with the senders' names. But one was different. It was a Valentine card with a traditional red heart on the front, surrounded by a garland of flowers. Inside, the verse read:

> The flowers are for you, my dear,
> The heart is just like mine.
> Remember I am always here
> And long to be your Valentine.

There was no name.

Boyce, who had shut the wardrobe door, came across to peer over the Chief Inspector's shoulder.

'Could be from the husband,' he pointed out.

'Somehow I don't think so,' Finch replied. 'He didn't strike me as the type who'd send his wife an anonymous Valentine card, not with a verse like that on it. Have you got something we can put it into, Tom? I'd like to have it fingerprinted.'

Boyce took a clear plastic envelope from his wallet and Finch, having slipped the card inside it, carried it downstairs where he showed it to Mrs Franklin.

'Have you any idea who might have sent it to your daughter?' he asked.

Mrs Franklin shook her head.

'It was in a box with some twenty-first birthday cards,' Finch added.

Her face cleared.

'It was Stella's twenty-first at the end of January. An envelope came here a few days later, at the beginning of February, with "Please Forward" written across the front. I posted it on to her, thinking it was another birthday card.

It could have been that one, I suppose. I remember thinking at the time: If it's for her birthday, she'll get it too late.'

'You didn't recognise the handwriting on the envelope?'

'No. The name and address were printed in capitals.'

'I see.' Finch's expression was blank. 'You don't mind if we take it with us?'

'Not if you need it. Has it something to do with Stella's death?'

'I don't know, Mrs Franklin,' Finch confessed. 'We still haven't finished our inquiries.'

Outside, Boyce said unexpectedly, 'Something's up. I can tell by the look on your face.'

His tone was almost accusatory.

They were standing in the road by the front gate to Mrs Franklin's cottage where Finch had paused to look up and down the street as if uncertain which way to go. He grinned at Boyce a little ruefully.

'Let's get in the car, Tom,' he replied. 'I don't want to stand out here talking about the case. Drive up to the church.'

'Well?' Boyce asked as he drew up at the churchyard gate.

'All right,' Finch agreed. 'There is something the matter and that Valentine card clinches it. What do we do with it, Tom? Have it fingerprinted? And what then? Fingerprint every man in the village who knew Stella Reeve and might have sent it to her? Where the hell do we draw the line? I didn't want to discuss it with you before because I wasn't sure myself. And I still haven't made up my mind. Stella Reeve could have died accidentally although the case smells to me of murder. No, don't ask me why,' he put in quickly as the Sergeant seemed about to open his mouth. 'I admit I have no real reason for thinking that. I hoped Pardoe's report would clear the matter up but it hasn't. Those bruises on her arm could be unconnected with her death. We're not even sure how she got them. I know Mrs Bingham's statement about seeing Stella Reeve and Alec Lawson quarrelling would suggest him but he denies this and his explanation seems plausible enough. The point he raised, too, about the car passing too quickly for the driver to have had more than a fleeting glimpse is a valid one.'

'So you're suggesting we cross him off the list?' Boyce asked.

Finch felt exasperation rise. It was this same literal-mindedness on the Sergeant's part which had been one of the reasons behind his reluctance to take Boyce into his confidence in the first place and he wished to God he hadn't been drawn into the discussion. Boyce lacked subtlety. As far as he was concerned, facts were all that mattered. Speculation was dangerous. In that respect, he shared Pardoe's approach to evidence.

And he was right, too, up to a point. But Finch could not help regretting that Marion Greave hadn't been involved on the inquiry. She would have understood his doubt over the case and his need to discuss it as an intellectual exercise without committing either of them to rigid conclusions as Boyce was doing. She might, or so he liked to think, have also appreciated his dilemma over his sense of divided loyalties which still disturbed him although, with his conscious mind at least, the choice had been made.

He wondered if he should phone her and then dismissed the idea. It smacked too much of a mere excuse to contact her again and he was anxious not to appear too eager.

It was better perhaps to remain aloof from her and try to explain himself to Boyce who was at least on the inquiry with him and ought to be fully involved, although he could hardly admit that his reluctance to do so was entirely due to the Sergeant's own limitations.

Trying to keep his voice even, he replied, 'That's the whole point, Tom. There isn't a list. Or rather there shouldn't be if Stella Reeve died accidentally. But if she didn't, can we prove it was murder? I don't think we can on the evidence we've so far collected even though I'm still convinced it wasn't an accident. Besides, there's something else that's bothering me.' He paused and for once Boyce had the good sense to keep silent. 'In a place like this we could stir up a lot of mud which could stick. Take Lawson as an example. Macey soon got rid of him. And that could be only a beginning. If it's a case of murder, we have no choice in the matter. But supposing it isn't?'

It was only an approximation of his real feelings, the nearest he could get to expressing himself out loud. As he finished, he glanced sideways at Boyce who was sitting with his arms folded. Seen like that, his heavy shoulders squared, he looked too positive and challenging, hardly in the frame of mind to listen sympathetically to Finch's tentative explanation.

His answer surprised Finch.

'I don't see we have any choice,' he replied. 'You've smelt a wrong'un so we go on with the inquiry.'

Finch nearly laughed out loud with relief and genuine amusement. After all his own uncertainty and mental anguishing over the dilemma, it was Boyce who had cut through to the heart of the matter with a few laconic sentences, typical of the man and yet expressing his complete faith in the Chief Inspector's judgement.

He realised something else as well: that Marion Greave would have given him exactly the same advice only expressed more cogently. He could almost hear her saying it: 'Trust your own instinct, Jack. There's no alternative.'

And it was the only possible answer. He saw that now.

'Right!' he said with new vigour. 'So we carry on. We'll get that card checked for prints and see if we can find out who sent it. We'll also check Lawson's statement this afternoon. In fact, we'll go over all the evidence again, Tom.'

'Okay by me,' Boyce replied in the same offhand manner. 'Where to now? Back to headquarters?'

TWELVE _____

Alec Lawson came out of Divisional Headquarters and paused on the steps to button up his coat before walking to his car.

It was still raining, a fine misty drizzle, and the air felt cold and damp after the centrally heated warmth of Finch's office.

During the interview, while his statement had been taken down and read over to him, he had managed to preserve an aloof, amused air as if he were indulging the Chief Inspector and his Sergeant in some ridiculous game they had chosen to play but the truth was that, despite himself, he had been impressed by Finch's quiet authority and his imperturbability which nothing seemed to shake.

At the end of the interview, after the statement had been signed, Finch had merely gathered up his papers, nodded pleasantly to Lawson and left the room with the Sergeant, sending in a uniformed Constable to conduct him downstairs.

Walking back to the entrance, Lawson had been aware of an atmosphere of activity and busy commitment about the place. Telephones rang in offices. Typewriters clattered. Passing an open door, he caught a glimpse of three men bent over a desk, examining a large sheet of paper spread out over its top.

He was reminded of Tierson's where he used to work and, for a moment, he regretted having lost that sense of belonging and participation which, in the good days before his disillusionment had set in, he had enjoyed.

It was absurd, of course. This was Finch's little kingdom, not his. All the same, he half-envied the Chief Inspector his familiarity with these corridors and rooms, the fact that the girl he passed, carrying a pile of folders, would no doubt recognise him and smile as she said hello.

For his own part, he got nothing; not so much as a glance. He was the outsider who had no place here.

As he emerged into the rain, this sense of alienation deepened as he realised that he had nowhere to go except back to the shop in Studham, to the cheerless upstairs room and the shop itself, stripped down to the plaster.

It wasn't until he had driven away from Divisional Headquarters into the one-way system that it occurred to him as he approached the traffic lights that, if he turned right, he could go home.

No, not home, he corrected himself. He no longer had the right to call it that. It was merely the house where he used to live.

The urge to revisit it was quite irrational although he told himself that, since he was so near, it would be stupid not to call and make arrangements for collecting his books.

Simon would be at school and for that he was grateful. He didn't want to meet the boy in such familiar surroundings. Joanna, too, might be out. If she was, he'd let himself in and leave a note for her.

But she was at home. As he turned into Claremont Drive, he could see her Renault parked on the hard-stand in front of the garage.

At the sight of it, he almost turned back. It had been a mistake to come, he realised. The house and its setting reminded him too painfully of the weeks of anguish which had preceded his decision to leave.

It stood in a small, exclusive development of what the planners called 'executive residences' – detached, four-bedroomed houses with white-painted cladding on the upper storeys, vaguely Swedish in conception although the brass carriage lamps at the front doors and the landscaped gardens were entirely English, neo-Georgian with a dash of Capability Brown.

It was their pretentiousness which he had rebelled against and the realisation that they represented a life-style which he had found increasingly antipathetic. They epitomised for him a safe, smug, middle-class conformity which dictated the make of car you drove and the brand of sherry you served before dinner; the upmarket image which Joanna had seized on so eagerly. She had wanted nothing more than to be an executive wife with an account at Harrods and a son at St Mark's prep school.

What the hell did any of it matter?

And yet the anger which had sustained him no longer seemed to matter either. He felt he had moved on to another plane and all he experienced now was a curiosity to observe once again what he had so violently rejected.

He rang the bell like any other visitor although he still had his own keys to the house in his pocket.

Joanna answered the door. For a few moments, he saw her with a stranger's eyes: an attractive, dark-haired woman, no longer young but carrying about her the unmistakable gloss of class. Then he noticed, with more familiar eyes, that she looked tired and unexpectedly harder as if something inside her had stiffened. Her hostility towards him was apparent.

'Oh, it's you,' she said coldly. 'I suppose you'd better come in.'

'I called to make arrangements about picking up the books,' he replied awkwardly, addressing her back as she preceded him down the hall to the drawing-room.

'They're packed,' she said. 'You can take them with you.'

The room, too, was familiar and yet different. The shelves which filled both fireplace alcoves were empty apart from a few books he recognised as hers. Piled up on the floor near them were supermarket cartons, printed with the names of the different products which they had once contained, neatly fastened down with parcel tape and labelled according to their contents: Biography, History, Fiction.

Seeing them, he felt oddly humble and grateful.

'You shouldn't have gone to all that trouble,' he said.

'I wanted them out of the way,' she replied. 'The house is on the market.'

'So soon?'

'Wasn't that what you wanted?' she retorted. 'I thought that was the idea. If there's anything else you want, you'd better take it while you're here.'

'There's nothing else,' he said, trying not to look about him at the furniture, the big chesterfield covered in buttoned velvet, the wing armchair which had always been his. He was aware suddenly of how comfortable and attractive the room was. Anyone who visited the house had always admired Joanna's taste. Hesitating, he added, 'Except perhaps the horse.'

It was a bronze figurine he had picked up cheap in a junk shop, one of his few contributions to the furnishings. It stood on the stripped pine mantelpiece, rearing up to flourish its front hooves. He had bought it because it seemed to symbolise freedom and an unwillingness to submit.

'I'll pack it up,' Joanna said.

When he returned from having carried the books out to the car, she had it ready for him, wrapped in several layers of newspaper.

'Give Simon my love,' he said as he took it. 'How is he?'

'He's well,' she replied.

They might have been talking about some distant relative in whom both of them had only a peripheral interest.

'Perhaps I could call another time when he's home and take him out,' he suggested.

'If you wish. But I'd be grateful if you telephoned first to let me know you're coming. It could be inconvenient if you just turned up.'

'Yes, I see that,' he agreed quickly. He felt some apology was needed for his unexpected arrival there that afternoon. Absurdly, too, he wanted to confide in her the reason in order to gain – what? Her sympathy? He wasn't sure. 'I had to come to Chelmsford to make a statement to the police so I thought I'd call on the way back.'

'The police?' she said sharply.

Now that he had her interest, he wanted perversely to treat the matter dismissively.

'A girl was found dead in the ford on Friday night. Funnily enough, you might have seen her on the Wednesday when you came with Simon. You probably passed her in the lane. She was young, blonde, a bit buxom.'

He could tell from Joanna's expression that she recognised the description although all she said was, 'Why did the police want a statement from you?'

'Because she called to see me on the Friday shortly before she died. It was almost certainly an accident although the police seem to view my relationship with her with some suspicion. They appear to think we were having an affair.' He paused before adding, 'We weren't.'

This time he aroused no reaction in her except withdrawal.

'If there's nothing else you want,' she said.

He tucked the paper-wrapped horse under his arm.

'No, thank you. Next time I'll phone before I come.'

She accompanied him to the front door as if she were showing a stranger out but shut it as soon as he crossed the threshold.

So that was that, he thought.

Joanna returned to the drawing-room. Alec's arrival had disturbed her more than she was willing to admit although, up to the time of his explanation for his sudden visit, she congratulated herself on having handled the situation well.

His admission about his statement to the police had shaken that self-assurance. It brought back the memory of that terrifying walk along the lane and her reason for making it.

Alec's denial that he had been having an affair with the girl seemed genuine. He rarely lied, she realised; a quality in him which she had not fully appreciated before although the reason for it was not so much a regard for the truth as an impatience with deceit, especially the socially conventional kind. It could at times be a form of cruelty, a stripping away of any covering of pretence.

In this particular instance, however, she felt he had used the truth in self-defence. He felt vulnerable and the realisation of this made her feel strangely protective towards him, the first time she had ever experienced such a reaction. It was always she who had turned to him for comfort and support.

Her suspicion of him and the girl now seemed mean-spirited and unworthy, more especially since the girl was dead.

It was absurd, of course, for the police to think that Alec was in any way involved although her own action in trying to spy on him the night the girl died seemed to place her, in her own eyes, on their side. However badly Alec had treated her, she felt that she nevertheless owed him some loyalty.

But what could she tell the police that would help him? She had seen nobody on that walk, only the headlights of a car in the distance. Could that be significant? Not knowing exactly when the girl had died made it impossible for her to judge.

On the other hand, even if what she had to tell them wasn't useful to Alec, she could at least make it clear to the police that she believed he was speaking the truth when he said his relationship with the dead woman had been innocent. She could also explain that Alec had never once, during their fifteen years of marriage, shown any signs of violence.

I'll go and see them, she decided and went immediately into the hall to fetch her coat from the downstairs cloak-room, pleased with her own decisiveness. Since Alec's desertion, she had learnt quite a few useful lessons in coping on her own.

Checking she had her keys with her, she let herself out of the house.

Her arrival surprised Finch, who had been discussing the Stella Reeve case with Boyce.

The first intimation he had of it was when the Constable on desk duty telephoned through with the information that a Mrs Lawson was downstairs and wished to speak to someone about the death of a young woman in Wynford. Finch immediately instructed him that she was to be brought up to his office.

The name Lawson had given him an idea of her relationship with Alec Lawson but, all the same, he was taken aback when the WPC ushered her into the room. She was not at all what he had been expecting.

Lawson was careless about his clothes and appearance. Mrs Lawson was smartly dressed and carefully made up although under the surface pose he detected a certain nervousness as she sat down opposite him.

She began speaking at once, as soon as he had introduced himself and Boyce.

'I really know very little about what has happened,' she said. 'Alec called on me about half an hour ago and said he'd been asked to make a statement about the death of a girl in Wynford on Friday evening. I don't know her although I think I may have seen her.'

'When was this?' Finch asked.

'On the previous Wednesday afternoon. I believe I passed her in the lane. Alec said she called on him. She was blonde, wasn't she? Quite young? I don't know anything else about her, not even her name.'

'Her name was Stella Reeve,' Finch explained. Intrigued to discover just how much she knew and the reason for her visit, he was reluctant to give away too much information. 'Can you describe the woman you saw in more detail?'

Mrs Lawson hesitated.

'She was dressed in jeans and a fur jacket; not real fur. As we were coming up to the footbridge, she was walking across it.'

'We?' Finch prompted.

'Simon, my son, was with me.'

'And you were calling on your husband?'

Mrs Lawson's chin went up in a defensive manner.

'I don't know if Alec has told you about us. We are separated. I went to see him to discuss a possible divorce.'

'I see.' Finch remained bland. 'So it was while you were on your way to the caravan that you passed this woman? Did you speak?'

'I didn't. Simon asked her if she knew where the caravan was and she told him it wasn't far.'

'So you didn't speak to her yourself?'

It was Boyce who asked the question. Mrs Lawson turned to look at him with a slight frown as if resenting his interference. Probably out of snobbery, Finch guessed. Boyce's rank of Sergeant didn't count for as much in her estimation as his own. As far as she was concerned, he was a mere hanger-on.

This superior attitude was confirmed by her reply.

'No, I didn't. I had no wish to become involved with anyone from the village where Alec was now living. Besides, she was a little . . .' She made a vague, deprecatory gesture with one hand before continuing, '. . . over-friendly, I thought.'

Common, she really meant, Finch suspected, although Mrs Lawson was too careful of her own image to use the word openly.

His own expression courteous, he resumed the questioning.

'Did you know she'd called on your husband that afternoon?'

Her reply came too quickly.

'I had no idea. Alec didn't say anything to me at the time.'

But she'd guessed. Finch was convinced of that although quite how she knew he could only surmise. Possibly something in her husband's manner had given her a clue; that, together with Stella Reeve's knowledge of where the caravan was to be found would have been enough. Mrs Lawson was no fool and it wouldn't have taken much intelligence to put two and two together.

He was curious also to discover exactly why she had turned up at headquarters that afternoon. So far she had said nothing to explain her purpose. It was time she was brought to the point.

He began with deliberate vagueness, letting the sentence remain unfinished in order to allow her to complete it in her own way.

'About what happened last Friday evening, Mrs Lawson . . .'

She seized on it eagerly.

'I was there!'

'*There!*'

Boyce was too quick off the mark and was rewarded with another of Mrs Lawson's quick little frowns.

'I mean I was in the village that evening.'

'I think,' Finch broke in smoothly, 'that you'd better tell

us exactly what happened in your own words, Mrs Lawson.'

And giving Boyce a small warning glance not to interrupt, he settled back comfortably in his chair to listen.

The explanation came so pat that he suspected she had rehearsed it on the way.

'I decided on the spur of the moment on Friday evening to see Alec again. The discussion we'd had on Wednesday afternoon hadn't been very satisfactory and, as I'd been to see my solicitor in the meantime, I'd found there were one or two points which I wanted to clear up.'

Lie number one, Finch thought, although his expression betrayed nothing more than official interest, polite but non-committal.

'I took Simon with me but left him in the car which I parked behind the Goat.' Even she seemed aware that this part of her story hardly stood up to close examination for she added, giving Finch a quick smile to invite his sympathy, 'I'm not a very good driver, you see, Chief Inspector. I was nervous of taking the car through the ford in the dark and then having to turn it in the lane. On Wednesday, I'd nearly driven it into a ditch. So I decided to walk.'

Lie number two, Finch decided, at the same time nodding pleasantly as if in perfect agreement with this explanation.

'I got as far as the S bend and then decided to turn back. It was darker than I'd expected and it was just beginning to rain. The whole idea suddenly seemed rather stupid.'

'What time was this?' Finch asked.

'I suppose about eight o'clock.'

If the answer meant anything to him, there was no suggestion of it in either his voice or manner.

'I see. So you turned back before you reached the ford?'

'Yes, as I said, at the corner. I realised the ford wasn't far off but it was too dark to see it.'

'Did you meet anyone on the way?'

'No, no-one.'

'Or hear anything such as footsteps which might suggest someone else was out and about at the same time?'

'No. All I saw were the headlights of a car coming down

the hill towards me. It was one of the reasons why I decided not to go on.' She smiled again, trying to win his approval. 'It may sound silly but I was rather frightened at being out alone in the dark with a car, driven by God knows who, likely to pass me at any moment.'

'Understandable,' Finch murmured sympathetically. 'And it was at this moment you turned back?'

'Yes. I thought I'd write to Alec instead or get my solicitor to contact him. I realised the whole idea of going to see him had been irrational and rather melodramatic.'

In this, at least, she was speaking the truth. There was genuine embarrassment in her manner which Finch could understand. Humiliated and distressed, no doubt, by her husband's desertion, she had felt the need to make some emotional gesture but not quite, he thought, in the manner in which she had described it.

She was adding, 'I don't know if any of this has helped you in investigating that girl's death but I felt I had to come forward and explain that I was in Wynford that evening in case it was of any use to you. I also wanted to say that I don't for a moment believe Alec had anything to do with it. We've been married for fifteen years, Chief Inspector, and, although I'm divorcing him, I'd like to make it clear that he's never shown any violence either to me or our son. The marriage broke up for quite different reasons.'

It was said not without a certain dignity which Finch responded to with a small nod of his head, acknowledging if not his official acceptance of her statement then at least his recognition of her loyalty to her husband.

'Thank you, Mrs Lawson,' he said. 'I'm grateful for what you've told me. All information is useful. In fact, I may ask you to make an official statement at some later date. There's just one further point I'd like cleared up. I assume you walked straight back along the lane to the Goat?'

'Yes, Chief Inspector, although "run" would be a better word.'

'Did you pass anyone on the way?'

'No, I met no-one, much to my relief, I might add. As soon as I got back to the car, I drove straight home.'

Finch rose to his feet and, after thanking her again, signalled to Boyce to escort her downstairs.

'Well, there's a turn-up for the books,' the Sergeant commented as soon as he re-entered the room. 'Who'd've thought Mrs Lawson was in Waterend Lane on the night Stella Reeve died?'

'She was lying, Tom,' Finch replied. He was standing staring down at the large-scale map of the area which one of the DCs had been sent out to buy that morning and which, while Boyce was out of the room, Finch had spread out on the desk. Boyce went across to join him.

'Lying? You mean she wasn't there?'

'No, she was there all right. I meant she was lying about the reason. My guess is she wanted to catch her husband on the hop. That's why she left the car at the pub and walked. She didn't want to warn him of her arrival.'

'But what was the idea?' Boyce asked. At times his naïvety could be astonishing.

'Looking for evidence for a divorce?' Finch suggested. 'I think she suspected Lawson of having an affair with Stella Reeve and she hoped to catch them at it. It was her way of getting a bit of her own back on him for walking out on her. But the point is this – how far was she lying? She said she turned back here, at the S bend.' Finch jabbed a finger at the map. 'We only have her word for that. Supposing she didn't? If she'd walked on, she'd've met Stella Reeve on or near the footbridge. The timing would have been right. Lawson said the girl left the gate of the caravan and started to walk down the lane seconds after the car Mrs Bingham was driving passed them. Mrs Bingham's statement corroborates that. Now, according to Mrs Lawson, she saw the headlights of a car coming down the hill towards her as she reached the S bend which is about thirty yards from the ford. That would place her within – what? a half-minute's walking distance from it. In other words she'd've arrived at the footbridge at roughly the same time as Stella Reeve who was approaching it from the other direction. If that's what happened, then Mrs Lawson would have been there when Stella Reeve met her death.'

'You think she could have murdered the girl?' Boyce demanded.

'I'm not saying she did,' Finch replied, feeling some of his former exasperation return. 'I'm merely putting the idea forward as a possibility. The bruises on Stella Reeve's arm suggest someone grasped her quite forcibly not long before she died, perhaps in a quarrel. On her own admission, Mrs Lawson already knew her by sight. She'd passed her in the lane only two days earlier. If, as I believe likely, she suspected her husband and the girl were having an affair, she'd have motive, especially if she thought the girl had come from another evening making love to her husband. She admitted in her statement that she was frightened and overwrought. It wouldn't take much to make her lose complete control. She might not even have intended to kill Stella Reeve deliberately. You remember the set-up, Tom? The evidence tends to show that Stella caught her heel in the planking of the bridge as she crossed over it. Supposing at the moment she was trying to free it, Mrs Lawson came up . . .'

'Hang on a moment,' Boyce protested. 'How did either of them know who the other one was? It was eight o'clock at night and pitch dark.'

'All right.' Finch conceded the point. 'Mrs Lawson could have recognised Stella Reeve's voice. She said the girl spoke to her son on Wednesday afternoon when they passed in the lane. As for Stella Reeve not knowing who Mrs Lawson was, that hardly matters although Mrs Lawson could have let slip some remark about Stella visiting her husband, Alec. The point is, Tom, a quarrel could have broken out in which Mrs Lawson grabbed the girl by the arm and pushed her off the footbridge. Or there's another explanation which is just as plausible – that Stella Reeve lost her balance when Mrs Lawson grabbed her. But whatever version is the true one, if Mrs Lawson *was* on that bridge on Friday evening, the outcome amounts to the same – she walked away and left the girl to drown in fourteen inches of water and did nothing to save her.'

'Except one's murder and the other's manslaughter,' Boyce pointed out. 'There's only one thing wrong with it as a theory, though. If Mrs Lawson was involved in Stella Reeve's death, why the hell did she come forward and make a statement? No-one knew she was in Waterend Lane on Friday evening. If she'd've kept her mouth shut, we would've been none the wiser.'

'Perhaps she thought she'd been seen. She said she left the car at the Goat so it's possible a customer from the pub saw her. Or the driver of the car, Mrs Bingham. There could be another reason which would apply if she's not guilty – she wanted to protect her husband or, at least, divert our attention from him. And if that's the case, it raises some interesting questions. Does she suspect he could be guilty and, if so, has she any evidence of her own to make her think that?'

'But aren't they getting divorced?' Boyce asked. 'I'd've thought the last thing she'd do is to stick up for him.'

'I don't know, Tom,' Finch admitted. 'Women do things sometimes for the oddest reasons.'

As he said it, he was ashamed of the chauvinism in the remark, more so when he saw Boyce smile in agreement. What would Marion Greave have thought of it?

'Anyway,' he added briskly to cover up the slip, 'there isn't just Mrs Lawson to consider. There's still Lawson himself, not to mention Reeve or whoever sent that Valentine. You took it along to be fingerprinted?'

'Yes, although it's a hell of a long shot, isn't it? Besides, what are we going to do if Wylie comes up with a set of prints which aren't Stella Reeve's? Check on every male in Wynford, like you suggested?'

Boyce seemed plunged into gloom at the possibility.

'Not necessarily, but we might make a start on the regulars who were in the Goat on Friday night and eliminate them first. I'll get that list off Mitchell tomorrow. At the same time, we could find out if anyone saw Mrs Lawson leave her car behind the pub. Get the file out, will you, Tom? It's on top of the cabinet. I just want to go over again exactly what Mitchell said when we interviewed him.'

Boyce fetched the file and laid it down on the desk, watching over Finch's shoulder with a casual air as if he considered the Chief Inspector's meticulousness unnecessarily pernickety.

He was quite unprepared for Finch's reaction.

'My God, look at that!' he exclaimed, holding out the typewritten report for the Sergeant to read, one finger pointing to a line a couple of inches from the bottom. 'How the hell did I miss it?'

Joanna sat in her car outside headquarters for several minutes before driving away, trying to persuade herself that the interview had gone well.

But it was no use. The truth was it had been a disaster. Finch had known she had been lying about her reason for being in Wynford on that Friday evening. Underneath his polite blandness, she had detected a scepticism. He hadn't been fooled.

God, what a mistake she'd made! She'd done nothing to help Alec; perhaps had even made it worse for him and, what was more, had involved herself.

Well, it was too late now. There was no turning back. All she could do was hope that nothing would come of it and the girl's death would turn out to have been an accident after all.

If it wasn't . . . But that didn't bear thinking about.

Starting the car, she drove slowly out of the car-park into the one-way system which led home.

THIRTEEN _____

Mitchell said, 'Oh, God, you don't want that list now, do you, Chief Inspector? It's the day the brewery delivers and I'm expecting the lorry any moment.'

Finch and Boyce had found him in the storeroom of the Goat where he was stacking up crates, trying to clear a space for the new consignment.

'No, not the list,' Finch replied. 'At least, not at this stage. There's just a couple of questions I want to ask you. Firstly, did anyone park a car behind the pub on the Friday Stella Reeve died and then walk away from it? There was a boy left sitting in the car while it was parked.'

Mitchell shook his head.

'Sorry, I can't help you there. I was busy in the bar that night from the time we opened till we closed so I've no idea what cars were parked out the back.'

'Did any of your customers mention seeing it?'

'Not to me they didn't. Mind you, that's not to say none of them noticed it. You'd have to ask them yourself.'

'It may come to that,' Finch agreed. 'In that case, the list would be useful, Mr Mitchell. I'll let you know if I need it. The second thing I want from you is a name. You said when I interviewed you the first time that you were going to follow Ken Reeve outside to warn him off but changed your mind because another customer left at the same time as Reeve or shortly after. Who was it?'

He said it casually although it was this part of Mitchell's statement which had excited his interest and to which he had drawn the Sergeant's attention. As he waited for Mitchell's answer, he avoided Boyce's eyes. The identity of the man could be important to the inquiry.

Mitchell looked from the Chief Inspector to the Sergeant who had taken up a position in the passageway just outside the storeroom, not only blocking out the light but preventing him from leaving. He put down the crate he had been in the act of moving, his expression wary.

'What is this?' he demanded. 'I thought Stella's death was an accident.'

'The name, sir.'

It was Boyce who spoke, looming in the doorway and almost filling it with his bulk.

Mitchell looked at him, sizing him up, and then shrugged.

'All right. I suppose I'll have to tell you. I don't want to stand in the way of any inquiries you're making. It was Reg Bartlett. I'll say this, though. If you think Reg had anything to do with what happened to Stella, you're barking up the wrong tree. He wouldn't hurt a fly although . . .'

'Yes?' Finch prompted as Mitchell hesitated.

'It's nothing much,' Mitchell continued, 'but I've just remembered something. On that Friday evening, Reg came up to the bar for a refill as Stella was standing there chatting to me. Only a moment before she'd said she'd wait in case Lawson turned up. Then suddenly she changed her mind and decided to walk up to the caravan to find him.'

'As if she were trying to avoid Bartlett?' Finch suggested.

Mitchell looked unhappy.

'It could be,' he admitted.

'Tell me a bit about him,' Finch asked casually as if his interest were only marginal. 'What does he do for a living, for instance?'

'He used to work for George Sutton, a local farmer, till he had an accident about two years ago and had to give it up. He does a bit of gardening now to earn himself a few bob although he's got a pension.'

'And he knew Stella Reeve?'

'Of course.' Mitchell seemed surprised that Finch should ask the question. 'Both of them have lived in the village all their lives. Reg must have known Stella since she was born. But look, Chief Inspector . . .'

'And where does he live?' Finch broke in.

'There's a pair of cottages on the left-hand side, just before you get to the church. Reg lives in the last one.'

He seemed about to add another protest but Finch thanked him briskly and walked away, Boyce following.

Bartlett was at home. A bike was propped up against the wall near the back door when Boyce and Finch tramped down the path past a front garden full of daffodils just coming into flower to the rear of the cottage. Here, a long vegetable plot, neatly dug and planted, extended down to the boundary hedge which separated it from the adjoining field; the same field, Finch noted, across which the foot-path ran from the church to the ford in Waterend Lane.

Bartlett must have heard them coming for he was on the back doorstep to meet them.

He was in his fifties, older than Finch had expected; a loose-limbed gangling man with a long, melancholy face, who was dressed in old working trousers and a waistcoat, worn over a collarless shirt open at the neck.

'What you want?' he demanded.

'Mr Bartlett?' Finch said cheerfully. 'I'm Detective Chief Inspector Finch and this is my Detective Sergeant, Boyce. Do you mind if we come in? We're making inquiries into the death of Stella Reeve and there's a few questions we'd like to ask you.'

Bartlett made no direct reply but merely jerked his head, inviting them inside. Walking with a pronounced limp, he went ahead of them into a small front room, full of old-fashioned furniture which was too large for it. Heavy curtains cut out most of the light. In the gloom, the large-patterned, floral wallpaper took on a sepia colour making the whole effect sombre and claustrophobic. Even the air seemed thick and stale as if it had been shut away inside there for years.

'Sit down,' Bartlett told them grudgingly.

They sat on either side of the fireplace on armchairs covered with worn velvet, Bartlett perching himself awk-wardly on a straight-backed chair with a horse-hair seat near the window. Of the three of them, he looked the most ill at ease.

'Well?' he asked.

During the short drive from the Goat to Bartlett's cot-tage, Finch had worked out a strategem with Boyce. If Bartlett seemed amenable to questioning, the interview would proceed slowly. If any problems seemed likely, then, at a signal from the Chief Inspector, Boyce would start straight in with the heavy guns.

Summing up Bartlett briefly and realising that the chatty, low-key approach was not likely to succeed, Finch gave the Sergeant a look and a nod at which Boyce produced the clear plastic envelope containing the Valentine card from the folder he was carrying.

'Do you recognise that, Mr Bartlett?' he asked.

Bartlett took it from him. It had been handed to him with the blank, reverse side uppermost, another ploy previously agreed on, so that the man had to turn the envelope over in order to see the front of the card.

Finch watched Bartlett's face closely as he stared down at the coloured picture of the heart and the garland of flowers but could read nothing in it except a look of sad bewilderment.

'Where did you get this from?' he asked.

'Never mind that,' Finch told him. 'Did you send it to Stella Reeve?' As the man was silent, he continued in a sterner voice, 'Look, Mr Bartlett, if you did, I'd advise you to admit it. It'll save us a lot of trouble. You see, whoever sent it, left his fingerprints on it and, if need be, we can take you into headquarters and have your prints checked on. I'm sure you wouldn't want that. It's the sort of thing that gets talked of in a place like Wynford. So, if it was you, you'd do better to tell us now while it involves just the three of us.'

Bartlett muttered something but in so low a voice that Finch couldn't hear the words.

'What did you say?' he asked sharply.

Bartlett lifted his head and looked at him, his expression closed.

'I said I sent it,' he repeated. 'What else do you want me to say? There was no harm in posting it to her.'

'What exactly was your relationship with her?'

The man appeared not to understand.

'Relationship?' he asked dully.

'Were you in love with her?'

'Love?' Again Bartlett repeated the word, this time as if testing it out. Then he shook his head. 'No, but I was fond of her.'

'Did you make her a proposal?' It was Boyce who spoke this time and Bartlett turned his head slowly to look at the Sergeant. 'Of marriage,' Boyce added as the man didn't respond.

'No,' he said at last. 'Marriage? Her and me? It never crossed my mind.'

'But you made her an offer?' Finch resumed the questioning as Boyce seemed taken aback by the denial. 'An offer of what?'

Bartlett's head swung back in the Chief Inspector's direction. It took so long for his reactions to register that it was like prodding some great farm animal, Finch thought.

'To help her out with money,' he said. 'I'd got some compensation, see, from the accident and I wanted her to have it. That was before she married Ken Reeve. I knew she wouldn't be happy with him. I'd seen them together in the Goat and I could tell by the way he treated her. It wasn't right. She knew it, too, 'cos she threw him over. Then the talk was that she was going to marry him after all . . .'

He broke off and looked down at his feet, planted side by side in their working boots on the worn carpet.

'Because she was expecting his child,' Finch put in to help the man out. Clearly Bartlett was unwilling to admit this fact out loud.

He looked up at the Chief Inspector, his expression oddly grateful for this assistance.

'I knew her mother wanted her to marry him. I'd heard the gossip about it. That's when I decided to say something to her.'

'To Stella, you mean?' Finch wanted this point quite clear.

'That's right. I saw her going into the Goat one evening. There was no-one about so I spoke to her.'

'And offered her your compensation money? What for?'

'What for?' Bartlett seemed surprised that Finch hadn't understood. 'So she wouldn't have to marry him, that's why.'

Finch left it there. It was pointless, he decided, to press Bartlett for an explanation of exactly how he had intended the money to be used. Probably he had no clear idea himself whether he had wanted Stella, had she accepted it, to spend it on an abortion or to support herself and the child. Bartlett's mind did not work on such clear-cut lines. To him, it was enough simply to offer the money.

'But she wouldn't take it?' Finch asked.

'No,' Bartlett replied. 'That's why I sent the card. It was to let her know that I hadn't forgotten her and the money was still there if she needed it. I knew she'd realise it was from me. I was fond of her, see. I'd seen her grow up and I didn't want her marrying *him*.'

'I understand,' Finch said. He did, too, although judging by Boyce's expression, the Sergeant hadn't fully grasped the situation. Bartlett had loved her although he was probably speaking the truth when he said marriage had never entered his mind. What he had felt for Stella Reeve had been the inarticulate longing of a lonely, older man for a young girl who was far beyond his sphere of expectation. So he had offered her all that he had, his compensation money, but she had refused even that. Finch could see the pathos in the situation. At the same time, it proved that Stella had possessed some special quality when she had been alive which so many people had found appealing – Mitchell, Lawson, even Hadley. And now Bartlett. Again he felt that sense of waste which he had experienced when he had looked down at her body in the mortuary. A light had been put out.

As for Stella herself, she must have been touched by Bartlett's gesture even though she had laughed about it to Lawson. She had at least kept his card.

'Now, Mr Bartlett,' he continued, 'I'd like to move on to more recent events. You were in the Goat on that Friday evening, I believe? You saw Stella come in? But she didn't stay long?'

Bartlett, who had merely nodded his head at the first two questions, expanded a little on the third by saying, 'About quarter of an hour. Then she left.'

'You knew where she was going?' Finch asked and when Bartlett didn't reply immediately, he went on, 'Come on, Mr Bartlett, you knew, didn't you? She told Fred Mitchell she was going to the caravan to see Lawson and you overheard.'

It was a shot in the dark but it had to be right. All the same, Bartlett's reply surprised him.

'I knew she'd been seeing Mr Lawson before that. I heard it from Mrs Bingham on the Wednesday.'

'From Mrs Bingham?' Finch asked sharply. 'She told you?'

Something like a smile passed over Bartlett's face.

'No, she didn't tell me. I heard. I'd been doing her garden, see, that afternoon. She went out, down to the post office she said, and when she came back she brought me out a mug of tea. When I was ready to finish work, I took the mug back to the kitchen. I knocked on the back door but she couldn't have heard me. But I heard her. I let myself in to leave the mug and pick up my wages from the window-sill.' He paused as if waiting for some sign from the Chief Inspector that he had followed the account up to that point and when Finch nodded, Bartlett resumed. 'She was in the sitting-room, talking to her husband. She said she'd seen Mr Lawson and then she said about Stella being back in the village, only it wasn't her mother she was visiting, it was him.'

'How did Mrs Bingham know?' Finch asked.

Bartlett lifted his shoulders.

'I dunno. But that's what she said and that's how I knew about Stella being friendly with Mr Lawson before that Friday night.'

'And that's all she said?' Finch asked as the man seemed to have finished his account.

'That's right,' Bartlett agreed.

Finch glanced at Boyce who raised his eyebrows, expressing the same idea that Finch had in his own mind – so what? The story, such as it was, had proved little except Bartlett's previous knowledge of the friendship between Stella Reeve and Alec Lawson, a point which the Chief Inspector picked up when he resumed the questioning.

'So on the Friday evening you knew where Stella was going when she left the pub?' Bartlett, who had reverted to his more inarticulate method of replying, merely nodded in agreement. 'And then a little later her husband, Ken Reeve, came in. I believe he didn't stay long?'

'Not much above five minutes,' Bartlett replied.

'And when he left, you followed him outside. Why, Mr Bartlett?'

'To see what he was up to. I thought he might be looking for Stella.'

'Did you speak to him?' Boyce asked.

'No. I just followed him.'

'Where did he go?'

'Back to his car which was parked outside Stella's house. He stood beside it to light a cigarette and then he got in.'

'And what about you, Mr Bartlett?'

'Me? I was stood outside the Goat watching him.'

Boyce had difficulty suppressing his impatience at the man's obtuseness.

'I mean afterwards. You didn't stand there watching him all evening, did you?'

'Course not!' Bartlett sounded unexpectedly derisive. 'I waited for a few minutes till he got settled in and then I came back here.'

'To the house, you mean?'

'That's right.'

'You didn't go up to the caravan?' Finch asked.

Bartlett turned to look at him with that slow, swinging movement of the head. He seemed to miss the point of the question for he replied, 'No, I didn't. There was no need. I could see Ken Reeve wasn't likely to go looking for her so I reckoned it'd be all right.' He began to add something more. 'She was . . .' But he broke off and stared down at his boots again, his expression morose.

'Yes?' Finch prompted.

Bartlett looked up and met his eyes.

'Perhaps if I'd gone after her I might have saved her. But I didn't like to push myself forward. She was a bit – I don't know how to put it – funny with me after I'd offered her the money; not as friendly as she'd once been.'

'Perhaps she was embarrassed at having to turn it down,'

Finch suggested to help the man out although he suspected that this was only partly the reason. Stella hadn't wanted to encourage whatever unspoken sexual longings Bartlett had felt for her.

'Could be,' Bartlett agreed. 'I don't know. But I'll miss her just the same. It ain't right that someone as young as her should die.'

'Yes,' Finch said. At least in that they were in agreement. There seemed nothing more to add and he got to his feet. 'Thank you, Mr Bartlett. We may need a written statement from you later. I'll let you know.'

Outside, Boyce could hardly wait to ask the question which he had obviously had in his mind throughout the interview.

'What the hell did you make of that?'

'I don't know, Tom,' Finch replied. He genuinely didn't and would have preferred to keep silent until he'd had time to consider it at greater length.

He walked on past the car which was parked outside Bartlett's gate towards the church which was only a short distance away, Boyce hurrying to catch up with him.

In the narrow entrance to the footpath, where it ran between the churchyard wall and the hedge of the rectory garden, he stopped to look up at the sign-post which read in white lettering on the green paint: 'Public Footpath to the Ford'.

Boyce put his thoughts into words.

'You think Bartlett could have gone to the ford after all?'

Finch humped his shoulders.

'It's possible,' he agreed.

'By the footpath?' Boyce persisted.

Finch merely nodded this time.

'What about the timing?' Boyce asked. 'If he followed Reeve out of the pub, would he have had time to get to the ford before Stella Reeve?'

Despite himself, Finch looked interested.

'We'll have to work it out, Tom. It took me nine minutes to walk it from here the other day in the opposite direction but that was downhill and in daylight. Bartlett's got a game leg as well so it would have taken him even longer.'

'He could have gone on his bike,' Boyce pointed out.

'Oh, hell!' Finch said. 'Yes, he could have done. That'd mess up the timing even more.'

'Come to that, Bartlett could have been speaking the truth,' the Sergeant put in. 'Ken Reeve could just as easily have met Stella at the ford and shoved her off that bridge. I know Bartlett said he saw him get in his car which would seem to corroborate Reeve's statement but there was nothing to stop him from getting out of it again and walking along the lane towards the caravan.'

'But Mrs Lawson was walking along it at roughly the time Stella Reeve died. She'd've seen him.'

'Would she? It was dark, remember. Reeve could have been just behind her. If he kept to the verge, she wouldn't have heard him and, when she turned back, he had only to keep close up to the hedge and the chances were she wouldn't have seen him either. Come to that, he could have used this footpath. He'd lived in the village for a few months with Stella's mother before they moved to Studham so he'd've got to know the area fairly well. He must have known about the path. Here, where are you off to now?' Boyce broke off to ask, as Finch had done a smart about-turn and was heading back to the car.

'Headquarters, Tom,' he said over his shoulder. 'We'll need to look up the statement and get the timings worked out. We'll also need that large-scale map.'

There was a message waiting for him when they returned to the office. It was lying on top of his in-tray and, as Finch glanced down at it, the name 'Dr Greave' seemed to stand out from the other words as if it had been written in larger letters.

Boyce, thank God, was on the other side of the room, fetching the map and the file on the case, and Finch was able to read it through quickly before the Sergeant came back.

In the event, the message was brief and businesslike, hardly designed to raise romantic illusions. It simply read:

'Dr Greave telephoned at 11.25 a.m. and said that, if you were free at 8 p.m. tomorrow evening, she would like to see you.'

That was all.

All the same, as he stuffed the piece of paper into his pocket, Finch felt a lifting of his spirits. She wanted to see him! Absurdly, he felt as excited as an adolescent about to embark on his first date.

'Here we are,' Boyce was saying, crossing to the desk and spreading out the map. 'I've got the reports as well so let's see what we make of them.'

They didn't make a great deal. After an hour and a half in which they pored over both in turn, they had reduced the information to a few facts which Finch jotted down. In all, they hardly filled one side of a page.

STELLA REEVE – victim. Died by drowning at approx. 8.03 p.m.
Possible Suspects:
1. ALEC LAWSON. Within a hundred yards of victim at time of death. Had possibly been quarrelling with her shortly before. May have been having an affair with her. MOTIVE – jealousy, fear, revenge?
2. MRS BINGHAM. Passed Lawson and victim in car at approx. 8.02. Knew victim. MOTIVE – none known.
3. MRS LAWSON. Lawson's wife. In lane within thirty yards of victim at approx. 8.02. Timing verified by Mrs Bingham's statement. May have suspected husband was having an affair with victim. MOTIVE – jealousy?
4. REG BARTLETT. Left Goat at approx. 7.40 p.m. Waited to observe Ken Reeve for a few minutes. Could have left for ford at approx. 7.42, either along lane or by footpath, on foot or by bike. Timings and distances to be checked. Was fond of victim. Knew of her relationship with Lawson. MOTIVE – jealousy?
5. KEN REEVE. Victim's husband. Separated. Known to want victim to return to him. Left Goat at approx. 7.40. Seen in car by Bartlett at approx. 7.42. Car still

in village at 9 p.m. – seen by victim's mother. Could have walked to ford by lane or by footpath. Timings to be checked. MOTIVE – jealousy, revenge?

'It's too wide open, Tom,' Finch pointed out, straightening up from the desk and grimacing as the muscles in his back protested. There was something else unsatisfactory about the report which he couldn't quite put his finger on but which was connected with the suggested motives, all of them involving jealousy which was acceptable in theory and yet he felt in some inexplicable way was inadequate. As there seemed no point in trying to express this further doubt to Boyce, he continued, 'We'll have to establish the timings much more accurately. For example, we must find out exactly how long it might have taken Bartlett to walk or cycle to the ford along the footpath. Then there's Ken Reeve. If we assume he was sitting in the car at 7.42, could he have got to the same place in time to kill his wife? We don't even know how long it would have taken him to walk from the gate of Mrs Franklin's house where he was parked along the lane to the ford.'

'What do you suggest?' Boyce asked.

'Going over the area on foot with a stop-watch?' Finch put the idea forward without much enthusiasm, an attitude which the Sergeant seemed to share.

'You mean tramp round it ourselves?'

'That's the general idea, Tom. I know it could be a waste of time if the case turns out to be accidental death after all but until it does, we're doubly in the dark.'

'All right,' Boyce conceded unwillingly.

'Look at it as an intellectual exercise, like doing a cross-word puzzle,' Finch told him, amused despite himself at the gloomy expression on the Sergeant's face as he retorted, 'I hate crossword puzzles but I suppose the timings will have to be checked. When were you thinking of doing it?'

'Tomorrow morning?' Finch suggested. 'That way, we can get it over and done with and spend the afternoon revising the provisional timetable we've drawn up. By the way,' he added with studied carelessness, putting his hand in his pocket to finger the folded sheet of paper with Marion Greave's message on it, 'I'm hoping to knock off reasonably early tomorrow. I've got an appointment.'

'To do with the case?' Boyce asked nosily.

'Could be,' Finch replied. It wasn't exactly a lie. He might very well discuss the inquiry with Marion. It crossed his mind to wonder why she wanted to see him, and then he dismissed the thought as useless speculation. He'd find out soon enough when he met her the following evening.

Tomorrow evening! A mere thirty-six hours or so away. Not long and yet it seemed like an eternity.

Anxious to get rid of the Sergeant before he asked any more awkward questions, he continued, 'Right, Tom! If you'd like to push off now, I'll get on with writing up my notes on the Bartlett interview. In the meantime, perhaps you'd expand these into a proper report.'

Knowing himself dismissed, Boyce took the proffered sheet of paper on which the timings were written down and went towards the door where he paused to look back.

But the Chief Inspector already had his head bent over his desk, seemingly absorbed in the new task, and, reluctant to interrupt him, Boyce walked away although he couldn't resist shutting the door behind him with more ostentation than was strictly necessary.

FOURTEEN

'Nearly home now,' Alec Lawson said with pretended cheerfulness as if the prospect held out Dickensian delights of log fires, hot punch and welcoming company.

Beside him in the passenger seat, Simon was silent.

As an outing, the afternoon had not been a success.

Alec had telephoned Joanna the previous day, suggesting a meeting with Simon whom he had not seen since the

Wednesday afternoon when Joanna had brought him to the caravan. He had meant to arrange to take his son out on the following Saturday for the whole day but Joanna, cold and distant on the telephone, had vetoed that idea. Other arrangements, she didn't specify what, had already been made for the weekend. He could, however, she said, meet Simon from school if he wished but the boy had to be home by seven o'clock at the latest as he had homework to do before he went to bed. It was like, Alec had thought, trying to make an appointment with some important stranger through an aloof and difficult receptionist. All the same, he had acquiesced.

Simon had been embarrassed at meeting him at the school gate, scuttling into the car before his friends could see him and sinking low in the seat.

As there was nothing suitable on at the cinema, they had gone instead to the park where they had walked about largely in silence; at least, Alec had made conversation and Simon had answered in monosyllables. Even the ducks hadn't co-operated. Discovering they were not going to be fed for Alec had not thought to bring any bread with him, they had waddled back into the water and swum silently away.

Tea had been only marginally better. In a last effort to introduce some joy into the occasion, Alec had ordered a double hamburger and a banana cream surprise for his son; not the type of tea he imagined Joanna would approve of. She had once followed a course of evening classes on diet, largely for her own benefit as she had been conscious at the time of putting on weight, but all of them had been subjected to a regimen of low-fat, high-fibre food in which he imagined, watching Simon munch his way steadily through the meal, chips and synthetic cream were not included.

But at least Simon's silence was more acceptable. With his mouth full and his eyes intent on his plate, his lack of conversation had not seemed so alienating.

It had been half past six when Alec paid the bill. Time to go.

The house, he noticed, as he turned into Claremont Drive, now had a For Sale sign outside it. It reared up out of the clumps of azaleas like a protest banner, much too obvious and challenging, as if advertising, in its strong black lettering, his desertion of his family for everyone to see.

He stared up at it as he turned the car into the entrance to the house. Of course, it was only what he should have expected. He had, after all, told Joanna to put the house on the market. Once the divorce went through, there was no reason why she and Simon should continue to occupy four bedrooms and two reception rooms, not to mention a utility room and a downstairs cloakroom.

And yet he was overcome with sudden guilt at the process of disintegration for which he was responsible. It would all be dispersed: the wing chair and the china, the little Victorian dressing-table mirror he had bought as a birthday present for Joanna in happier times, Simon's books and toys and precious models which he had helped the boy to glue and fit together so painstakingly.

For some absurd reason, he imagined them living as he did, crammed into some substandard accommodation with rattling windows and a damp kitchen which smelt of rot and sour food.

Simon was saying, turning in his seat to look up at him as he drew up in front of the house, 'Are you coming in, daddy?'

'No,' Alec replied, 'but I'll see you to the door.'

All the same, after he had rung the bell, he waited although, if he had really not intended entering, he should have walked away as soon as he saw Joanna's figure, looking oddly distorted through the reeded glass, coming towards them along the hall.

She looked surprised and then disdainful on seeing him standing with Simon on the doorstep. Ignoring him, she spoke to Simon first asking, as he stepped into the hall, 'Did you have a good time?' her voice too bright and at the same time faintly commiserating as if she knew the outing had been a disaster.

Alec followed him into the house, one hand on the boy's shoulder and almost treading on his heels in his eagerness to get inside before she shut the door on him.

'I want to talk to you, Joanna,' he said.

He had to admire the way in which she coped with the situation but then Joanna had never been lacking in social poise. It was one of the qualities which had first attracted him to her. Without showing the slightest hesitation, she said to Simon, 'Go upstairs and start your home-work, darling,' before turning and leading the way into the sitting-room where she closed the door behind them.

'Sherry?' she asked as if he were a guest who, while not exactly welcome, had to be shown some sign of hospitality for the sake of mere politeness.

'Yes, please,' he replied.

Standing just inside the door, he watched as she crossed to the side table on which the sherry decanter and glasses were placed. He was aware of an unfamiliar and disconcerting assurance about her. She even walked differently as if something inside her had tightened, stiffening her back-bone and giving a more positive tilt to the angle of her head. She had had her hair cut, too, in a new, shorter style. Seen from the back, she looked almost boyish in jeans and a loose, red sweater.

'Well?' she asked, handing him his glass and looking into his eyes with a challenging air in which he seemed to detect amusement.

In fact, her attitude towards him was very largely a pose. Since the interview with Finch, her feelings had changed. She had been frightened by the Chief Inspector's response to her and this had put her on the defensive. It was far better, she had decided, to keep aloof both from Alec and the situation regarding the dead girl. As it was, she had no intention of telling Alec that she had been to see Finch. She saw it now as foolishness on her part which had done neither of them any good and she regretted her impulsive-ness. She would involve herself no further. After all, they were now quite separate people, responsible only for themselves, as Alec had made very clear to her when they had talked together that Wednesday afternoon in the caravan.

Aware of the change in her, Alec didn't know what he was doing there or what it was he had wanted to say.

'I just wondered how everything was going,' he said awkwardly.

'Going?' She raised her eyebrows. 'If you mean the house, it's going splendidly. I already have someone interested in buying it. If you mean the divorce, that's all in hand, too, or so my solicitor tells me.'

'I'm sorry,' he said, looking down into his glass.

'About what?' she asked sharply.

'About everything; you, Simon, the marriage . . .'

'Isn't that water under the bridge, as you put it?'

'I am still concerned about you,' he said.

She was silent for a moment before replying, 'I can understand your feelings, Alec, but you can't have it both ways. You lost the right to be concerned when you walked out. What you really mean is you like the idea of being a warm, caring husband and father without having to accept the real responsibility of the roles.'

'That's not fair, Joanna!' he protested, although as she spoke he remembered Stella Reeve walking away from the gate alone into the darkness because it hadn't occurred to him to offer her a lift.

'Fair?' she repeated. 'No, it probably isn't but a lot of things aren't exactly fair. Your desertion wasn't fair. My having to bring up Simon on my own isn't fair either. If I said that all of this appears to be what you want, I suppose I could also be accused of being unjust. If so, I'm sorry but that's how I see it.'

'I didn't want it to happen this way!' he exclaimed.

'Then in what way was it supposed to happen?' she demanded. 'For God's sake, it's your doing, not mine. What *do* you want, Alec?'

'I don't know,' he said. And suddenly he didn't. It had all seemed so glittering before – the prospect of freedom, of owning the bookshop, of being his own master at last. But it had been, as Joanna had pointed out, only an idea after all. The reality had turned out to be very different, sad, tarnished, reduced to a For Sale notice in a front garden, a silent walk through a park with his son, splintered floorboards piled up in a back yard.

'I don't know,' he repeated. 'If only . . .'

'If only what?' she asked.

'I honestly don't know that either, Joanna,' he confessed. 'I just wondered if perhaps we might somehow start again. Not in the old way but as if we were just beginning . . .'

He stopped, unable to articulate what he wanted to say because he wasn't sure himself.

She turned away to put her glass down on the mantelshelf so that he could only see her face in profile. It looked suddenly tired and old. She was silent for so long that he wondered if she were weeping and he said her name in quick anxiety.

'Joanna?'

'I'm sorry, Alec,' she said at last, still not looking at him. 'I think it's too late. I've changed but not enough for you, only for myself. You see,' and as she said the words, she turned to look at him, 'unlike you, I do know what I want and you're not part of it any more. I've learnt to do without you. You spoke of your concern for us and that was considerate of you. But the truth is, I'm not concerned about you any more. If I didn't see you again, it wouldn't really matter. Does that sound unkind? I'm sorry if it does. You see, I'm picking up the pieces you so carelessly scattered and I'm putting them together again. I've got a job with a good salary which I'm starting after Easter. I've found rather a nice house which I'll be able to afford. My father's lending me the money for Simon's education. It's all coming together into a new pattern.'

'In which I haven't any place,' Alec said, finishing the sentence for her.

'I'm sorry,' she repeated.

He walked across the room to put his empty glass down on the side table.

'But I'll be able to see Simon?' he asked, his back to her.

'Of course,' she replied. 'Whenever you want.'

'Thank you,' he said. 'I'll see myself out.'

'Hell!' said Finch. He was standing, stop-watch in hand, on the step of the stile. 'This isn't going to work.'

'Why not?' Boyce demanded. He had been sheltering in the lee of the hedge near the ford, having walked up Waterend Lane from the direction of the Goat, timing himself with his own stop-watch. As the distance was shorter than Finch's own timed walk from the public house to the same destination along the footpath, the Sergeant had been waiting for the Chief Inspector's arrival for several minutes and, in consequence, he looked pinched with the cold.

Spring, promised earlier in the week in the sudden burst of sunshine, had retreated and, if it weren't for the leaves on the bushes and the celandines sprinkling the banks, it might have been February again. An overcast sky hung low over sullen-looking fields and a chill little wind, with the breath of winter still about it, was blowing down the lane, ruffling the brown water of the ford into tiny, white-capped waves.

'It took me eight minutes and thirty-five seconds to walk from the car-park of the Goat,' Boyce continued in an aggrieved voice as if Finch's comment on the failure of the experiment reflected on his own part in it. 'I timed it exactly.'

'That's not the problem, Tom,' Finch explained, climbing down from the stile. 'Although the individual timings are important, it's not that I'm complaining about. It's something else. It struck me as I was walking across the footpath. I happened to catch sight of you passing that gateway further down the lane and it was then it occurred to me.'

'What did?' Boyce demanded, only partly mollified.

'That it's the way the timings coincide that really matters. We've got, what? Four people who could have been approaching the ford just before Stella Reeve died – Lawson, his wife, Reeve and Bartlett; five if we count Mrs

Bingham in her car. And that doesn't take into account Stella Reeve herself. I know we could work it out on paper but that's not going to give us a proper idea of how the timings mesh together. I want to actually *see* it happening.'

'What do you mean?' Boyce asked, shifting from one foot to the other to get the blood moving.

'A reconstruction,' Finch said.

'Oh, God!' the Sergeant muttered under his breath.

'It shouldn't take too much organisation,' Finch continued, ignoring Boyce's interpolation. 'We'd have to block the lane off at both ends to make sure no other traffic used it so we'd need a couple of men posted on that duty, plus two WPCs to take the parts of Stella Reeve and Mrs Lawson. Lawson's timing isn't a problem. As we know he'd've had plenty of opportunity to follow Stella Reeve to the footbridge, we shan't need to cover his movements. But we'll have to have a couple of PCs to be Reeve and Bartlett and to come across the fields by the path, one on foot, one on a bike.'

'Won't you want a third in case Reeve came by the lane?' Boyce asked.

'Not now you've timed it and we've established it takes roughly nine minutes. We've already worked out that Bartlett last saw Reeve sitting in his car outside Mrs Franklin's cottage at approximately 7.42 on that Friday evening so, assuming Stella Reeve died a couple of minutes after eight, he'd've had over a quarter of an hour to walk to the ford along Waterend Lane which is more than enough time. It's the other route, across the fields, that bothers me. Because it's uphill, it took me nearly eighteen minutes to cover the distance from the Goat to the footbridge, six minutes longer than it takes in the other direction, which is cutting the time down to a very close thing for both Reeve and Bartlett if they came along the path. It's that timing which I'll want checked.'

'What about Mrs Bingham's?' Boyce put in, looking interested despite himself. 'You'll want someone in a car to cover hers.'

'Right!' Finch agreed. He seemed pleased at the Sergeant's apparent willingness to co-operate.

'So when were you thinking of setting it up? Tomorrow night?'

'No. I'd prefer it to be done in daylight. I know that won't be the right conditions but I want to see what happens.'

'How are you going to manage that?' Boyce asked.

Finch grinned at him as he remounted the stile.

'If I stand up here, I'll have a good view in both directions, as far down as the S bend where Mrs Lawson says she turned back as well as up the lane towards the gate of the caravan. The footpath's no problem. Anyone coming in that direction will be easily seen. You know, Tom,' he added, climbing down, 'I think we'll ask the witnesses we know were in the area, Lawson and his wife as well as Mrs Bingham, to come along and watch the reconstruction. It could jog their memories. There could be something they saw or heard which they've forgotten to tell us about.'

'Could be,' Boyce said without much enthusiasm. 'On the other hand, it could turn out to be a complete waste of time and manpower. Still.'

He didn't complete the sentence although the implication behind the last word was apparent to both of them; still that was Finch's decision and, ultimately, his responsibility.

Ignoring the remark, Finch started to walk away.

'Come on,' he said over his shoulder. 'Let's get back to the car. We've got a lot of sorting out to do this afternoon and I don't want to work late tonight.'

'Oh, of course, your appointment,' Boyce remarked, catching up with him. He gave the Chief Inspector a sideways look, full of curiosity, which Finch pretended not to see. It had never been easy to deceive the Sergeant.

Dorothy, his sister, was less suspicious. When Finch arrived home soon after half past six that evening, announcing that he had to go out again to interview a possible witness in the case he was working on, she expressed nothing more than commiseration on his behalf that his free time should be taken up with official duties.

So it was that at eight o'clock precisely, showered,

shaved and wearing a clean shirt, Finch, feeling elated but also a little guilty at lying to his sister, presented himself at Marion Greave's house, a detached Victorian villa at the end of a quiet, tree-lined cul-de-sac in the Springfield area of the town.

He had not seen her for several weeks. Both of them were busy, professional people and their relationship, if that's what it was, had never been committed on the part of either of them to regular meetings although the decision was hers rather than his.

All the same, as she answered the door to him, she showed that warmth of welcome which made him feel that perhaps she did care for him more than he dared believe at his lowest moments.

'I'm so pleased to see you again, Jack!'

He smiled but said nothing, following her down the hall to the large, book-lined sitting-room at the back of the house, where the lamps were switched on and bowls of hyacinths scented the air.

Coffee was ready on a low table.

'You wanted to see me, Marion?' he said as he sat down opposite her, watching as she poured the coffee and familiarising himself again with her features.

He had been right in thinking that she was not beautiful. Not even the love he felt for her could persuade him otherwise. For him, her attractiveness lay entirely in her inner self-containment, a still centre of being, so quiet and composed that it was easy for the casual observer to dismiss her without a second glance. It was only after he himself had worked with her on a case that he had realised that her face with its smooth, high planes above the cheekbones and the little humorous puckers underneath the eyes had a beauty of its own, not apparent to most people.

She passed him his cup of coffee and then sat back in her chair, her short dark hair, tucked behind her ears, as glossy as a blackbird's wing in the lamplight.

'My news can wait until later,' she said. 'Tell me about your case first.'

He told her, knowing she would be interested but largely

for his own sake because he was able to explain to her more easily than he could to Boyce the doubts he had felt throughout the investigation.

'So you're convinced the girl didn't die accidentally although there's no evidence apart from the bruises on her arm.'

She had, of course, uncovered the root of his dilemma at once.

'The taint of violence,' he said, although it wasn't just the bruises he was referring to; it was also the atmosphere which had been present at the scene of Stella Reeve's death and which was too subjective to put into words. She understood that, too.

'But sufficiently strong to make you want to carry out the inquiry as if it were murder,' she continued. 'You don't have any choice, do you, Jack? You must trust your instincts.'

The advice was, as he had expected, much the same as Boyce had given him yet it was good to hear her say it. It swept away any last lingering doubts he might have had.

'Yes, I have to go on,' he agreed, 'if not for my sake, then for Stella Reeve's. When I saw her lying in the mortuary, I thought . . .'

He broke off, unable to articulate his feelings even to her.

'What? You must try to put it into words, Jack. What did you think when you saw her?'

'What a damned waste!' he said, smiling at her ruefully.

'A waste of what? Her life?'

'No, not just that. I feel that every time I get called out on a case which involves a death. With Stella Reeve it was different. She had an interesting face; not particularly beautiful although it would have been attractive in life. Talking to people about her, too – Hadley, the local PC, the girl's mother, Lawson as well—I got a strong impression of her personality. She was very likeable, friendly but positive, prepared to stand up for herself although she'd taken a few knocks in her time but, in spite of it all, she was still on the side of life.' Like you, he added silently, addressing

Marion Greave as she sat opposite him across the low table. 'That's why her death seemed particularly – oh, I don't know – inapt, unkind . . .'

'And deliberate?' Marion suggested. 'Because of what she was?'

He stared at her astonished. She had expressed an idea which even he had not been fully aware of although he realised it had been lingering at the back of his mind when, on drawing up the timetable with Boyce, he had been struck by the apparent inadequacy of the motives.

'Exactly! Someone wanted Stella Reeve dead because she had the courage to be herself—a bit common, I suspect, and not very subtle in her relationships with other people but honest and therefore vulnerable. Does that make sense?' He paused to look across at Marion, searching for her agreement, and, when she nodded, encouraging him to go on, he continued, 'I feel that someone killed her not just out of jealousy, although that seems to be the most obvious motive. But underneath there was a less apparent and more subtle reason which probably even her killer doesn't fully recognise – an envy or a resentment of that special quality which Stella possessed.'

'Her name means a star,' Marion said.

'Of course!' Finch exclaimed before adding, half to himself, 'The giver of light!'

It seemed to crystallise his feelings.

'So,' he continued, rousing himself, 'I've set up a reconstruction for tomorrow morning. God knows if it will prove anything but at least I'll have a clearer idea of the movements of the various suspects on the night Stella died. Boyce thinks it'll be a waste of time and manpower but I'll know I've done everything I can towards solving the case. There's no other line of inquiry I can follow up. If nothing comes of it, we'll have to drop the investigation and it'll probably be written off as an accidental death at the inquest.'

'The coroner may bring in an open verdict,' Marion pointed out.

Finch shrugged but didn't seem very convinced.

'On just the evidence of the bruises on her arm? I doubt it.' He smiled, trying to appear unconcerned. 'But I've talked for long enough about my own affairs. What about you? You wanted to see me about something in particular?'

Even before she spoke, he knew it was going to be bad news and he felt a hollow sensation in his chest as if all the breath had suddenly been sucked out of him.

She was too honest not to come straight to the point.

'I've been offered the post of pathologist at Leeds General Hospital so I'll be selling the practice and moving there.'

'When?' he asked. The word seemed to come involuntarily and, after he said it, he ran his tongue over his lips. They felt dry and stiff.

'In June.' When he didn't speak, she continued, 'I'm sorry I didn't tell you about it before, Jack. I only heard I'd been accepted on Monday. It seemed pointless to speculate before I had definite news.'

'Yes, of course I see that,' Finch replied. Under the circumstances, what else could he say? All the same, he would have been grateful for some warning which would have prepared him for the shock. But was it really any of his business? She had her own life to lead and he had no claim on any of it. And in not telling him until now she had acted as she always did, not out of heartlessness but out of that untouchable sense of self-containment and independence which had made her reject him as a lover – clean, sharp, as bright as a diamond or the blade of a knife.

Realising this didn't make it any easier. He felt the edge cut deep although he struggled to conceal the wound.

'Congratulations! It's what you've always wanted,' he said. 'After all, you trained to be a pathologist, not a GP. I'm pleased you've got the post.' He hesitated before adding, 'I suppose we'll still be able to meet from time to time? It isn't as if Leeds is the other side of the world.'

'Yes, of course we must keep in touch.'

He smiled and nodded, grateful at least for that although he knew, and suspected that she did, too, that their relationship would never be quite the same again and that, of the two of them, it was he who would have lost the most.

So what was left? Not a great deal, Finch thought bleakly. Perhaps an occasional telephone call and an exchange of letters or cards at Christmas. He didn't hold out much hope for anything more.

'I must go,' he said, trying to act normally as he rose to his feet. 'I've got this reconstruction organised for tomorrow morning and I still have to write up the final instructions for those who'll be taking part.'

She made no attempt to keep him, realising that he wanted to be alone although on the doorstep, when he turned to offer his congratulations again before they parted, she said, holding out her hand, 'I'm sorry, Jack.'

They had never touched before except to shake hands when Pardoe had first introduced them and on that occasion the contact had been a mere social gesture. Now their hands met to express something more complex which neither of them wanted to put into words but which, on Finch's part at least, included regret, gratitude and the depth of affection which no woman before and, he suspected, none later, would ever again rouse in him.

The next moment, by mutual consent, their hands parted.

'One thing before you go,' Marion added as he began to walk away. 'That envy you were speaking of. Remember? Your victim was a woman. I think you'll find in that case it's more likely to be another woman who felt it although I could be wrong.'

'Thanks. I'll bear it in mind,' he said. As he drove away, catching a glimpse of her in his driving-mirror in the act of closing the front door, he wondered what had prompted the remark. Some special experience of her own? Or a reaction she had noticed in someone close to her? He didn't know and he doubted now if he would ever ask her. The process of separation had already begun. It was better that way.

Driving home, he turned his thoughts to the investigation. For what else was left? The world hadn't come to an end, after all; only some warm, secret place inside himself had shrivelled and died but not any part that Boyce or his sister or any of his colleagues would ever be permitted to see.

A woman, Marion had suggested and, despite it all, he still trusted her judgement.

Mrs Lawson perhaps? She seemed the most likely candidate.

FIFTEEN ────────────────────────────

From his elevated position on the step of the stile, Finch glanced across at Mrs Lawson. She was standing a few yards away from him where he had instructed Boyce to place her, on the side of the ford nearest to the village within sight of the stream and the footbridge in one direction and the S bend in the other.

She seemed ill at ease, he thought, and quite unsuitably dressed for the occasion in court shoes and a pale grey cloth coat, too lightweight for such a chilly morning, with a wide silver-fox collar which she had turned up against the wind. He could see the pastel fur shiver as the breeze ran across it, ruffling the fine, silky surface. Cocooned in its texture, her face looked drawn and tense.

A little further along the verge, Mrs Bingham, in a more sensible tweed skirt and calf-high leather boots, was moving restlessly from foot to foot as if impatient at the delay, her hands thrust deep into the pockets of a sheepskin jacket.

The cars belonging to the two women were drawn up on the other side of the lane where they would not obscure the view.

Neither woman spoke to the other, the distance between them being too great for conversation, another deliberate stratagem on Finch's part. He wanted his witnesses visible to him but incommunicado except, when the time came, to himself.

Alec Lawson's position had been chosen with the same care, this time on the other side of the stream nearest to the caravan and on the verge facing the footbridge where the lane began to turn before starting the long climb up to Macey's farm. The caravan and the stretch of lane leading up to it were therefore out of sight of him and the others, Lawson's car, drawn up behind him, acting as a further shield to any activity which might be taking place near the gate to the caravan.

Lawson looked strained, Finch thought, turning briefly in his direction to check his position. He had evidently come straight from working on the shop without bothering to shave or change his clothes and the dark stubble on his chin gave him a hollow, starved look.

He had reacted strongly when his wife first appeared, starting forward as if eager to talk to her, but Boyce had bustled him into his place without giving either of them a chance to speak to one another. Since that initial shock, Lawson had looked across at her several times as if appealing to her for some response but she had ignored him, turning up the deep collar of her coat and averting her face. The gesture and their physical separation, with the stream running between them like some Rubicon, seemed to express a deep alienation which Finch, in his turn, found symbolic of his own mood.

As a professional policeman, he was alert and acutely aware of the reactions of those about him but, on a deeper and more personal level, he functioned as if in a coma, all feelings deadened, the conscious world a mere transparency.

'We're ready, sir.'

It was Boyce, moving across to speak to him, timing schedule in hand, the microphone of his radio telephone attached to the lapel of his coat. He seemed suddenly aware of the Chief Inspector's distraction for he added with quick concern, 'Are you all right?'

Finch made an effort to rouse himself, straightening his shoulders.

'Yes, Tom, I'm fine, thanks.'

'Well, you don't look it.'

There was nothing Finch wanted less at that moment than the Sergeant's solicitude. It seemed to bore into him like a probe, piercing the deadened nerve ends and teasing them back to life. For a moment, as he gazed down into Boyce's face, he remembered Marion Greave's expression of concern as she had sat opposite him in the lamp-lit room the previous evening, a memory which he had managed to thrust into some small, hidden corner of his mind but which now came peeping out at him.

'I said I'm all right,' he snapped.

Boyce's expression turned from one of commiseration to the closed formality of the subordinate.

'Sorry, sir,' he said, and, turning his back, took up his position at the foot of the stile.

It would have been easy enough for Finch to apologise in his turn. Glancing at his watch, he saw he had two minutes to spare before the reconstruction was due to begin, time in which to touch Boyce on the shoulder and offer some excuse. But the effort seemed too much to make.

Instead he looked about him as if unaware of the Sergeant who was standing immediately in front of him, his shoulders squared and his spine rigid, expressing even in this back view of himself his sense of injured pride.

Madge Bingham witnessed this brief exchange between the Chief Inspector and his Sergeant and, although its full significance was lost on her, took it to mean that the reconstruction was about to begin.

It was about time.

The whole affair struck her as absurd. What on earth did Finch hope to prove by this ridiculous charade? The girl had died accidentally. That much was obvious and no other evidence to the contrary could possibly be discovered at this late stage in the investigation.

A few feet away from her, Mrs Lawson shivered and

drew the collar of her coat closer about her face. Madge glanced at her quickly.

God knows what she was doing there. As far as Madge was aware, only she herself and Alec Lawson had been anywhere near Waterend Lane when the accident happened. She could only suppose that Lawson's wife had been somewhere in the area on her way to visit him at roughly the time Stella Franklin died and that Finch had called her in to check on her movements. There was no other explanation.

On the other side of the ford, Lawson, too, glanced across at Joanna and wondered why the hell she was present at the reconstruction. He had not been in contact with her since his disastrous attempt at a reconciliation although several times he had been tempted to phone her.

Her unexpected arrival on the scene that morning had totally bewildered him and, like Madge Bingham, he could only conclude that Joanna had been in or near Wynford on that Friday evening and the purpose of her visit had been to see him.

But why, for God's sake?

He wanted to believe that her intention had been to persuade him to come back to her and Simon. At least, that interpretation would have given him some hope for the future. But he wasn't sure. Her refusal to look at him or even acknowledge his presence seemed to rule out that possibility. She was aloof, like a stranger. And also, he realised, afraid. Her tension communicated itself even across the several yards of space which separated them.

Aware of this, he was afraid on her account.

Joanna stood rigid, keeping her face deliberately turned from her husband. It was the only way she was able to keep herself under any pretence of control. Alec's physical presence had disturbed her more than she dared show. He looked so ill, she thought; a mere shadow of his former self as if in the few days since she had last seen him the strength had gone out of him. Seeing him, she felt her resolve, built up so painstakingly day by day, begin to weaken. She had persuaded herself that she could cope without him and, had she not become involved in the girl's death, she might have found the courage to carry on alone.

Now she felt that confidence drain away. The return to the scene of that terrifying walk in the dark had aroused the same irrational sense of fear which she had experienced then.

What did Finch know? What did he hope to prove?

She had seen nothing, heard nothing that night, only the wind booming in the trees. She heard the sound again as the branches stirred overhead and she shuddered with a mixture of fear and physical discomfort as she clutched her coat collar tighter to her throat, aware of Finch's eyes turned towards her with that look of cool, sceptical appraisal with which he had regarded her when she had gone to see him in his office.

Too late, she thought. Too late for everything; for denial that she had been anywhere near the ford on the night the girl died; for her and Alec. It had all gone beyond the point where she might have chosen another, safer path.

For the reconstruction was beginning. The Sergeant was checking his watch before glancing back over his shoulder to address the Chief Inspector.

'We're ready, sir,' Boyce was announcing.

'Then get the men moving,' Finch replied.

As he spoke, he glanced at his own watch and his copy of the time schedule which he had fastened to a clipboard. It was 10.40 a.m.; the approximate minutes to the hour when he estimated that Bartlett and Reeve had left the Goat on that Friday evening. The two Constables, Marsh and Johnson, who were to take their parts, would be setting off at any second from the door of the public house to walk through the village to the church.

He heard Boyce pass on the instruction through his radio microphone and looked back across the meadow towards the footpath although he did not expect either man to appear for another five minutes, the time it would take them to cover the distance from the Goat to the far end of the village street, including the two minutes he had estimated Bartlett had spent watching Reeve as he stood by his parked car.

Until they appeared, it was a question of waiting and he humped his shoulders, alternately glancing at the second hand on his watch as it swept round the dial and then across at the church tower where the two men would shortly come into sight in the gap between the trees.

10.50 a.m.

Boyce was again murmuring into his radio microphone, this time to WPC Drake who was re-enacting Mrs Lawson's role and was waiting in the car-park of the Goat to walk to the ford along Waterend Lane as she had done on that Friday night.

He exchanged a nod with the Sergeant who passed on the order.

'Right! You can start now.'

It had been Finch's intention to concentrate on the timings and to ignore the witnesses until the plainclothes men and women appeared in sight. It was then that their reactions would be worth observing. But he could not resist looking round quickly at the three of them, at Lawson, over to his right, shabby and unshaven, and, to his left, Mrs Bingham, upright and trim, aware that events were about to happen and glancing this way and that with a quick, intelligent interest. And then, past her, to Mrs Lawson who, anticipating the next stage in the reconstruction, had turned her head to watch the bend in the lane where, at any minute, the figure of the policewoman who was taking her part would come into view.

He wondered what was going on in their minds, especially Mrs Lawson's. Before assigning them their positions, Boyce had instructed each in turn to observe the reconstruction carefully and then to report at the end of it if anything they saw or heard differed from their memories of the events which had happened on the night that Stella Reeve died.

It was a long shot but one which he hoped to God was worth playing. Otherwise, he would have to admit defeat and close the investigation, letting Stella Reeve's death pass unpunished into the catalogue of unsolved crimes.

Not if he could help it, he thought grimly, turning his glance lastly at the stream, its water running fast and flashing brightly in the sudden sun and shadow of that windy morning. Someone was responsible and, even if the reconstruction proved nothing, as far as he was concerned, the file on Stella Reeve would never be closed.

But the action was speeding up at last and needed his immediate attention. Boyce was looking round at him for further orders. It was 10.56, time for the car to set off from Macey's yard; time, too, to alert the last participant in the events.

He gave the instructions with an increasing sense of exhilaration. The play had begun in earnest for, as if across a huge stage, the actors were now beginning to converge on this one small arena where the final enactment was to take place.

A quick glance over his shoulder confirmed the arrival into sight of Marsh and Johnson on the footpath which led from the church, Marsh still on foot, Johnson now riding the bike which he had picked up at the gate of Bartlett's cottage. Finch saw him dismount half-way up the slope and start to push it. The two men were only yards apart.

So far so good. The timing seemed to be working.

As they approached, the car also came into view, the sunlight flashing briefly on its windscreen as it began the long descent from Macey's farm towards the ford, as Mrs Bingham's had done on that Friday night.

When it reached a point mid-way down the hill, almost opposite the caravan which was out of sight behind the hedge, the figure of WPC Drake suddenly appeared at the other end of the lane where the S bend straightened out before the road dipped down towards the ford.

She stood in the middle of the lane for several seconds, only thirty yards away from them, conspicuous if only by the solitariness of her position under the trees, the wind blowing the scarf she was wearing about her head.

Mrs Lawson registered her presence. Finch saw her start visibly as if she had been confronted by her own ghost.

Mrs Bingham had also noticed her sudden appearance and was straining forward to get a better view, puzzled, no doubt, at her arrival. After all, like Lawson, she knew nothing of Mrs Lawson's involvement in the events of that Friday evening. Finch could not see her face clearly, only part of her profile outlined against the dark mass of the hedge, her chin raised and the whole set of her head watchful and intent.

The next moment, the figure turned and began walking rapidly away in the direction from which it had come towards the village, disappearing from sight beyond the curve in the lane.

At the same time, the other figure appeared.

She was a young WPC whom Finch had chosen for her similarity to the dead girl. They were of the same height and build and possessed certain features in common, particularly a fullness about the mouth and chin.

Now, dressed in jeans and a fur fabric jacket of the same colour as the one Stella Reeve had been wearing, a satchel handbag slung over one shoulder and a blonde wig covering her own short brown hair, she stepped from the place where she had been kept hidden behind the caravan out of sight of the witnesses and came walking into view.

Finch had intended her appearance to be sudden and dramatic. Lawson's car, parked strategically against the verge, effectively blocked off any sighting of her until the last moment so that it seemed as if she had been conjured up out of the air. But even he had not bargained for the reaction of the witnesses.

As she walked past Lawson towards the ford, her high heels clipping smartly on the hard surface of the lane, the blonde hair bouncing on the shoulders of her jacket, the man put out a hand as if to touch her and convince himself that she was real.

Mrs Bingham, too, took a step forward in startled recognition.

Mrs Lawson was the last to register the girl's presence. She still had her head turned away in the direction of the S bend round which WPC Drake had, a few moments earlier, disappeared from sight, as if her interest were centred solely on the re-enactment of her own movements.

The sudden shudder which passed through the others, almost audible in the strength of the reaction, drew her attention back to the ford and to the scene which was taking place there.

The car, which had passed the young WPC as she set off to walk from the gate of the caravan towards the footbridge, was now edging its way slowly across the ford in bottom gear, sending long, slow ripples lapping out to touch the banks and to slap up against the wooden supports.

But no-one seemed interested in it as, having reached the other side of the stream, it picked up speed and disappeared up the lane towards the village in the same direction as WPC Drake.

Nor was any attention paid to the two plainclothes policemen, Marsh and Johnson, who had by this time reached the stile by the footpath and were standing just behind the Chief Inspector, spectators themselves now, although Finch had noted down the time of their arrival.

Everyone was watching Stella; even Finch thought of the young policewoman by that name as if, in assuming her appearance and actions, she had taken on the dead woman's identity and, by some mysterious process of metamorphosis, had become the victim herself.

She was only seconds from the moment at which she had died, mounting the worn concrete steps to the footbridge before stepping forward on to the bridge itself.

There was no other sound or movement, Finch noticed. Everyone stood silent and immobile. Even the wind seemed to drop so that the trees were motionless as, in the great silence, Stella's footsteps rang out on the planking with a hollow insistence, clearly audible above the sound of running water as the stream slid under the bridge.

In the centre, she stopped abruptly and, bending down, began pulling at her shoe as if the heel had become caught in a gap between the planking before, straightening up, she turned to grasp the rail, twisting the upper part of her body and leaning forward so that her reflection appeared suddenly on the surface of the water beneath her, blonde hair glinting, the oval of her face disintegrating into patches of paler colour as the ripples caught it and swept it away.

'Oh, God, no! Don't let her fall!'

It was Mrs Lawson who had cried out. She had run into the centre of the lane and stood facing the ford, her arms held out in protest.

As if on a signal, the scene began to break up.

Lawson, who until that moment had stood transfixed, also started forward, shouting out, 'Joanna, stay where you are!' before setting off at a charge for the bridge.

'Bloody idiot!' Finch heard Boyce bellow and he, too, ran forward a few paces in warning as Lawson pushed roughly past the young WPC who, alerted of the danger, clung to the rail.

The same thought was going through the Chief Inspector's mind as he scrambled down off the stile.

Bloody idiot, indeed!

The answer was so damned obvious that he couldn't think why he hadn't seen it before.

'Boyce!' he shouted furiously.

But it was too late.

The Sergeant's sudden movement had served as a further catalyst to the others although he could hardly blame the man. If he hadn't acted, the girl might have lost her balance and fallen face downwards into the stream as Stella Reeve had done and that was too dangerously close to reality.

All the same, the damage had been done.

As Boyce, looking shamefaced, turned back towards him and the WPC straightened up and walked a little shakily to the end of the bridge, Finch saw Lawson, who had run past him, seize his wife by the shoulders and draw her on to the verge where he stood, his arms round her and his head lowered protectively against hers.

Mrs Bingham, too, had moved out of her position. Until the moment when Boyce had called out and started forward, she had remained where she had been placed, a few yards from the stile, her hands still plunged into the pockets of her sheepskin jacket.

Now, as Boyce walked back, his expression contrite, she seemed to hesitate and then, making up her mind, crossed the lane towards her car and, getting in, started the engine.

'Sorry about that,' Boyce was saying, raising his voice above the sound of Mrs Bingham's car as it made a neat three point turn and headed off towards the village. 'I thought the girl was going to fall. God knows what Lawson thought he was playing at. Still, no harm's done.' He broke off to repeat in a tone of exasperated amusement, 'Bloody idiot! Just look at him now!'

Finch followed his gaze to where Lawson and his wife were still standing in one another's arms at the side of the lane and felt a brief jolt of emotion pass through him although quite what his feelings were even he wasn't sure.

Envy? That certainly played a part. He was aware also of a sense of loss which was like a physical pain under his ribs. But he was conscious mostly of a mixture of anger and exhilaration – anger that the reconstruction had ended in this confusion; excitement that he had, after all, been proved right. Stella Reeve's death was no accident.

He shouted briefly, 'Get yourselves organised!' to Marsh and Johnson who, together with the young WPC, were milling about near the end of the bridge, talking too loudly and, as they fell silent, he pulled Boyce to one side out of earshot, jabbing at the timing schedule with his forefinger to emphasise his point.

Boyce listened, his face impassive although, as Finch finished his explanation, he looked across at the Lawsons who were still standing on the verge some distance away, unaware of anyone else's presence except their own. They had broken free from one another's arms although Lawson was now holding his wife by the elbows as, head bent, he talked to her quickly and urgently. She appeared to be crying.

'Which of us is going to break it up?' Boyce asked. From his expression, it was clear he preferred it not to be him. Almost as an afterthought, he added, as if aware for the first time of her absence, 'And where the hell's Mrs Bingham?'

'Left a few minutes ago,' Finch said succinctly. He tucked the timing schedule under his arm. 'Okay then,

Tom? You agree it couldn't have happened any other way?'

As Boyce nodded in confirmation, Finch touched him lightly on the arm before turning away. As a gesture, it could have meant anything or nothing – an indication to the Sergeant to remain where he was, a recognition of Boyce's agreement with the facts as presented to him, a mere 'wish-me-luck' token. But, as far as Finch was concerned, it was the gesture he should have made before the reconstruction began when he had spurned the Sergeant's sympathy and which he offered now as his own form of reconciliation.

The Lawsons were still too concerned with themselves to be aware of Finch until he was only a few feet away from them.

He heard Mrs Lawson say, 'I don't know, Alec, I honestly don't know,' and Lawson's reply, his voice rough and urgent, 'For God's sake, Joanna, we can make it work, I promise you.' He broke off suddenly, conscious of Finch's presence. 'What the hell do you want?'

'To speak to your wife,' Finch replied. He deliberately used his official voice, flat and unemotional, but all the same he saw the look of alarm on her face. Lawson had taken her by the arm, showing every sign of remaining with her. 'On her own, Mr Lawson,' Finch added, this time with the full weight of his professional rank, and was human enough to feel a sense of satisfaction as Lawson, after hesitating for a second, stepped back in deference to that authority.

SIXTEEN

Boyce was saying, 'So it wasn't a waste of time, after all.'

It was meant, Finch realised, as an apology on the Sergeant's part for having doubted the Chief Inspector's decision to hold the reconstruction.

They were on their way by car to the outskirts of the village to make the arrest, another police car containing a uniformed woman Sergeant and a WPC following behind them.

'I'm not so sure about that, Tom,' Finch confessed. 'If I'd been quicker off the mark in the first place, there'd have been no need to hold it. I could kick myself for not noticing the discrepancy in Mrs Lawson's statement at the time she made it. It stood out a mile.'

Boyce kept prudently silent. After all, he, too, had failed to pick up the omission in her evidence. He was aware also of a moroseness about the Chief Inspector's mood which, while he wasn't sure what had caused it, he felt had nothing to do with the case.

In this, he was right. Once the elation at establishing the identity of the guilty person had passed, Finch had descended rapidly into the trough of despair on the other side. The excitement was over. All that remained was the formality of the arrest, a duty which he had never looked forward to with much pleasure. And after that – what?

Nothing very much that he could see apart from the usual routine of professional duties which was little consolation. He was suddenly sick of crime. He wanted to be assured that other human qualities such as love and tenderness and compassion were as important and as widely practised as greed, revenge and violence. But once Marion had gone, would he be able to sustain such a belief? It seemed impossible.

Looking ahead, he could see no reason for optimism. The future stretched out in front of him like a barren landscape across which he would have to toil with no promise of any celestial city at the end of it.

'Here we are,' Boyce announced, stating the obvious as usual as he turned into the driveway of the Binghams' house.

Dr Bingham met them at the door. It was the first time Finch had seen him and he found himself facing a tall, rumpled, middle-aged man, wearing an expression of dignified grief, sick with worry but trying not to show it. However much one's own distress, it was bad form to inflict it on others.

'Come in,' he said. 'We've been expecting you. My wife's through here.'

Avoiding his eyes, Finch stepped past him into the hall, standing to one side as the doctor went ahead into the large, comfortable drawing-room at the back of the house.

Mrs Bingham, who was sitting in an armchair drawn up to the fire, got to her feet as they entered, her husband crossing the room to take up his position beside her, Finch, Boyce and the two women police officers remaining just inside the door and placed according to rank, the Chief Inspector a little in front of the others.

The piece of ritual which followed might have been rehearsed. As Dr Bingham took his wife's hand, Boyce, with a glance at Finch, moved forward a pace and began to announce the formal words of the official caution.

'Mrs Bingham, you are not obliged to say anything unless you wish to do so but whatever you say will be taken down in writing and may be given in evidence.'

As he listened, Finch fixed his gaze on the neutral space between himself and the Binghams although, just before Boyce finished, he took a surreptitious glance at Mrs Bingham's face to reassure himself that she would not break down and could not help admiring her self-control.

She was frightened but she wasn't going to admit it in front of others. Head up, lips pressed together, she didn't once take her eyes off Boyce's face.

Finch was touched, too, by her husband's concern. As they stood there hand in hand, he comforted himself with the thought that, whatever happened to Mrs Bingham, she would not have to endure the punishment alone. Bingham would remain loyal to her and Finch found himself half-envying her that assurance of unchanging love.

As Boyce finished and stepped back, leaving Finch to take over, a small rustle and stir of movement ran through the group as at the end of any ceremony.

It was Dr Bingham who suggested, 'Shall we sit down,

Chief Inspector? I know my wife would like to explain what happened.'

They took their places, Dr Bingham on the arm of his wife's chair, Finch and Boyce side by side on one of the chintz-covered sofas, the two women police officers on the other.

Finch began in his formal voice.

'Although you are not obliged to say anything, Mrs Bingham, I should like to go over the evidence with you. If you prefer, however, we could do this at headquarters where a written statement will have to be drawn up later. But I take it that you wish to make a verbal account first?'

'Yes, I do,' she replied.

'Very well.' Finch glanced down at his notes before continuing. 'We have reason to believe, Mrs Bingham, that you were present when Mrs Reeve died. The reconstruction which took place earlier this morning would seem to confirm this. Mrs Lawson has made a statement in which she says . . .'

'So she was there on that Friday evening?' Madge Bingham broke in. 'I thought she must have been somewhere in the area when she arrived at the reconstruction but I had no idea she was in Waterend Lane until that woman suddenly appeared at the bend in the lane. I realised then that she must be taking Mrs Lawson's part. That's why I left as soon as it was all over. I knew you'd discover the truth.'

'Mrs Lawson was on her way to visit her husband,' Finch explained, grateful for the opportunity her interruption gave him to drop some of his official manner although he was careful to keep his voice guarded and impersonal. This account of Mrs Lawson's presence in Waterend Lane would have to do. He had no intention of explaining her real motive which anyway he only suspected. At the same time, he could not help silently applauding Mrs Bingham's intelligence. It hadn't taken her long to grasp the significance of the evidence against her. 'She saw the headlights of a car coming down the hill towards her as she reached the S bend in the lane; your car, Mrs Bingham. As soon as she saw the lights, Mrs Lawson turned and began walking back towards the village but the point is,' and here he gave Boyce a small, sideways glance to confirm the admission he'd made earlier that he should have noticed this fact much earlier in the case, 'no car passed her on the way back. I spoke to her after the reconstruction and confirmed this with her. The only possible conclusion that we can draw is that you stopped somewhere along the lane before you reached the bend—I believe at the ford.'

Finch paused, inviting her to comment, and, thinking that she was going to remain silent, was about to continue when he saw Dr Bingham put a hand on her shoulder, encouraging her to speak.

'As I told you in my statement when you first came here,' she said, 'I passed Stella and Mr Lawson at the gate of the caravan and I thought they were quarrelling. That was a genuine impression, Chief Inspector. I had no wish to make it appear that Mr Lawson was in any way involved in Stella's death.'

Finch let it pass, merely nodding to her to continue although he had his doubts about the statement. Mrs Bingham had seen what she wanted to see which was another matter altogether. Even quite impartial eye-witnesses are notoriously prone to put their own interpretation on events, without intending to twist the facts, and Mrs Bingham had, he suspected, her own reasons for convincing herself that Stella Reeve and Lawson had been quarrelling.

'It had begun raining,' Mrs Bingham went on, 'and as soon as I passed them, it occurred to me to offer Stella a lift home.'

That, too, was passed over without comment although Finch guessed that this wasn't her only reason for stopping. Curiosity to find out exactly what had been going on between Stella Reeve and Lawson had also been a motive.

Her statement raised another issue which he blamed himself for not having considered before. Of course she would have offered Stella a lift. In a village, it went without saying that, if you passed someone you knew, you stopped the car as an accepted courtesy. You didn't ignore the person and drive on.

'So you pulled up?' Finch asked. 'Where exactly?'

'On the far side of the ford. I left the engine running while I waited.'

'Which was how long?' Boyce put in.

She glanced at him with a slightly impatient look, similar to that which Finch remembered Mrs Lawson giving the Sergeant during her interview, as if Boyce's inferiority of rank made him less of a human being. Boyce, thank God, was not thin-skinned enough to notice.

'At most, two minutes. Then I saw her coming across the footbridge. I opened the car door and called out, " Do you want a lift?" she said she did and thanked me.'

'And then?' Finch prompted as Mrs Bingham hesitated. He knew why, too. She had come to that difficult part of her account where she would have to admit the truth of her subsequent actions. To give her her due, she was courageous enough to face it. Finch saw her chin go up.

'It was one of those ridiculous situations, Chief Inspector. As she walked across the bridge, she caught her heel between the planks. I had the passenger door open ready for her to get in. When she called out that her heel was stuck, I got out of the car to help her. She was trying to wriggle the shoe free while she was still wearing it. I said, "Don't be silly, Stella. Why don't you take your foot out? It'll be easier." She didn't reply but went on trying to free it. I admit I was annoyed. I'd stopped to offer her a lift when I needn't have bothered. It was beginning to rain more heavily by this time, too. I didn't see why I should have to stand there getting wet while I waited for her. But she'd never been willing to take advice even when it was well meant, had she, Gordon?' She turned to her husband in quick appeal but he did not respond apart from making a slight, deprecatory gesture with one hand which seemed to Finch to convey a warning as well although Mrs Bingham appeared to be unaware of its full significance.

Finch kept his own expression neutral. It was important, he realised, that he expressed no sense of moral judgement.

At this stage in her account, Madge Bingham's overriding need was one of self-justification. If he criticised that by showing even the slightest flicker of disapproval, she would not admit to the full truth.

She seemed disappointed at her husband's apparent lack of response for she turned instead to Finch, speaking more rapidly now, her eyes fixed on his. He was aware of the force of her personality and that quality of self-righteousness which kept it charged as if a current were constantly passing through it, driving her forward.

'I told her to hurry up. I said, "If you're not ready in one minute exactly, Stella, I shall leave you here."' Although her eyes did not leave Finch's face, she hesitated for a moment and he saw her gaze shift focus slightly to a point mid-way between them and he knew she had come to that part of her statement which even she found difficult to defend. 'I suppose, strictly speaking, it was none of my business, Chief Inspector. But I had seen her quarrelling, as I thought, with Alec Lawson and I knew she was the type of girl to get herself into all kinds of trouble without thinking what she was doing. I mean, she was expecting a baby before she was eighteen and had to get married. And it wasn't just herself who suffered. Her mother was worried to death about her and Gordon was run off his feet at the time caring for them all. I could see that, if she were having an affair with Alec Lawson, it would only lead to more problems. But, of course, I should have known she wouldn't take kindly to advice.'

Finch, who had decided to say nothing during her account, refrained from pointing out that Lawson and Stella had not been lovers. It was Dr Bingham who broke in.

'What did you say to her, Madge?'

He had sat silent during the first part of his wife's statement, gazing down at the floor, his expression pained and oddly humiliated as if he found the revelations embarrassing. Now he raised his head to look at her.

She reacted at once as if still annoyed at his earlier lack of sympathy.

'What I thought she needed to be told, of course. I

said, "I think you're very unwise to get involved with Mr Lawson, Stella. In a small place like Wynford, people are bound to gossip." Which was perfectly true. If I'd noticed them together, others were certain to do so sooner or later. 'I'd left the car headlights on so I was able to see her quite clearly. She had straightened up and twisted round to grasp hold of the rail as she tried to pull the shoe free. I suppose what I said angered her. I can only excuse her reply on that account although I'm not used to being talked to in that manner, Chief Inspector.' She again addressed him directly and Finch saw the colour had risen in her face. 'She said, "Just because you're the bloody doctor's wife, it doesn't give you the right to interfere. What's the matter? Do you fancy him yourself?" It was quite inexcusable! As far as Alec Lawson was concerned, I'd done nothing more than try to welcome him into the village. But I could hardly expect someone like Stella Franklin to appreciate that.'

'I see,' Finch said in the same, non-committal voice.

But he saw more than the simple, unemotional statement implied. In reporting Stella's reply, Madge Bingham had mimicked the girl's voice, emphasising not only the local accent which she must have used but the irreverent and mocking tone in which the words had been spoken. It explained a great deal about Mrs Bingham's attitude of social superiority towards Stella as well as her sense of her own esteem which, in speaking those words, the girl, who had learned to stand up for herself in a harsher world than Mrs Bingham's, had dared to attack.

As for Lawson, in questioning him after the reconstruction, Finch had learned for the first time of Mrs Bingham's visit to the caravan and his rejection of her overtures of friendship out of pique at what he, too, called her sense of superiority. 'As if', as he had explained, 'being the doctor's wife gave her a special recommendation.'

And yet it was because of such trivial-seeming circumstances that Stella's death had occurred.

'I mean, they had nothing in common,' Madge Bingham continued. 'She wasn't the type, I should have thought, to appeal to a man like that, obviously educated and interested in books.'

More your type, Mrs Bingham?

Although Finch did not ask the question out loud, she must have been aware of the unspoken thought which perhaps she had enough sensitivity to see in his face or even to ask herself for she avoided his eyes.

'I had started to walk back along the bridge towards the car. It was my intention to drive off and leave her there. As I did so, the heel of her shoe snapped off and she lost her balance. I tried to save her. I turned back and caught her by the arm but there wasn't time to take a proper grip and, besides, she was too heavy for me. She fell face downwards into the stream and must have hit her head because she didn't move. I called her name and ran down the steps at the end of the bridge. I was going to pull her out and then . . .'

'And then, Mrs Bingham?' Finch repeated gently as she hesitated.

She lifted her chin and met his eyes again.

'I went over to the car and drove home.'

'And left her there? For God's sake, why, Madge? I still don't understand.'

Dr Bingham asked the question, his voice expressing the pain and bewilderment which so far had shown only in his face.

'I don't know,' she said flatly. 'At the time, it didn't seem wrong. I remember thinking: Even if I hadn't stopped to offer her a lift, she'd've fallen. It would have been an accident and no-one's fault except her own.'

'Her fault?' Finch asked.

Although it had been his intention to say nothing, the words came involuntarily.

'Because she had no business being there in the first place,' Mrs Bingham said sharply. 'And because, being the sort of girl she was, it seemed inevitable. But I told you, I really don't know why.'

Finch got to his feet. He had heard enough. If Mrs Bingham did not fully understand her own motives, he felt he had a glimmer of perception. She had left the girl to die as a punishment, not just because of what she had said or done but simply because she was Stella, too bright and individual a star in the little firmament of Wynford in which Madge Bingham was accustomed to shine supreme.

Put out the light and then put out the light.

He left the woman police Sergeant to explain to Mrs Bingham the arrangements for taking her to headquarters and went with Boyce into the hall.

Dr Bingham caught up with them at the front door.

'What will happen now, Chief Inspector?' he asked.

'Your wife will be charged, sir.'

'With murder?'

'No; with manslaughter.'

'I see.' The man stood in silence for a moment before adding, his pleasant face rigid with the effort of controlling his emotions, 'I'm sorry.'

It seemed a ludicrously inadequate comment to make under the circumstances but Finch had noticed before the inability of people under stress to find the words to express their feelings.

Sorry for what, in God's name? he wondered.

For everything, he supposed. For Stella's death; for his wife's involvement with it; perhaps even for himself.

At the same time, it crossed his mind that Mrs Bingham herself had not so far uttered even the most banal apology for her part in the tragedy.

'What will you do, Dr Bingham?' he asked. It was not mere curiosity. He was genuinely concerned for this large, crumpled, kindly man.

'I shall stand by her, of course,' Dr Bingham replied. 'Afterwards, when it's all over, I shall sell up the practice here and move somewhere else; make a fresh start for us both.' He held out his hand. 'Goodbye, Chief Inspector. I'd better get back to her. She's going to need all my support.'

As they got into the car, Boyce asked, 'What do you reckon she'll get on a manslaughter charge?'

'I don't know, Tom. It'll depend on the court,' Finch replied. 'It could be two years, I suppose.'

Boyce started the engine.

'Two bloody years for leaving someone to drown? It doesn't seem enough.'

'No,' Finch agreed.

But only half his mind was on Mrs Bingham's future. His own had begun to re-occupy his thoughts, jogged into fresh awareness by Dr Bingham's parting comment. The parallel between his decision and Marion's was painfully obvious.

'Where to?' Boyce was asking as the car approached the end of the drive. 'Back to headquarters?'

Finch came to a sudden decision.

'No, not straight away. I want to stop off in Studham for a few minutes to see Alec Lawson.'

'What the hell for?'

'To tidy up a few loose ends, that's all.'

He was grateful that Boyce didn't press the point and that, when they drew up outside the shop, he accepted the Chief Inspector's order, 'Wait here!' without any argument. It wouldn't have been easy to explain that the only loose end he hoped to tie off concerned himself, not Lawson.

Lawson was less easy to fool.

'I've dropped by to let you know we've made an arrest,' Finch said when the man let him in. 'I assume you can guess who it is.'

'Yes, I can,' Lawson replied and waited.

He seemed aware that this wasn't the only reason for Finch's visit for he was watching the Chief Inspector with a speculative, inquiring air, encouraging him to continue.

To cover up his awkwardness, Finch looked about him. Some progress had been made with the interior. The missing floorboards had been replaced with new timber, looking very pale against the old wood and smelling sweetly of pine. The ceiling, too, had been painted white and several light flexes dangled down.

'So you'll be staying on here after all?' he asked.

He thought Lawson would not understand the purpose

behind the question for, in his anxiety to appear casual, he had put it too obliquely. But Lawson seemed to catch the drift for he replied, 'If you mean, will my wife and I get together again, I don't honestly know, Chief Inspector. I assume that's what you're getting at. You must have seen what seemed like a reconciliation this morning.'

'It's none of my business,' Finch began, hoping that Lawson would not take the remark at face value.

To his relief, the man seemed eager to talk.

'I've made a cock-up all round, haven't I? First my marriage and then the relationship, such as it was, with Stella. Even though it was totally innocent, I feel partly to blame for the whole tragic business. If I hadn't met her that day in Studham, if I'd been a little less arrogant towards Mrs Bingham, if I hadn't bloody well been in Wynford in the first place, none of it would have happened. Well, I began the God-awful mess when I walked out on Joanna so it's up to me to clear that part of it up at least; pick up the pieces and try to fit them together again. I'm willing but Joanna won't commit herself at this stage and I don't blame her. I wouldn't if I were in her place. So, as far as the future's concerned, only time will tell.'

It was hardly worth waiting for and yet, as Finch held out his hand, he felt oddly appeased.

Only time would tell.

There was nothing else he could do except wait, like Lawson, for events to happen. The end hadn't been tied off, after all, but contrary to his expectations, he found it a source of hope rather than disappointment.

'So?' Boyce asked as he climbed back into the passenger seat.

'Nothing much, Tom. I just thought I'd let him know what happened.'

'Well, I suppose we owed it to him,' Boyce agreed reluctantly. 'After all, he was one of our suspects and that got him chucked out of the caravan.'

Finch let it pass. If that was the interpretation which the Sergeant put on the visit, then it was better he left it there.

'Back to headquarters?' Boyce added.

'Yes,' Finch said.

There was nowhere else to go and it was, after all, his world. He knew no other. Like Lawson, he would have to pick up the pieces of his life as best he could. Whether Marion, his own particular bright star, would ever again form part of the pattern, he did not know. Only time would tell.

'Treat you to a beer tonight?' Boyce was asking. 'Sort of celebration now that the case is over.'

Finch was about to refuse and then changed his mind. Why not? he thought. Life had to go on.

'Yes, I'd like that, Tom,' he replied, adding after a pause, 'Thanks.'

It was meant to convey more than just the mere surface meaning of the word. Whether Boyce realised this, Finch wasn't sure but, as they slowed down at the roundabout on the outskirts of Studham before taking the right-hand fork for Chelmsford, the Sergeant turned to grin at him before concentrating his attention again on the road ahead.

Close
Her Eyes

DOROTHY SIMPSON

Winner of the Silver Dagger Award

News that an innocent young girl like Charity Pritchard is
missing will pierce the armour of policemen far more
hard-bitten than Inspector Thanet. And his concern deepens
when the first thought of her family – strict religious
fundamentalists – is to leave the matter in God's hands.

Of course no detective worth his salt will put much faith
in outward appearances. And he is hardly likely to pay much
heed to first impressions. But it will be a good while after
Inspector Thanet finds Charity's poor broken body before
he realises just how wrong his preconceptions can be . . .

0 7221 7874 3   CRIME   £2.50

Also by Dorothy Simpson in Sphere Books:
PUPPET FOR A CORPSE

A LETHAL COCKTAIL OF VIOLENCE,
DEATH AND BLACK HUMOUR . . .

The Secrets of
Harry Bright

JOSEPH WAMBAUGH

Nothing much lived in the desert around Mineral Springs.
Just lizards and motorcycle gangs and a few dopers.
A corpse with a bullet hole in a burned-out Rolls Royce was
kind of unusual.

For a homicide cop like Blackpool this was a case to pass on to
some other poor sucker. Except he'd been hauled out of LA
by the victim's own father. Told to handle it personally as a
private commission. And promised a nice fat backhander at
the end of the day . . .

'So much energy . . . a detective no other writer could have
cooked up, a resolution no other could have ordained'
NEW YORK TIMES

0 7221 8914 1 **GENERAL FICTION** £2.95

Also by Joseph Wambaugh in Sphere Books:
NEW CENTURIONS
THE BLUE KNIGHT

A selection of bestsellers from Sphere

FICTION

THE PRINCESS OF POOR STREET	Emma Blair	£2.99 ☐
WANDERLUST	Danielle Steel	£3.50 ☐
LADY OF HAY	Barbara Erskine	£3.95 ☐
BIRTHRIGHT	Joseph Amiel	£3.50 ☐
THE SECRETS OF HARRY BRIGHT	Joseph Wambaugh	£2.95 ☐

FILM AND TV TIE-IN

BLACK FOREST CLINIC	Peter Heim	£2.99 ☐
INTIMATE CONTACT	Jacqueline Osborne	£2.50 ☐
BEST OF BRITISH	Maurice Sellar	£8.95 ☐
SEX WITH PAULA YATES	Paula Yates	£2.95 ☐
RAW DEAL	Walter Wager	£2.50 ☐

NON-FICTION

NEXT TO A LETTER FROM HOME: THE GLENN MILLER STORY	Geoffrey Butcher	£4.99 ☐
AS TIME GOES BY: THE LIFE OF INGRID BERGMAN	Laurence Leamer	£3.95 ☐
BOTHAM	Don Mosey	£3.50 ☐
SOLDIERS	John Keegan & Richard Holmes	£5.95 ☐
URI GELLER'S FORTUNE SECRETS	Uri Geller	£2.50 ☐

All Sphere books are available at your local bookshop or newsagent, or can be ordered direct from the publisher. Just tick the titles you want and fill in the form below.

Name_____

Address_____

_____

Write to Sphere Books, Cash Sales Department, P.O. Box 11, Falmouth, Cornwall TR10 9EN

Please enclose a cheque or postal order to the value of the cover price plus:

UK: 60p for the first book, 25p for the second book and 15p for each additional book ordered to a maximum charge of £1.90.

OVERSEAS & EIRE: £1.25 for the first book, 75p for the second book and 28p for each subsequent title ordered.

BFPO: 60p for the first book, 25p for the second book plus 15p per copy for the next 7 books, thereafter 9p per book.

Sphere Books reserve the right to show new retail prices on covers which may differ from those previously advertised in the text elsewhere, and to increase postal rates in accordance with the P.O.